DATE DUE

Larry McMurtry

LOOP GROUP

SIMON & SCHUSTER
New York • London • Toronto • Sydney

SIMON & SCHUSTER
Rockefeller Center
1230 Avenue of the Americas
New York, NY 10020

SIMON & SCHUSTER and colophon are registered trademarks
of Simon & Schuster, Inc.

For information about special discounts for bulk purchases,
please contact Simon & Schuster Special Sales at 1-800-456-6798
or business@simonandschuster.com

Designed by Dana Sloan

Manufactured in the United States of America

10 9 8 7 6 5 4 3 2 1

The Library of Congress Cataloging-in-Publication Data
McMurtry, Larry.
   Loop group / Larry McMurtry.
      p. cm.
   1. Middle-aged women—Fiction. 2. Los Angeles (Calif.)—Fiction. 3. Female friendship—Fiction. 4. Automobile travel—Fiction. 5. Women travelers—Fiction. 6. Texas—Fiction. I. Title.

PS3563.A319L66 2004
813'.54—dc22   2004052216

ISBN 0-7432-5079-6

For Diane and Dorrie

LOOP GROUP

Book One

HOME

1

MAGGIE WAS rummaging fretfully in her small pantry, wondering why in the world she could never remember to buy tea bags, when she happened to glance out the window just in time to see her daughter Kate's enormous SUV whip into her driveway and stop. That was a little surprising—it was Sunday morning, only about ten o'clock, and Kate was a lazybones who normally did not bestir herself much on Sunday morning. Besides which, Kate lived in Marina del Rey—what was she doing in Hollywood at such an early hour?

Maybe it's some excursion with the kids, Maggie speculated, but she watched and no grandkids bounded out. No one had bounded out—Kate had not even killed her motor. But finally she did kill it, after which, to Maggie's mystification, all three of her daughters emerged: Kate, Jeannie, Meagan, three competent, appealing, go-for-it young women; they were the best daughters anywhere, Maggie believed, though it was odd that they had not called to let her know that they intended to pay her a visit. All three had cell phones and, of course, *had* had cell phones from the minute cell phones came on the market.

Their sudden appearance in her front yard gave Maggie the beginnings of a ganged-up-on feeling, but she opened the door anyway; she had never not been glad to see her daughters, even when they chose to strike without warning on Sunday morning.

"Mom, don't you even bring in your paper anymore?" Kate asked, handing Maggie her big fat Sunday L.A. *Times,* which had been reposing in the middle of her sidewalk, thick as a log.

3

Kate's tone made Maggie's hackles rise a little.

"I bring in my paper every day, and what's more, I read it," Maggie assured her. "Is there a law that says I have to bring it in by ten A.M. or something?"

"A wino could walk by and steal it," Jeannie pointed out.

Maggie shrugged.

"What's the big deal about my morning paper?" she asked.

"Just forget the fucking paper, you two," Meagan told her sisters. Kate was the oldest, Meagan the youngest, and Jeannie in the middle. Kate and Meagan frequently tangled; Jeannie glided around conflict whenever possible.

Kate grew red in the face—she looked like she'd enjoy slapping her younger sister. She also looked as if she might soon burst into tears. The Sunday *Times* got pitched onto the couch; several of the fat classified sections slid off onto the floor. Maggie thought she might check out the classifieds later, to see if there were any promising garage sales within walking distance; but that would have to wait until her daughters left.

"Mom, we're doing an intervention," Jeannie informed her quickly. "You're worrying us all too much. We love you and we can't let you go on this way."

For a moment Maggie wanted to laugh, something she now rarely did; but she was alert enough to realize that her daughters wouldn't appreciate levity, not at this time. They had screwed up their courage and come to confront her about a serious problem; and to be honest, there *was* a serious problem. The worst thing she could do at the time would be to laugh.

"I wish we could be having tea while you were intervening," she said mildly, "but for some reason I can't seem to remember to buy tea bags."

"That's it, Mom . . . no tea bags!" Meagan said loudly. Meagan had a big voice and often spoke more loudly than she intended to.

"See, you've totally given up," Meagan added, in a more moderate tone.

Maggie turned on her heel and walked into the kitchen. She might lack tea bags but she had plenty of oranges. If they couldn't have tea while this intervention was taking place, at least they could have fresh-squeezed orange juice. She cut several oranges in two and began to squeeze them.

"Ma, will you please stop *doing* things?" Kate asked. "We need to talk." They all trailed her into the kitchen. Kate seemed more keyed up than the other two—perhaps because she was the oldest, she had been chosen to be spokesperson.

"We've been thinking about this for weeks," Kate went on.

"No, we've been thinking about it for *months,*" Jeannie corrected. "You have to confront your problems—none of us can take this anymore."

Maggie kept squeezing oranges, until she had enough juice for four good-sized glasses. Kate and Jeannie took sips, but Meagan, who had a big appetite to go with her big voice, immediately glugged hers down.

"I thought interventions were for alcoholics or drug addicts or something," Maggie said, washing the orange pulp off her hands. "All you've accused me of is being slow to bring in the paper and not remembering to buy tea bags."

"No, no, no—it's not *those* things!" Kate insisted.

"Mom, those things are trifles—we need to keep things in perspective," Jeannie told her.

"It's your condition," Kate said.

"Your state," Meagan added, by way of clarification.

"The way you are," Jeannie insisted.

Maggie was silent for a moment.

"Oh," she said, finally. "You must be referring to my despair."

"That's *it*! You finally said it yourself, your despair!" Kate said, sounding suddenly much less tense.

"I don't know that interventions are recommended for despair, my dears," Maggie said quietly.

Then mother and daughters fell silent. They could get no further, but Maggie was glad, at least, that she had squeezed the oranges. A little OJ never hurt.

2

"Don't I go to work every day? Don't I?" Maggie mentioned, in her own defense, once things were calmer. Kate had rushed up to the big grocery store on Sunset, returning with a bag full of teas, some Danish, and a lot of corned beef. She also bought some St.-John's-wort, which she didn't suppose her mother would take, but why not try?

Then they all went into the small leafy backyard and had their tea, while Jeannie painted her toenails. Jeannie had always been fussy about her feet—had to have just the right sandals and the like. She spent, in Maggie's opinion, far too much money on pedicures and foot care in general—but then Jeannie was a grown woman, thirty-five years old, and could pamper her feet if she wanted to.

"Mom, we *know* you go to work," Meagan said, her tone only slightly patronizing. Their mother's professional reliability was not the point—not what caused Meagan to leave her bungalow in Echo Park, and Jeannie to leave her large house in Silver Lake, or Kate to leave her new place in Marina del Rey; and all this at a time—Sunday morning—when all of them preferred to do as little as possible. After all, they had jobs, they had husbands, they had kids—who couldn't use a little downtime?

"Mom, you raised us—it's because of you that our lives have sort of worked out," Kate said, in a gentler tone.

"It's the truth," Jeannie agreed. "If it wasn't for you we'd all probably be whores or dopers or shoplifters or something."

"It's true your father wasn't much help . . . I apologize," Maggie admitted—Rog had never been any help, but why get into that?

"It's just that I miss my womb," Maggie added quietly, telling them, again, what she had already told them a hundred times.

"It was *my* womb—I should never have allowed them to take it out," she said. "I lost an important part of myself. How else can I put it?"

"But, Mom, you got two scary Paps in a row—you were flirting with cancer!" Meagan reminded her.

"Flirting's not always fatal," Maggie pointed out.

"Hey . . . you could be dead by now if you hadn't had that hysterectomy," Jeannie insisted.

"Millions of women have hysterectomies and get over them," Kate reminded her. "They go on to live perfectly healthy lives."

Maggie shrugged. It was about the nine hundredth time that her daughters, or a friend, or a doctor had mentioned the millions of women who had hysterectomies and made full recoveries and went back to living excellent lives.

"My hat's off to them," Maggie told her daughters. "They're my heroines, believe me. I wish I was just like them, but I'm not. I haven't made a full recovery, or any recovery. The best I can do is go to work. I support myself. I pay my bills."

"You do, but you're not *interested* in anything now. You were always so interested in stuff," Meagan told her.

Maggie didn't deny it.

"You're not even interested in your own grandkids," Jeannie pointed out. "They all wonder what happened to their granny."

It was a low blow, words Jeannie immediately regretted saying, but her regret didn't change anything.

Maggie began to cry, silently but copiously.

All the girls at once hugged her and told her they were sorry. The intervention just didn't seem to be working.

"Don't you understand? I feel guilty about everything now," Maggie said. "I feel guilty about everything and everybody, but I feel most guilty about my grandchildren."

She stood up, still crying, and went into the house.

"Now we've just made things worse," Kate said.

"Plus wasting Sunday morning," Meagan said.

"I told you we should just have left it to her shrink," Jeannie said.

"Dr. Tom, the Sicilian midget?" Kate said, with a shrug of contempt.

"Be kind," Meagan said. "He's not a midget. I've dated shorter men myself."

"And he loves Mom," Jeannie said. "Besides, people from Sicily have just as much right to be shrinks as anybody else.

"Why shouldn't a Sicilian be a shrink?" she asked, but no one bothered to answer the question. The daughters went back in the house and tidied up the kitchen. There was not much to tidy. Kate, who had an oral fixation, polished off the Danish.

As her daughters left, Maggie was sitting on the couch, painstakingly reading the classifieds in the *L.A. Times*. There was a pile of soggy Kleenex beside her.

"I'm sorry I brought up the kids," Jeannie told her.

Maggie shrugged. "I *know* I'm guilty, you know," she said—why deny it?

They all hugged her, but no one could think of much else to say.

"ARE YOU GOING to see your boyfriend?" Kate asked Jeannie as she was driving her sisters back to the Denny's on Santa Monica where they had left the other two cars.

What had prompted the question was a certain look in Jeannie's eye.

"I might," Jeannie said.

In fact she couldn't wait to get to Glendale and yank her boyfriend's pants off.

"Is Fred at all suspicious?" Meagan asked.

"Look, I'm not in the mood to discuss my marital situation," Jeannie said. "Mostly I treat my husband fine."

"Don't be so touchy," Meagan said.

3

FOR A WHILE, after the girls left, Maggie felt even more depressed. Her daughters had made a big effort to jerk her out of her gloom, but the effort had misfired. The more they demanded that she cheer up, the more impossible it became for her to feel cheerful. Life just seemed to be perverse that way. Kate, Jeannie, and Meagan were complete women; they had husbands and sex lives and children and friendships and decent jobs. Kate played softball with her office team and Meagan liked to Rollerblade. Jeannie, of course, was into balling rather than softballing; she was no doubt already up in Glendale, fucking her boyfriend's brains out, what few the poor sap had, while Jeannie's big jovial husband, Fred, was probably sitting home watching baseball, letting the kids run riot.

Maggie understood exactly how her daughters felt: after all, for fifty-nine years, she had been as complete as anybody. She had mainly worked as a script girl until all the directors began to do large amounts of cocaine, which made most of them even more difficult to work with. After two directors fired her, Maggie felt she'd held scripts long enough; she switched to managing a loop group. Prime Loops was the name she finally settled on for the company. Her loop group specialized in Westerns, action movies, and comedies, and from the first did pretty well, mainly because Maggie was popular with a lot of producers and the managers of quite a few of the mix studios.

Meanwhile, of course, she was busy being a complete woman: fighting with Rog, the worthless horse's ass she had for some reason married; she took lovers when it suited her, got drunk when the affairs ended—but drunk or sober, happy or unhappy, there was never a day's work missed—never. In the movie industry it took very little sluffing off to get oneself marked down as unreliable. Once that happened there would soon be no work, and Maggie had always had bills to pay, particularly after Rog died, making the Clarys a one-income family: her income. It took her two years just to pay off Rog's coffin, a fancy one the girls had insisted on. Being his daughters, they were better able to overlook Rog's flaws than Maggie was. In fact they soon became very sentimental about their father—in his absence, of course—and lit into Maggie if she let slip the least critical word, once Rog was gone.

What Maggie knew her robust, normal daughters just couldn't grasp was how it might be for a woman to feel incomplete, so incomplete that she no longer felt herself to be the woman she had been for almost sixty years. She felt like someone else—a someone she scarcely recognized.

"I mean, has it hurt your sex life?—I've heard hysterectomies can do that," Meagan asked, trying to understand.

"Honey, I'm not having a sex life right now," Maggie had reminded her. "I kicked Terry out, remember?"

Then Kate came over one day and tried to give her a pep talk. "Mom, you're still a good-looking woman," she said. "You could easily get a guy."

Kate was sort of geared to the pep talk—perhaps it was from having coached so many peewee soccer teams.

"I wasn't complaining, honey," Maggie said. "Every time the phone rings it's some man I don't want."

Maggie had never really had raving looks—what she had was just a shine, mostly. When she happened to switch her brights on, a lot of guys wanted her—even young guys—*especially* young guys, in fact. Art directors seemed to be particularly susceptible: the gay ones became her chums and the ungay ones tried to fuck her.

Probably another factor that added to Maggie's appeal was that she really liked working as a member of a movie crew. Just driving up and seeing all the bustle, with people moving cameras and lights around, made her feel on top of the world. Usually she arrived at the set with a big grin on her face, thrilled to be working in the great American film industry. Even the gloomy A.D.'s—usually the gloomiest people on any movie set—brightened a little when Maggie favored them with a smile, or a punch on the shoulder, or something innocent like that.

What she had to figure out now was why the loss of one little over-the-hill uterus could change so much, could dim her lights so. Wasn't she still Maggie Clary, a woman who had raised three fine daughters after burying her Billy, a tiny son, aged only three days at his death?

Billy was buried in Hollywood Memorial Cemetery, just a short walk away. She had endured a dopey marriage, paid her bills, worked all over town, from Fox to Warner, Universal to Paramount. She kept her house pretty neat, though to be truthful, she had never gone overboard on the neatness thing—after all, some of the best things in life were a little messy, sex for one. Barbecue might be another.

For the moment, though, what she felt was that she was tired of sitting on her couch with a pile of damp Kleenex beside her. In ten seconds she got up, doffed her pajamas, and grabbed a blouse and pants; then she brushed out her hair and was out the door on a sunny morning into what, to Maggie's mind, was the most beautiful place in the world: Hollywood, California. And of course she didn't mean North Hollywood, over the hills, or West Hollywood, where things began to get fancy and expensive; she meant Hollywood proper, the Hollywood that had probably once been the most glamorous place in the whole world—in fact it still seemed so to Maggie, though it had to be admitted that some shabbiness had crept in.

Her own bungalow, the Clary home, was on Las Palmas, a few houses down from De Longpre Avenue; apart from a few months here and there, spent lolling in the apartments of various lovers, Maggie had lived in the bungalow her whole life. Her parents, taking their hearts in their hands and every penny of their savings out of the bank, had bought the bungalow in 1946, and the Clary family had lived there ever since. Of course, Maggie and her little sister, Tanya, had grown up supposing they would fall in love and move away; and of course, both of them did fall in love lots of times; but before either of them could move out, their parents had the misfortune, one foggy morning, to have a head-on with a truck while on the Rim of the World Scenic Byway on their annual camping trip to Big Bear Lake. Both were killed instantly and the bungalow became the possession of Maggie and Tanya; but Tanya, never lucky, was killed in a car wreck too; this one happened in El Segundo: somebody ran a light and Tanya was gone. That was that. Maggie became an orphan with a nice bungalow on Las Palmas, where she had lived ever since, where she had had her children, and where, in due course, she expected to die.

But not this morning, which was on the whole a sunny one, just a bit of haze. It amused Maggie that no one called the white summer skies in L.A. smog anymore: it had been upgraded to haze. Usually the haze didn't bother her—just occasionally she might get a little stinging in the eyes.

4

Not expecting much—it was late to be hitting a garage sale in L.A.; usually the good stuff would be snarfed up in about three minutes— Maggie nonetheless hurried over to one she had noted on Cherokee, just a block away, where, to her amazement, she bought a lovely coral necklace for only two bucks. The find was so unexpected that Maggie took it as a sign that her luck was bound to change. A nice coral necklace usually wouldn't last five minutes, not in L.A., where a lot of women seemed to wear coral.

Cheered by her unexpected acquisition, Maggie put the necklace on and wandered up to Musso Franks, the famous old movietown restaurant on Hollywood Boulevard, where she planned to indulge in a secret culinary passion, a sardine sandwich, a taste treat she was careful not to indulge in unless she felt it unlikely that she would be kissing anybody for a while. She loved the oily taste of the sardines, but was less enthusiastic about the aftertaste, which tended to linger for a while: even a good gargle with Listerine couldn't necessarily get rid of it.

Terry Matlock, her last boyfriend, a tall young actor from Alabama, would certainly have dropped her immediately if he'd caught the least whiff of sardines. Terry wasn't working much, so he filled in with Prime Loops a few times, when Maggie found herself shorthanded—Solomon, her best grunter, having collected one too many DWIs, which meant jail for six months. Terry Matlock proved much too condescending to fit in as a loop grouper, but he was tall and cute, so Maggie decided to seduce him, which she promptly did. What might have been behind it was a desire to find out if her surgery had made any difference vis-à-vis her sexual response; she had heard disquieting rumors that everything sexual was apt to go kind of slack after a hysterectomy.

Fortunately, in Maggie's case, that didn't turn out to be a problem—Terry was really an attractive young guy and sex seemed to work about as well as ever, a fact that didn't cheer her up as much as she had hoped it would. She still liked fucking: what could there be to get so depressed about?

Of course, the affair with Terry, who was only twenty-four, was not likely to last forever, but so far none of Maggie's affairs had lasted forever: why should the one with Terry be any different? Back in Alabama Terry had belonged to some fraternity; he seemed to feel that membership in the fraternity sort of elevated him above the common man. Pretty soon he started insisting that Maggie be on top, which now and then she didn't mind, but being an older woman, she didn't want to be on top *all* the time.

What cut it with Terry, though, wasn't anything sexual—it had to do with money. Loop groupers were frequently apt to find themselves in desperate straits financially, so Maggie made a habit of keeping several hundred dollars in cash, in case she had to bail someone out of jail, or maybe make a little emergency loan or something. Now and then, once Terry moved in, she began to have the disquieting feeling that maybe the kid was stealing from her. It seemed that she always had fifty bucks less than she thought she had—sometimes even a hundred bucks less. So one day after sex she peeked through the crack in the bathroom door and saw Terry slip out of bed still naked and make straight for her purse, where he coolly extracted three one-hundred-dollar bills.

"Put it back, Terry," she said matter-of-factly, stepping out from behind the door. She was by then fully clothed.

"No way," Terry said, with his superior little smile. "Us gigolos have to live too."

"Hurry up, leave—I'm tired of looking at you," Maggie told

him. He didn't have much stuff: just a few T-shirts, a few jeans, and lots of CDs. Soon enough Terry Matlock was driving away, in a little green pickup that still had Alabama license plates.

Later, thinking about it, Maggie decided that the gigolo remark wasn't all that unfair. She *had* been running a little test, to see if she was still okay in one particular way. Terry was a snobby kid, but he hadn't beat her or anything, or been rough; the thing to do was let it go, which she did without crying over it much—maybe just once or twice, when she remembered the disdain in his eyes as he was leaving.

5

Right away Maggie saw that Paolo, the headwaiter, wasn't going to let her drink her Bloody Mary and eat her sardine sandwich in peace. It was lunchtime on a Sunday and Musso's was buzzing as usual, but Paolo obviously had no intention of letting that keep him from enjoying a chat with his old customer Maggie Clary. Paolo, after all, had been with the restaurant something like thirty years, longer than any waiter except old Mario—nobody could remember how long old Mario had been at Musso's, but he was so old and shaky that he was no longer allowed to serve soup because he couldn't get it to the table without spilling half of it. Maggie felt sorry for old Mario—after all, he was doing his best not to be a burden to society, or even to the restaurant where he had worked most of his life.

Paolo, much younger, was a different matter. Maggie had known him the whole time he worked there, and all along she'd had the sense that Paolo was the kind of guy who wouldn't mind fraternizing with the customers a little—at least he wouldn't mind if the customer happened to be Maggie. He had a wife and lots of kids, plus even more lots of grandchildren, whose pictures he was fond of showing to Maggie.

"It takes a pretty virile guy to produce twenty-two grandkids and seven greats," he said, sidling up to her and spreading out the photos in his wallet. Sure enough, there seemed to be two or three more puzzled-looking babies in the crowd.

"That's right—pretty soon you'll have to get a bigger wallet, Paolo," she said, keeping her voice strictly neutral. Nothing in the world could be much worse than to have Paolo make some kind of pass at her while she had sardines on her breath.

"What's the matter with you? You look low," Paolo asked, adopting the gentle approach.

"I'm not low, honey . . . I'm in despair," Maggie said pleasantly. Lately, whenever someone told her that she looked low, Maggie pointed out that she wasn't low, she was in despair—her hope was that they'd take it as a joke and let her alone.

Paolo, to her surprise, took the comment seriously.

"Despair? Come on. Why?" he asked, which annoyed her.

"Frankly, I'd rather not discuss it while I'm eating," she told him. "I'm working it out with my shrink, if you don't mind."

"Dr. Tom ain't going to cure you," Paolo informed her, twirling his finger around his ear to indicate his low opinion of Dr. Tom's sanity.

From time to time, after a session, she and Dr. Tom wandered up to Musso's to refresh themselves with a plate of fettuccine with clams. Naturally the fact that Maggie arrived with a man, albeit an old man, made Paolo as jealous as hell.

"Sicilians are never too old to fool around," Paolo had hinted darkly, the next time Maggie showed up at the restaurant.

"Lay off, Paolo—he's my doctor!" Maggie retorted. She didn't like comments like that from anyone, much less from an overly aggressive headwaiter.

This morning Paolo wisely contented himself with a little finger twirling. She knew perfectly well that most people found Dr. Tom a little weird, but he was her own beloved shrink, who had been helping her get through emotional crises for nineteen years: she was not about to let Paolo or anyone else say bad things about him.

Besides, Paolo was from Milan, which she understood was in a different part of Italy from Sicily—why did he think he knew so much about Sicilians?

Paolo immediately backed off about Dr. Tom, but the fact was, Maggie Clary stirred desires and had been stirring them the whole time she had been coming to the restaurant. He wanted her when she was in her fresh-faced thirties and still wanted her now that she must be hitting sixty; he had a crush on her, and twenty-two grandkids and seven greats hadn't made it go away. Paolo had had plenty of crushes on good-looking lady customers, but usually the feelings waned as the ladies aged. Maggie was the one exception; though nothing was happening, nothing had waned. Paolo had often tried to work up the nerve to ask Maggie to see him outside the restaurant; after all, seeing him after work could lead to only one thing. It occurred to him that showing her pictures of his family might have been a stupid move. Maybe she had scruples about married men—even in Hollywood there were still a few women who had scruples about married men.

Maggie was getting a little riled—she wanted Paolo to go away and leave her in peace; she was about to tell him so in no uncertain terms when the guy surprised her. He came out with a totally weird suggestion.

"Ever lived anywhere but Hollywood?" he asked.

"Of course not, Paolo," she told him. "I was born here and I hope to die here."

"I wasn't saying you had to *live* someplace else—think how we'd all miss you," Paolo told her. He had seen the angry gleam in Maggie's eye and knew that this was not the day to ask her to take a walk or something.

"I just meant maybe you should take a trip," he said. "Maybe a little change of scene would cheer you up."

"I like to be in my own home at night, thank you," Maggie told him, and it was true—she liked to be in her own home at night and somewhere in her own hometown, Los Angeles, during the day.

In fact, all the Clarys were homebodies—none of her girls really liked to travel, either. Maggie had been to Tahoe twice; she had once had to go to Oklahoma City for a wedding, a horrible experience, and a boyfriend who liked to shoot doves took her with him to a big ranch in Mexico, south of Mexicali, where he shot a whole bunch of doves before he brought her back. When the kids were little there had been talk of a vacation to the Grand Canyon, but for one reason or another they always settled for Disneyland. The mere thought of riding several hundred miles in a car with Rog caused her to scuttle the Grand Canyon expedition while he was alive—even Disneyland was a long way to drive in a car with Rog. Even on a short trip Rog's bad attitudes reminded her of at least a hundred reasons why she should never have married him, much less live with the jerk for eighteen years.

Since Paolo seemed to have backed off, at least for the day—he was actually waiting on a customer—Maggie decided to indulge in another Bloody Mary. Pretty soon she had downed five, although she was not particularly in the mood to drink—when she was in the mood to drink, five Bloody Marys would have been nothing: just the windup, not the pitch.

When she got up to leave she couldn't resist giving old Mario a hug—she could just imagine that not being allowed to serve soup must have been a big blow to the old man's pride. Paolo was standing two feet away, adding up a check, but she didn't give him a hug; he'd gone too far again, leering at her while all she wanted was to be left alone to eat her sandwich and drink her drink. She thought she might just give Musso's a pass for the next few months, until Paolo had time to cool down.

6

SINCE SHE WAS SO CLOSE, Maggie crossed the street and spent a few minutes checking out the mannequins in the window of Frederick's of Hollywood. The lingerie was pretty silly, maybe, but Maggie still felt a certain affection for the old place. Long ago she'd had a boyfriend who thought pink lingerie was the hottest thing under heaven, at least if Maggie was wearing it. You had to allow for a little silliness now and then, if you wanted much of a sex life.

Just as she was wandering off, a white Mercedes convertible cruised by, with two young guys in it—for some reason she happened to notice the license plate, which said New Jersey. A minute later she saw a Texas license plate, and one from Indiana. It made her proud that so many people drove long distances from remote places in America to admire her hometown. She felt a little throb of civic pride, though undoubtedly what the young guys from New Jersey were looking for was a few sexy Hollywood teenyboppers—they probably hadn't driven all that way to admire art deco architecture or something like that.

Maggie wandered down to Sunset Boulevard, where she also noted quite a few out-of-state license plates, even one from Massachusetts, which was completely across America. To her it seemed kind of amazing that anyone would actually drive that far—after all, there were airplanes now, why not just jump on one? Even on De Longpre Avenue, which was not a particularly prominent street, she spotted another Texas license plate, and one from Idaho. Seeing all the license plates from other places reminded Maggie that she herself had never visited any of the places the cars came from. Maybe Paolo, despite his leering, had actually formulated a pretty good idea. Maybe she *had* stayed strictly in one place a little too long—sixty years in all, now that she thought about it. Why not just take a trip? She couldn't really claim any burning desire to see the Grand Canyon or the Old Faithful geyser or whatever scenic wonders might pop up along the road—but that didn't mean it wouldn't be fun to go somewhere.

She was at her door, key in hand, when a hugely radical thought occurred to her: *if she went away to places where no one knew her, she wouldn't have to pretend to be the woman she no longer felt she was!* She could drive along and miss her womb as much as she wanted without worrying her daughters to the point where they got in her face about it.

Just having the idea made Maggie feel better than she had felt in weeks. Sundays five to seven she had her weekly session with Dr. Tom, after which they always had dinner—Chinese or Thai or whatever they decided they were in the mood for. Maggie could hardly wait for it to be five o'clock so she could tell Dr. Tom her amazing new idea.

It was while she was in her bathroom, gargling mouthwash and doing what she could to combat sardine aftertaste, that Maggie suddenly realized that there was one huge obstacle to her new plan to drive off into America, where no one would be likely to ask her questions about her "state," as her daughters put it.

The big obstacle, of course, was her loop group, Prime Loops, which just happened to be booked solid for the next two weeks. The fact that she had completely forgotten about the loop group, even for a few moments, made her wonder if she was really going crazy, as her daughters seemed to think. Such a lapse was upsetting: the mere sight of a few out-of-state license plates had caused her to forget that she was a woman with responsibilities. What did that say about her mental state?

Before she could much more than spit out the mouthwash, her agitation began to mount. She had been about to shower; she had no clothes on but she grabbed a bathrobe and hurried out into the backyard, where she began to dip leaves out of her tiny swimming pool—dug by her father with his own hands. She had her dip net at the ready; usually dipping out whatever leaves were floating in her pool helped Maggie calm down, if she happened to be agitated.

This time the dipping process did nothing to relieve her agitation. It seemed incredible to her that she had just contemplated driving off, leaving the loop groupers to their fate, a grim fate that might involve overdoses, massive hangovers, evictions from apartments whose rent had not been paid, homelessness, AIDS, beatings, and all the other bad things down-on-their-luck actors were likely to experience.

But there it was: such had been her intention. She had even been sort of planning her route: her plan had been to slip down to the Coast Highway and flip a coin, heads south, tails north; a coin flip was sometimes the easiest way to come to a decision.

Standing by her pool with the dipnet in her hand, Maggie wondered if she was really going to flip out, go bats, go crazy; the level of her agitation was still rising, which was not a good sign, not a good sign at all. It suddenly seemed lonely in her backyard—lonely as if the ghosts of all her loved ones had decided to flee. The ghosts were all the people Maggie had lived with in that backyard: her parents, Tanya, the girls when young, Rog, various lovers, Connie, her best friend since the sixth grade, plus a few other friends. Usually she felt rather supported by her memories, many of them good memories; but today she was whirling, with no access to good memories at all.

The one good thought Maggie had to hold on to was that it was already four P.M.—in one hour she could seek safety with Dr. Tom, one of the few shrinks in L.A. who had office hours on Sunday, which he probably did because of an unhappy home life. Ninotchka, his wife, happened to be a bodybuilder, which meant she took bad steroids, of course, and as a result had fits, violent fits, during which she sometimes beat the crap out of Dr. Tom. Long ago Ninotchka had been Miss San Bernardino; that was before her bodybuilding days.

It seemed a long hour, the hour from four to five. Maggie got dressed, but even so, still had forty-five minutes to kill. She tried TV but didn't look at the pictures—she contented herself with reading the CNN crawl. She liked it that CNN mentioned celebrities on their birthdays—who would have thought that Joan Collins was that old?

The forty-five minutes finally ticked away and Maggie stood up to leave, only to have the phone ring just as she had her hand on the doorknob. The caller was undoubtedly Connie, who was most likely calling to report her latest romantic disaster, which, like most of Connie's disasters, seemed to occur on Sunday afternoons around four forty-five. Maggie knew that the main reason Connie called just at that time was because she was jealous of Maggie's devotion to

Dr. Tom. Connie, despite her hundreds of boyfriends, never really liked to share Maggie with anyone. Maggie knew she should just steel herself and go on to her shrink, but she could not quite bring herself to reject Connie or her last-minute calls, so, for better or worse, she picked up the phone.

"It's me," Connie announced. "Are you busy?"

"I'm on my way to my shrink. Can we talk later?" Maggie asked.

There was a silence—obviously Connie was offended at being asked to wait. In her world, best friends took precedence over shrinks any day.

"Are you there?" Maggie asked, after a bit.

"I've never known anyone to go to the shrink as often as you do," Connie said.

"Listen, I'm a troubled person, I nearly had a hysterical fit today," Maggie informed her. "I really need my session with Dr. Tom."

"Go, then!" Connie said. "Call me the minute you get home."

But Connie didn't hang up—she stayed on the line, nursing her resentment. Maggie knew her too well to be fooled.

"Look, I'm sorry I can't talk right now," Maggie said. "Can't you just tell me what happened in three words maybe?"

"Billy left me," Connie said.

"That's three words, all right," Maggie said. "Don't do anything rash. I'll call you when I get home."

7

FROM THE POINT OF VIEW of security, going to see Dr. Tom was never exactly a piece of cake. He was the only tenant left in a crumbling World War II–era office building on Highland; the fact that he was the only tenant didn't mean that he was the only person a visitor had to contend with. Among the people who might be congregated around the small foyer of the building were hookers and dopers, pushers, hippies, backpack bums, and, always, wild-looking kids with gang tattoos. Every time she made it past the crowd outside, Maggie felt almost afraid to ring Dr. Tom's bell, for fear she'd find him murdered, or at least beaten to a pulp. After all, in Los Angeles, people were constantly being murdered in buildings a lot safer than his building would ever be. She herself carried pepper spray when she went to her sessions; sometimes some of the kids on the steps looked as if they might try to pull her down.

Dr. Tom, as usual, was as dapper as if he had just come from a wedding. He wore a beautiful old gray flannel suit, with a blue scarf at the throat rather than a tie. When Maggie had first come to see him he often wore a tie with a diamond stickpin, but soon enough he realized that he probably would be murdered if he didn't leave the diamond stickpin at home.

When Maggie taxed him about the dangerous crowd outside, he just smiled and told her that when he first set up on Highland, in 1948, it was as safe as the lawn of heaven, an answer that didn't satisfy Maggie at all. In 1948, when Dr. Tom set up practice, most of Los Angeles was as safe as the lawn of heaven; but it wasn't anymore.

Dr. Tom insisted that Maggie lie on a couch—while she babbled, sliding along from recent problems to things that might have occurred in the remote past, Dr. Tom polished his military medals; he had a huge collection, all Russian, he claimed. Why a Sicilian psychoanalyst would collect Russian medals was just one of the mysteries about Dr. Tom. Why he would marry a female body builder was another mystery—but Maggie didn't dare ask him. Dr. Tom made it very plain that she was there to talk about herself—not about him. On his desk was a signed picture of Anna Freud. Once or twice it occurred to Maggie that Dr. Tom might not be a shrink at all—what if he were really a drug kingpin of some sort? Maybe that was why the gangs let him alone. When she felt desperate one time and asked him to prescribe her Prozac, he refused. "It will only make you constipated," Dr. Tom assured her.

"So what's worse, constipation or suicide?" she asked, one of those questions to which Dr. Tom chose not to reply. Scare tactics didn't work with him—later he shifted his ground from constipation to lowered sexual response as a reason for rejecting antidepressants. Not taking antidepressants left Maggie feeling a little left out; practically everyone she knew took either Prozac or Paxil, particularly the guys who worked in the big twenty-four-hour mix studios who lived in sealed rooms breathing other people's germs while being sunlight deprived as well.

What Maggie got into this time in her session was why the women in her family—her mother, her aunts, her three daughters, and herself—mainly liked blue-collar guys. All the time that Maggie had been a script girl she hung out with the carpenters and the grips—never with the writers. Her father had been a construction foreman; Rog became head electrician at Paramount; Kate's husband, Howie, was a crane operator, and not just a little crane either. Howie spent his days high up atop the tallest possible crane, helping build skyscrapers. Jeannie's Fred was a set carpenter at Warner or wherever Warner chose to send him; Fred was on location a good bit of the time, which suited Jeannie fine: she could have affairs galore without having to bother with too much subterfuge. Meagan's husband, Conrad, ran a forklift at a big lumberyard in Van Nuys. All three of her daughters' husbands were big, good-looking guys—the Clary women just seemed to like men with a little heft. Rog had not been tiny, and her father had been six four.

Before she knew it Maggie had spent nearly the whole hundred minutes talking about her sons-in-law; in a way it was an elaborate lead-in to the subject she really wanted to talk about, which was that her daughters had done an intervention. Near the end of the session she let that news slip out, causing Dr. Tom to put down the medal he had been polishing in order to make a note in his notebook, a small notebook covered in a strange bluish leather; she asked him once what the leather was and he said moleskin. Maggie had never seen a mole and was none too clear about what they did—what was interesting was that Dr. Tom was such a man of taste that he bought moleskin-covered notebooks.

As for forgetting the loop group when she was making plans for a trip . . . well, that was the kind of small lapse that Dr. Tom wouldn't mind discussing over dinner. Analysis, as he did it, was about something deeper, something older, events that left their mark way down in Maggie, at a depth she couldn't see, until Dr. Tom gradually prodded them out of hibernation. What amazed her was that even after nineteen years, things just kept bubbling up from deep in her past—rather like the sourdough that her father had brought to California before World War II; for years the sourdough just kept bubbling up little biscuits.

The sad thing was, though, that when her father went away to World War II—he had landed on Omaha Beach and had been almost as big a hero as Audie Murphy; he too had won a Congressional Medal of Honor—her mother, Sally Clary, let the sourdough die. Sally Clary constantly worried about her figure, which meant that she was not a big biscuit eater; she just sort of let it die, which was a big shock to her father when he finally returned from the war. Being a big hero, he was soon making good money as a construction foreman, but Maggie still had the sense that he never stopped feeling sad about his wife's neglect of the sourdough. Maggie had just the dimmest feeling that about the time the sourdough died, something was going on between her mother and Aunt Ruth's husband, Big Joe as he was called. Aunt Ruth was sickly; maybe Big Joe needed a little more sex than he could get at home and maybe Sally Clary supplied it; but it was all in the dim past, and Maggie knew she would never be able to be sure what happened or didn't happen between her mother and Big Joe Thomas, who had been exempt from the draft because of flatfeet.

Sometimes it crossed Maggie's mind that, despite her penchant for working-class guys, she had paid thousands and thousands of dollars over a space of nineteen years babbling to a Sicilian psychoanalyst who collected Russian medals and kept notes in moleskin notebooks and had a signed picture of Anna Freud on his desk. Her daughters, who charged through life like horses, thought it was a huge waste of money—and Connie thought it was a huge waste of money and also creepy besides.

Maggie blithely ignored them; she maybe didn't understand why she needed Dr. Tom so much, but that she *did* need him was not in doubt.

The minute the hundred-minute session was up, she and Dr. Tom were free to concentrate on the pleasant question of where to have dinner, a weekly occasion they both looked forward to.

"Chinese?" Dr. Tom suggested—he was always deferential and accepted Maggie's choices even if they differed from his.

"I was thinking Chinese but now I'm thinking Thai," Maggie said, and off they went, driven by Dr. Tom's driver, Sam, in a spotlessly clean if none too new Lincoln Town Car, to a little Thai place on Santa Monica Boulevard, where the food was excellent.

8

WHEN, AFTER NINETEEN YEARS of totally correct shrink-patient behavior, Maggie and Dr. Tom decided they could allow themselves the pleasure of dining together on Sunday night, she soon realized that she had begun to think of their dinners as dates. Nothing improper happened on the dates, except that they began to stay later and later in whatever restaurant they had chosen for the evening; they also tended to drink a lot while enjoying one another's company—it might be wine or sake or Thai beer or ouzo or tequila or vodka or whatever liquor went with the food. Dr. Tom had the most wonderful manners with the help at these restaurants. Maggie was quick to notice that. He never became impatient or rude, even if the order, when it arrived, was not exactly what he had specified.

Once when they were both a little tipsy Dr. Tom admitted that if he had stayed in Sicily he would have had the right to call himself a prince. He hadn't wanted to be a prince, though, so he went to London and studied with Anna Freud and became a psychoanalyst instead. It came as no surprise to Maggie that Dr. Tom could have been a prince; just the graceful way he handled his knife and fork really won her admiration. One reason they ate so much Chinese food was that watching Dr. Tom handle his silverware made her self-conscious about her own crude table manners. She even thought once or twice of going to Miss Manners's school or something, to improve her deportment. Sometimes she even felt that she might be falling in love with Dr. Tom just because of the courteous way he behaved in restaurants.

His other winning touch was that he never allowed her to walk home, not even if the restaurant was only a few blocks from her door. Always, Sam would be waiting, in neat chauffeur clothes, with his spotless Town Car, and soon she would be home.

On top of that, Dr. Tom didn't just sit in the car like a lump, he walked her right to her door and waited until he was absolutely sure that no rapist or murderer was going to jump out at her.

A long time ago a writer on *I Love Lucy* told her that it was absolutely common for patients to fall in love with their analysts. Maggie remembered that and was not upset when she realized she was beginning to have falling-in-love feelings for Dr. Tom. What she had forgotten to ask the writer was whether the analysts sometimes fell in love too. When she tried to call the writer and ask him, she discovered that the man had died. His widow hadn't exactly welcomed the call, either; obviously she thought Maggie was someone her husband had been fucking, somewhere along the line.

Of course, if Dr. Tom *had* happened to fall in love with her, Maggie would have been delighted; but, so far, it didn't seem that he was going to, though he certainly appeared to enjoy their dinners. On this occasion it was nearly one A.M. when Dr. Tom walked her to her door. He himself lived on Yucca, near the wax museum, which was not far—it wasn't the safest part of town, but then, presumably, he had a lady bodybuilder to protect him.

For about the last year Maggie had been sort of thinking about kissing Dr. Tom some Sunday night, in hopes that it might be something he'd like. Of course, kissing was unpredictable: you never knew if it was going to work until you did it. In her opinion a kiss would be a nice way to end the evening, although, of course, if it really worked, it wouldn't end the evening.

Maggie had never held to the view that the guy should be the one to make the first move; she didn't see a thing wrong with the woman doing the seducing—after all, these were modern times. Why should a woman have to wait around until some clumsy oaf made the first move? What held her back with Dr. Tom wasn't that he was old—it was that he was special. What if he played by rules she didn't understand—how would she know what the rules might be for a Sicilian man who could have been a prince? One day, maybe, she'd gamble and do it, but this was not the night—after all, she had to be up and on the road by seven, rounding up her loop groupers, and before that there was still Connie and her recent breakup with Billy to deal with. Connie, she well knew, was sitting with her cell phone in her hand, waiting for Maggie to call, which she did the minute she said good night to Dr. Tom and stepped in the door.

"IF YOU SAY ONE WORD about how beautiful his table manners are I'm going to upchuck," Connie said, in her resentful voice.

"Did I mention table manners?" Maggie asked. She knew that Connie was insanely jealous of Dr. Tom and everybody else who was close to Maggie. Nobody hated Rog—to take one example—like Connie hated Rog, and her hatred never flagged during the whole eighteen years Maggie had been with him.

"I can't believe you," Connie went on. "So you run off a beautiful twenty-four-year-old who could probably fuck all night and now you're thinking of getting it on with an eighty-year-old wop."

"Hey, none of that!" Maggie said. "Don't you call Dr. Tom a wop. It's after midnight—let's not be racists at this late hour."

Connie lived on Afton Place, the other side of Cahuenga, which wasn't very far. Like Maggie she was a true Hollywood girl. Connie would never dream of living in what she called the burbs, which in her opinion was every community between Santa Barbara and San Diego except Hollywood itself, the center of Connie's universe, just as it was of Maggie's.

Since Connie was a member of the loop group, and would have to be rounded up, like the guys, no later than seven-thirty in the morning, Maggie considered asking her to spend the night, which she did most nights anyway. Besides, a few nights at Maggie's was the traditional remedy for getting Connie over a breakup.

"Why did Billy leave?" Maggie asked, realizing even as she did it that she might be in for a long story.

In this instance, though, it proved to be quite a short story.

"He doesn't want to fuck me anymore," Connie admitted, in the meek voice she sometimes adopted when she was about to cry.

"He says we wore it out," she added. "He says I'm no longer desirable to him."

That, of course, was the very worst reason for being left by a guy.

"Sweetie, come on over," Maggie told her, relenting at once.

"I'd love to but my car won't run," Connie said.

"Billy says it needs a new fuel pump, because this one's shot," she added.

"Now, Connie—I seem to remember that Billy was a mechanic," Maggie said. "If your car needed a new fuel pump, which is an easy part to find, why didn't he just get busy and put one in for you?"

"Well, because he's a dickhead, that's why," Connie replied. "Billy Coombs is just not the kind of guy who's going to install a new fuel pump in a car belonging to a woman he no longer wants to fuck. It's as simple as that."

Maggie sighed.

"I hate men who attack a woman's self-esteem," she said. "I'll be right over to get you."

"I'll be ready," Connie said.

9

THERE WAS A LITTLE LATE-NIGHT MIST in the streets of Hollywood by the time Maggie drove over to Afton Place to pick up Connie. But the lights still shone at the Capitol Records tower, and a fairly steady stream of traffic was moving east on Cahuenga—partyers from the Valley heading home, or working folks just getting off their shifts.

Beautiful blonde Connie came waltzing out of her old condo building, sporting her Jean Seberg haircut and carrying a fashionable Prada bag she had talked a rich producer out of just before things heated up with Billy, the dickhead mechanic, who worked at a muffler shop in West Covina. There had probably never been five minutes in Connie's life when she hadn't considered herself desirable; if her many conquests stood in line, they would stretch all the way to Beverly Hills.

"I love to see the Capitol Records tower in the mist," Maggie said. "Or Hollywood in the mist, for that matter."

Connie looked as if she had things on her mind other than Hollywood landmarks such as the Capitol Records tower—after all, she had just been cruelly rejected by a stupid mechanic who didn't know a good thing when he had it in his arms.

But then a beat later Connie grew nostalgic.

"Mag, do you ever wish we could do it all over again?" Connie asked. "The cruising, I mean. Think of all the guys we caught that way. Maybe we didn't keep 'em, but by golly we caught them."

It was true. From the time the two of them were fourteen or so she and Connie had had the habit of cruising the streets of Hollywood at night, trolling for good-looking guys. As soon as they got their driver's licenses and could persuade their parents to let them have the car, they were out on the streets looking for adventure. Once they both had cars it was almost an every-night pursuit. Sometimes they would even go all the way out to Santa Monica and stroll the beach, ogling guys. Once in a while they tried downtown L.A., but downtown, for two white girls in a jalopy, was a little too scary;

generally they just cruised Hollywood Boulevard, or maybe the Sunset Strip, which wasn't even called the Sunset Strip when they first began to cruise it.

For old times' sake, probably, Maggie eased up to Hollywood Boulevard, scene of their former triumphs, even though she knew they ought to get to bed. The fact was, neither of them had ever been able to resist the call of the night. Going to bed alone was no fun for either of them: what could you do but thrash and turn until it was time to get up? But the streets of L.A. were always fun; they always held a hint of excitement. Maggie and Connie had cruised as teenagers, as young women, as young wives, as not-so-young wives, as widows, and as mature women, which is how they preferred to think of themselves now that they had both hit sixty. At sixty you were a mature woman if you were ever going to be one: and yet the late-night streets still held something of the promise they had had for them as teenagers.

"We're lucky we get to live in Hollywood," Connie commented. "No matter how many pricks you get involved with, there could always be a better guy tomorrow."

"Yeah," Maggie said, tearing up a second at the thought of how much she loved the place, although just at this particular moment in time Hollywood Boulevard was not looking its best—it was pretty scuzzy, really—too many crackheads had trashed it, up one side and down the other.

Over the years the two of them had picked up some pretty sweet guys on Hollywood Boulevard—country guys from Texas or some-where, come to Hollywood to try to be actors. But neither of them, adventurous as they were, would be so foolish as to try that today. Pick up the wrong crackhead and you'd be dead in a jiffy. The Boulevard wasn't so innocent now, and neither was the Strip. Prob-ably Melrose was the nearest place where there was a little street life that wasn't entirely murderous yet.

"I don't want to give up," Maggie said suddenly—inexplicably she found herself crying.

Connie looked annoyed—she never liked it when Maggie cried. If anyone got to cry it should be herself, Connie believed, not Maggie, who was the universal shoulder to lean on and always had been. After all, *she* hadn't been told she was no longer desirable by a stupid mechanic from West Covina.

"What do you think you've got to cry about?" she asked in her tough-love voice. "Didn't you just have dinner with a Sicilian prince?"

"I'm not really crying—it was just a splash or something," Maggie said.

"Do you think we're matrons now, Connie?" she added—the question had been on her mind ever since her operation.

The question took Connie totally aback—not for one minute had she considered herself a matron.

"Are you fucking crazy? Of course not," Connie replied in a startled voice.

"We're old enough to be matrons, though," Maggie reminded her.

"It's not about age, it's about attitude," Connie assured her, backpedaling as fast as she could from the notion that either one of them could be matrons. She noticed quite a few ratty-looking kids wandering along Hollywood Boulevard—the street was pretty riffraffy now, which had not always been the case.

"What makes you so sure we're not matrons?" Maggie wanted to know. "We've been married; we've got kids. I've even got grandkids."

"Yeah, but think about what we're doing right this minute," Connie replied. "We're in a car, cruising for guys—the same thing we've been doing since we were fourteen years old."

"We're still looking to get laid," Connie emphasized, so there could be no mistake about their unmatronly intent.

"You, maybe—I'm just sort of enjoying the mist," Maggie told her.

"I don't think you know how foxy you are," Connie said.

"It's nice of you to say that," Maggie told her, as she turned down Las Palmas.

"Hey, how long did it take you to seduce Terry, the little jerk?" Connie asked, omitting to mention that Terry had given her a call that very afternoon, ostensibly to see if there was any carpentry she needed doing—but Connie did not suppose it was really yard work he had on his mind. She had been cool with him at the time—not realizing that Billy was about to break up with her.

"Terry? About ten minutes," Maggie said.

After all, wasn't a big part of Hollywood's appeal the fact that it seemed to hold some immediate sexual promise? People who grew up there, like herself and Connie, always nourished at least the slight hope that they might be getting laid in the not too distant future. Their own midnight rambles, from age fourteen to sixty, had always sort of been about that. Even when they were married women with young children they had still managed to sneak off now and then and look for guys in the night. Hollywood just wasn't a puritanical place to grow up in, that was for sure.

"Connie, have you ever felt unavailable, except to one guy?" Maggie asked, as she was pulling up to her house.

"You mean from being married or something?"

"Not from being married—from being so in love you couldn't imagine doing it except with the guy you were in love with?"

"You mean *totally* unavailable except to just one guy?" Connie asked—it was obviously not a question she had had to think about before.

"Yep, that's what I mean," Maggie said.

"Gee, I don't think so," Connie said. "Which is not to say I haven't been pretty wrapped up with the guys I was in love with."

"But not so wrapped up that you were absolutely one hundred percent unavailable while the big affair lasted?"

Connie shook her head.

"You've got to stay just a little bit open," Connie said. "After all, there could always be somebody better.

"Do you think that makes me promiscuous?" she asked.

"Nope, I feel the same," Maggie confessed.

"I'll tell you what—I'd rather be promiscuous than be a matron," Connie told her.

"I'll second that," Maggie said.

10

MAGGIE ABSOLUTELY REFUSED to let Connie take the Prada bag with them to the mix studio.

"Are you nuts?" she asked her friend. "One of the guys would steal it and run outside and sell it to the first woman he meets, probably for about ten bucks."

Connie resisted at first—she loved her Prada bag.

"Carrying it gives me confidence, though," she explained. "Having a nice bag sort of makes me feel something might work out after all."

"Yeah, like what?" Maggie asked. She was shaving her armpits at the time; actually the fact that she still grew hair under her arms gave Maggie a little confidence. It meant her hormones were still putting out a little juice.

Certainly Connie knew better than to take an expensive handbag to a loop group session, most of the members of which had habits to support—drugs, alcohol, AIDS cocktails, you name it. Petty theft was something they would resort to in an eye blink, and a Prada handbag wasn't so petty. The one Connie sported must have cost at least six hundred dollars, a fortune to a loop grouper.

Anyway, in Maggie's opinion, Connie already looked like a million bucks—even without a handbag, she'd soon have all the male sound engineers eating out of her hand.

"Frenchwomen don't shave under their arms," Connie informed her, as they were going out the door. "They think having a little bush under there is sexy."

"Am I French? Should I care?" Maggie replied, in a snippy tone.

The last thing she wanted to discuss on a hectic workday was underarm hair.

"Why do you have to be so difficult in the mornings?" Connie asked, and then, with hardly a pause, she revealed her big secret, which was that Terry Matlock had called her the previous afternoon.

Maggie was driving, of course—the Prime Loops van, which it had taken her four years to pay off. She was hurrying down to La Brea at Fourth, where they hoped to find Jeremiah Moore waiting at the bus stop. Jeremiah was the sweetest of the loop groupers, but thanks to multiple drug habits, he was also the most likely not to show up. Maggie couldn't relax until she got to the designated bus stop and saw Jeremiah's slender form waiting for them there. It was Monday morning and the traffic was fierce, so fierce that, in her anxiety to gather up the loop groupers and get out to West Pico, where the mix studio was, she didn't immediately take in what Connie had just told her, which was that her former boyfriend had seen fit to call her best friend about carpentry. Just as Connie's little revelation registered, Maggie drew up to the bus stop, where, to her relief, Jeremiah was waiting. She wouldn't have to dig him out of any drug dens, not this morning at least.

"Hop in, Jeremiah—have a good weekend?" Maggie asked. Jeremiah was a sweet boy from Oregon who just needed to get a handle on his drug problem; he frankly confessed that he would do any drug at any time, which was honest at least.

"Oh, Maggie, I had a wonderful weekend," Jeremiah said, carefully buckling his seat belt.

"I got a ride to Arizona and did the toad poison . . . oh man, what a sweet high," Jeremiah said. He was always ready to talk about drugs, just as Connie was always ready to talk about sex.

Maggie decided to table the question of Connie and Terry—it had begun to drizzle and she had to fight her way over to National Avenue to pick up Auberon Jarvis, who was English and probably the most versatile member of the loop group. The little matter of

Connie and Terry would have to wait until a calmer moment presented itself.

"Toad poison? You took toad poison?" Connie said, recoiling in horror. For some reason Connie hated frogs—she invariably had a panic attack every time some cute little frog showed up in Maggie's swimming pool.

"Oh, sure—lots of folks in Tucson do the toad drug," Jeremiah assured her. "The upper Sonoran Desert is where the toads live, after all."

"That's the creepiest thing I ever heard of," Connie said. "Why'd you even come to work today if all you can talk about are things that give me the heebie-jeebies?"

"Will you give it a rest?" Maggie asked. "We need Jeremiah, and you know it."

Connie looked sulky—she never welcomed even the mildest reprimand; no doubt for revenge she was probably planning to go right home and jump in the bed with Terry. Maggie decided just to banish all that from her mind, which became easier to do once she pulled up in front of Auberon Jarvis's miserable smelly apartment building and saw Auberon come hobbling out on crutches, a big cast on one of his ankles.

"Oh my God, he's hurt himself—I had a premonition," Connie cried, jumping out to help Auberon. She adored Auberon, who was small, gay, and British, though as dapper as his income permitted him to be. He wore a polka dot bow tie, for example, though his black coat looked as if he'd slept in it for several years. His pants had seen better days too, something that would usually have put Connie off, but somehow she rose above her cleanliness fetish where Auberon was concerned.

Maggie was beginning to get a little nervous about the time—the drizzle wasn't helping matters, trafficwise. Now she had to zig over to Eldorado Hospital, on Olympic, to pick up Jesús, who should be just getting off his shift as night janitor; once she secured Jesús, that left only Christophe and Hugh, who lived together on Normandie

Avenue—for them it was just a straight bus ride down Normandie to Pico. Surely they could manage one simple bus ride—at least they could if their work ethic hadn't been damaged by the weekend, something that often happened with loop groupers.

Meanwhile it took Connie and Jeremiah both to load Auberon into the van—he was not very expert with his crutches yet.

"Thanks, chaps," he said, once he was in. "Took rather a tumble Friday night—fell off my balcony. Happily I only broke my foot."

Maggie was trying to decide whether to gamble on the freeway or stick to the avenues in order to pick up Jesús, the loop grouper in charge of what used to be called Mexican whoops but now were called Hispanic whoops.

"So can we assume you were drunk when you fell off your balcony?" Connie asked. Sometimes Connie's questioning could be pretty aggressive; once in a while Auberon had to get all icy and English to back her off, but today he seemed to welcome the question.

"Drunk as a lord," Auberon admitted. "Three sheets to the wind and all that."

Fortunately Maggie made six lights in a row, a rare thing for a Monday morning; fortunately, too, Jesús was waiting at the curb when Maggie pulled up behind the hospital. He looked a little glassy-eyed as usual; probably Jesús relieved the tedium of janitorial work by nipping a few uppers out of the pill room when nobody was looking. He was sort of shaking his head and mumbling, as if he might have a big high coming on, but at least he was in the van, which was what counted just at the time. Maggie knew he probably had a pocketful of stolen pills, which he would discreetly sell to Connie or Auberon or Jeremiah as the day went on; of course he wouldn't indulge in his little trades unless Maggie was in the bathroom or maybe busy with the sound engineers.

Like most loop groups, Prime Loops always hung by a thread—if there was any trouble with the law, beyond the level of a traffic ticket, there would soon be no Prime Loops—so Maggie tried to insist on a no-drugs-in-the-van policy. She was not always right on time to get the van its annual inspection; sometimes she took a month or two to get the emission levels tested, and in California there was nothing traffic cops liked better than stopping a van whose inspection sticker had expired. Maggie lived in dread of getting pulled over by a hostile cop, since almost everyone in the loop group was illegal to some degree, plus most of them had a few arrests to their credit, misdemeanors involving drugs mostly. Auberon's green card had expired about twenty years ago; Hugh and Christophe were Canadian; Jesús had no papers; and Jeremiah, sweet though he was, just looked like a druggie. A traffic cop with any savvy would haul them all in and run a check, which is why Maggie was extremely careful not to speed. She drove so slowly that Connie—who paid no attention to speed limits—invariably grew irritated and complained.

"I can walk faster than this," she claimed, when they hit the inevitable slowdown at Pico and the 405.

"You cannot, shut up!" Maggie said—it irked her that Connie could never understand the necessity for conservative driving practices.

"Dearies, dearies!" Auberon said. He hated it when Maggie and Connie got into it—sometimes his hands began to shake.

"Why should I shut up?" Connie inquired. "There's still freedom of speech in America, isn't there?" Connie always wanted the last word in any dispute.

"I wish I had some toad poison, I'd get high right now," Jeremiah said; he too was unnerved when Maggie and Connie began to bicker. The only one in the van who didn't care how much Maggie and Connie quarreled was Jesús; to him they were just two crazy gringas. Who cares what they said?

Finally, once past Barrington Avenue, the traffic began to loosen a little. Maggie's spirits improved, and they shot way up when she whipped into the parking lot of the mix studio with five minutes to spare and saw Hugh and Christophe sitting on the curb, obviously proud of themselves for having performed the enormous feat of getting themselves to work on the bus.

To encourage their competence with the mass transit system, Maggie jumped out and gave them each a big hug. They were very presentable young men, really—cute, in fact—who just happened, unfortunately, to have heroin habits.

Meanwhile Connie and Jeremiah were easing Auberon out of the van; he almost poked Connie in the eye with a crutch, prompting her to yell at him, although she basically adored him.

The big young guard at the entry desk was new—most of the guards had known Maggie for years and just waved her and her group on through. The young guard had to thumb his way through the paperwork for a while; he took his time about it, enough time that Maggie had to give Connie a look asking her to be patient with the kid, who looked pretty corn-fed and prairielike. Connie's patience with security guards was severely limited, but fortunately the young man found Prime Loops in the paperwork.

"*Death Walks in Laredo,* is that the film you're looping?" he asked.

"That's us," Maggie said, giving him her warmest smile. In Hollywood being friendly with security guards saved a lot of time—they definitely held your fate in their hands.

"Studio Four, downstairs to the left," the guard said, but impatient Connie had breezed right past him and was already at the bottom of the stairs.

11

"You know what? This sucks!" Connie said, when she discovered that the sound engineers who were going to be working with them on *Death Walks in Laredo* were all women, one of whom was much younger and at least as pretty as she was.

Meanwhile the loop groupers, having been told they were looping a Western in which there was much sudden death from guns and arrows, were wandering around singly, trying out grunts, groans, and dying gasps; they hoped to master the sound a man might make if an arrow had just thudded into his breastbone.

The only loop grouper who wasn't practicing sounds associated with violent death was Jesús, who sat in the front row, obviously high as a kite. Jesús was practicing nothing. Maggie might have been worried had she not watched Jesús come down from his high and make some excellent south-of-the-border sounds.

"Connie, it's just a job, and we were right on time thanks to my careful driving," Maggie told her.

"I thought Rocky Rosetti was mixing this picture—you told me that yourself," Connie said, spitefully.

"Rocky called in sick—so what?" Maggie informed her. Rocky Rosetti was a pushover for Connie, of course; no wonder she reacted negatively to the fact that he wasn't there to flirt with her.

"He's not sick, he's just chasing pussy," Connie complained.

Karen, the woman who was postproduction manager for the German film company that was to distribute *Death Walks in Laredo*, came over to Maggie looking a little concerned.

"Is that a Mexican kid, or is he the Indian?" she asked, nodding toward Jesús.

"Mexican," Maggie confirmed.

"Then where's our Indian?" Karen asked.

"Nobody said anything to me about needing an Indian," Maggie told her.

"Oh shit, then somebody fucked up, somewhere along the way," Karen said. "There are some Comanche war songs right at the end of the film—think any of your guys are up to doing Comanche war songs?"

"No," Maggie said—why lie? She was desperately looking through her own paperwork for this particular job—she was hoping it wasn't her fault that they were missing an Indian, which is to say a Native American. She showed Karen the fax confirming the count and there was not one word in it about needing an Indian.

Karen, a short, rather stout brunette in her forties, was beginning to look panicky. Working for punctilious Germans was no piece of cake—the absence of an Indian if Indians were in the picture was no small screwup, and Karen was a single mother of three, working her ass off on cheap miniseries, mostly for German television. Being a postproduction supervisor meant that her job was never quite done. The last thing Maggie wanted was to see a single mother lose her job, which in any case was one of the most stressful jobs in the movie business.

"Maybe we can find you an Indian by the afternoon," Maggie said, fishing in her big canvas bag, not Prada, not even Banana Republic, just a big canvas carryall purchased at Sam's Club way out on Van Nuys Boulevard—so far out, in fact, that it felt like she was driving to Arizona. Maggie had weathered hundreds of such screw-ups, for which reason she always had her laptop with her, snug in its little black padded case. As soon as it was obvious that the computer age was unavoidable, Maggie had bought herself a top-of-the-line laptop and immediately transferred her giant Rolodex onto it. Her Rolodex had more than one thousand names on it, with phone numbers, of the hundreds of loop groupers she had worked with over the years. The unfortunate aspect, so far as helping Karen find an Indian, was that loop groupers tended to be rolling stones, meaning that maybe ninety percent of the phone numbers were defunct.

Since Prime Loops had always looped a good number of Westerns, naturally Maggie had the names and addresses of a number of Indians, or at least of dark-skinned guys who could try to be Indians for an hour or two. Maybe most of them had never been east of Ventura Boulevard, but looping wasn't rocket science and standards were not too high. If she could just find a couple of guys who could try some Comanche-like yells, the job would get more or less done.

"While you look up Indians we better get started," Karen said. "The war songs come last—try to find somebody who can get here by maybe three-thirty."

The picture came up on the big mix screen and the loop groupers began to circle in front of a little dangling mike—they said their names or counted to ten so the engineers could establish correct sound levels. The enterprise got under way while Maggie sat in the corner with her laptop, patiently pulling up lists of Indians she had worked with and calling them on her cell phone.

In the first scene in the movie that was being mixed a little wagon train poking across the prairie was massacred by a roving bunch of Indians, who killed all the men and raped two or three of the women right on the spot. The men, of course, were moaning and groaning as they died, and the women screamed and grunted as they were being raped. The loop groupers circled the mike, trying out moans and groans and the sound a person might make who had just been hit with a big tomahawk.

Maggie, working her cell phone, thought the first round of moans was a little tentative—it always took the guys a while to get into the dying-moan mood. Auberon, as usual, was best, but then Auberon was a classically trained actor who had once acted at the Old Vic; he could be counted on to be in good voice from the get-go; but the other guys needed a little time to warm up. Connie, who was looping the raped women, was a little tentative too—she was doing the kind of scream she might do if she discovered a toad in her shower. Fortunately Jesús came off his high and proved to be a real trouper— he was doing gurgles and other death sounds that could be heard halfway to Tijuana.

The women sound engineers were patient enough with the guys—they knew that loop groupers couldn't necessarily summon their best moans and groans in the first scene or two.

Lanelda, the foxy engineer Connie was jealous of, stopped the picture for a minute and gave the guys a nice pep talk.

"You're doing good but I know you can do better," Lanelda said. "This movie is mostly just one massacre after another, so you don't want to moan yourselves out too soon—we don't want anybody to get hoarse or lose their voice."

While the picture was stopped Connie wandered over to Maggie, who was feeling a little discouraged. So far every single phone number she had called was no longer in service.

"What kind of hick name is Lanelda?" Connie complained.

Connie considered all female sound engineers uppity feminists, mainly because they possessed skills she didn't have—and for that matter, didn't want.

"Connie, it's just a name," Maggie said. "Try to scream louder, honey."

"What was wrong with my screaming, anyway?" Connie asked. "What if I get tortured or something? I need to be able to go up a few decibels."

Maggie didn't argue—let Karen or Lanelda deal with Connie if they thought they needed louder screaming. Right now finding an Indian who could approximate Comanche war songs was her main concern, and with so many disconnects already, prospects were not good.

Then, out of the blue, she remembered something she should have remembered immediately, which is that not long ago, Connie had had a boyfriend who considered himself an actor.

"Remember that boyfriend you had who was wearing all the turquoise?" she asked. "Wasn't he supposed to be some kind of Indian?"

"You mean Johnny Bobcat? I don't think so," Connie said. "He grew up in North Hollywood.

"The prick," she added, reminding Maggie that Johnny Bobcat had punched Connie a time or two during the course of their stormy breakup.

"But Johnny Bobcat's not a normal Anglo name," Maggie pointed out. "And he did wear a lot of turquoise. Maybe he started life on a reservation or something and moved to North Hollywood later."

"I doubt Johnny Bobcat was even his real name," Connie admitted. But then she sighed and fished her own meager address book out of her big canvas bag—hers was identical to Maggie's and had been purchased on the same expedition to Sam's Club.

Connie's address book was no rival to Maggie's—she just preserved the phone numbers of maybe the last dozen boyfriends, among whom, luckily, was Johnny Bobcat, who seemed to live in

East Whittier, or had, at least, at the time he and Connie had been a number.

Maggie immediately called the number and, by a miracle, actually got Johnny Bobcat on the line. The man was perfectly pleasant and said he would be glad to hurry over to Pico and help with the war songs—besides that, to be helpful, he offered to bring a Choctaw friend who might know something about Comanche music. Johnny Bobcat promised to be at the mix studio by three, in case the war songs came up a little early.

Maggie told Karen that luckily she had been able to contact two Indians who had done a little acting who would come and try to belt out the war songs. Karen, of course, was overjoyed, so overjoyed that she gave Maggie a big hug.

"I knew you'd save my ass," Karen said. "The great thing about you is that you're just so dogged. You just keep on trying no matter how bleak the prospect."

Karen's compliment, though well intended, threw Maggie into one of her little despondencies. Was dogged really what was left for her to be? Dogged Maggie Clary, the boss of Prime Loops. How many dogged sixty-year-olds like herself were perched with her on the lowest rung of the movie industry's ladder? She wanted to think of herself as graceful, appealing, foxy—anything but matronly and anything but dogged. The feelings Karen had unwittingly released got Maggie down to the point where she had to retreat to the bathroom to get a grip on herself.

She didn't cry, though; this was one of the dry depressions that had become all too common since her hysterectomy. It was weird that a single word could upset her so, but it had. She even retreated into one of the stalls in her effort to get a grip on herself.

Before she could draw any conclusions about her sudden sinking spell, who should come barreling in but Connie, who seldom allowed Maggie to mope for long.

"Come out, I know you're here, Maggie," Connie said. "There are big troubles on the mix floor."

"Is it Auberon?" Maggie asked, still hiding.

"How'd you ever guess?" Connie asked.

"Because it's always Auberon—who'd he bite this time?"

"Christophe," Connie informed her.

"But he bit Christophe last time—you mean he bit him *again?*"

"Yep," Connie said. "And he broke the skin too."

12

"YOU KNOW WHAT'S WRONG with you, you fucking little faggot?" Christophe was saying to Auberon when Maggie hurried over. "You've looped so many stupid Dracula movies that you think it's normal to bite people."

"I only bite Canadians, and then only when they're intolerably rude," Auberon said, in his iciest British voice. "You shoved me away from the mike just when I was doing my best groan. You deserved to be bitten."

The women in the engineers' booth stopped the picture and waited for this not particularly unusual conflict to play itself out. They were already on the third reel and thought they could allow a short break while the quarrel was being resolved.

"Auberon, just don't *bite!* How many times do I have to tell you that?" Maggie asked. Fortunately Christophe, who was twice the size of Auberon and could easily have cleaned his clock, stood on his dignity and walked away. Maggie followed and made him let her examine the bite, which was only a small dent on his hand. Connie, as usual, had exaggerated. It hadn't broken the skin.

"I should sue the little fucker—what if I get rabies or hep C or who knows what the little jerk might have?" Christophe told her.

"Christophe, I know it was his fault, but please don't sue," Maggie said. "If we start suing one another, Prime Loops is done for. Auberon has some bad habits but I doubt he's got rabies—anyway, it didn't break the skin."

Then she went over and had a little tête-à-tête with Jeremiah, explaining that she wanted him to be behind Auberon in the loop line, because Jeremiah was the calmest member of the group and would not be likely to provoke Auberon into one of his biting fits.

"I'll tell him that if he bites me he'll get hep C—that ought to back him off," Jeremiah said.

"Honey, do you have hep C?" Maggie asked, stricken.

"They think I do but they haven't done a liver biopsy yet, so maybe I don't," Jeremiah said. At that point the women in the booth decided that the break was over; the picture started running again and Jeremiah—he had the sweetest smile—hurried over and got in line behind Auberon, a man Maggie intended to have a stern talk with when the opportunity arose.

In fact Maggie was so shaken by the prospect that Jeremiah might have hep C that she abrogated her responsibilities for a while; she flopped in a seat and let the looping go on without her. Generally, low-grade though the work might be, she kept a close eye, or maybe it was a close ear, on the looping—after all, Prime Loops provided her with a livelihood of sorts; if she felt one of the guys was getting lazy, not putting enough timbre into his groans or whatever, she would nudge him a little, maybe make him do a scene over. But for a time, Jeremiah's problem was all she could think about.

"Why wouldn't he have it? Most addicts have it," Connie reminded her.

Of course, that was true, but Maggie, at the moment, was at such a low ebb that she could not think rationally.

"What is the matter with you?" Connie asked.

Maggie, wearing a kind of lost expression, just shook her head.

What she felt like doing was leaving the mix studio, leaving the loop group, leaving the van, leaving Connie and her daughters and Dr. Tom, leaving everyone she knew. She wanted to wander off into America, or maybe just some far, remote part of L.A. where she didn't know a single soul.

"It's too much, I'd like to go," she said.

Connie's eyes suddenly grew wide and fearful.

"Are you having one of your bad spells?" she asked.

Maggie didn't answer—she had no answer.

"Mag, you have got to snap out of it," Connie said, a panicky look in her eyes.

"I know, but what if I can't?" Maggie asked.

13

BY THE TIME THE LUNCH BREAK was upon them the whole loop group was in a panic about Maggie—Karen, Lanelda, and Cherry, in the mix booth, were feeling anxious as well. In a long day of mixing and looping, anyone might sag—anyone, that is, except Maggie Clary. Through all the silliness of looping—the moans and groans and dying gasps—Maggie had somehow always managed to remain attentive, quick with a suggestion or a criticism—not always of the loopers; after all, engineers could make mistakes too.

But now there was a different Maggie, sitting alone in a front row seat; she made no suggestions and hardly seemed to be looking at the picture, which in a way was understandable—*Death Walks in Laredo* was admittedly not Oscar level stuff—but then if loop groups sat around waiting for Oscar level pictures, every loop grouper in L.A. would starve. The fact that the picture was not particularly watchable didn't explain what was happening with Maggie Clary.

"Maybe she had a little stroke—she's kind of that age," Lanelda said to Karen.

"Don't you even think in those terms," Karen said. "We're gonna need her at full strength when those Indians get here. I don't want to sound prejudiced against Native Americans or anything, but in my experience they can be difficult."

"Karen, everybody can be difficult," Lanelda said. "You should see me on a bad day when my period's about to start."

Karen left the booth and went over to talk to Connie and the guys, all of whom had become very subdued.

"What do you think, Connie?" she asked. "How big a crisis is this?"

"Let's let Auberon try to talk to her," Connie suggested. "He's educated."

"No, dear—I'm *not* educated," Auberon admitted. "But I *am* an actor, remember? I can *act* educated—it's mostly the voice," he said. "Whether it will fool our Maggie is anybody's guess."

Christophe had forgotten his animus against Auberon in his anxiety about Maggie.

"You're nominated—you must try, mate," he said, giving Auberon a scared look.

"All right—I'll try to get her interested in a shrimp taco or something," Auberon said. He skipped briskly through the seats until he came to Maggie. He thought a show of jauntiness might rub off—at least he could try.

"It's lunchtime, dearie," he said. "We're going to that little Mexican shack around the corner. Want to come? After all, it was your discovery."

"I'm trying to lose weight—I think I'll skip lunch," Maggie said.

"Can't I at least bring you a shrimp taco?" Auberon asked. "We've got a long afternoon ahead of us."

Maggie favored Auberon with some direct eye contact. Far from being jaunty, he looked nervous and scared. He was hoping she'd hop up and be her old cheerful self—probably everybody in the mix studio nursed the same hope. What would happen to all of them if Maggie Clary suddenly went under? And it was mainly her fault that they were worried. She had been the caregiver too long, to all of them. It wasn't just light care she gave, either—it involved two A.M. trips to the emergency rooms in Hollywood and elsewhere.

But suddenly life had taken an unexpected turn—the caregiver needed care—and not a single person in the building, all of them adults, had any idea what to do in such an unheard-of situation. They wanted her to snap out of it and keep on giving care.

For almost the first time, Maggie found that she resented their collective need. *She* was the needy one now, and the best Auberon Jarvis could come up with was the offer of a shrimp taco, which was an insult. She had lost her womb, she would never be her real self again. Fuck a shrimp taco!

"I know you mean well but just go away, Auberon," Maggie said. Then she put her head in her hands. She wasn't crying but she definitely felt herself to be at a turning point. She wanted to give up, let go, sink. She wanted to stop managing the loop group, stop paying her bills; soon enough they'd turn the water off, then the electricity. The house on Las Palmas was paid for: they couldn't evict her, but maybe she'd evict herself, just put a few belongings in her big canvas bag from Sam's Club in Van Nuys and wander off and give herself up to the streets—sleep in doorways or parks, whatever.

It seemed like such a sweet solution—she'd been responsible, indeed overresponsible, all her life; now it was time to let responsibility slide away, like the outgoing tide. Maybe it would even be better for the others—Connie, the loop groupers, her daughters—if she just quietly checked out. Maybe they'd learn to stand on their own two feet.

In her heart of hearts she didn't really believe it would work that way. She had no worries about her daughters—they had good jobs and good enough husbands, and they'd survive—but her loop groupers were a different matter. Some of them would perish. Of course, some of them might perish even with her help.

In the darkness, with her head in her hands, Maggie found that the most irritating part of her dilemma was that *she couldn't stop thinking about other people!* She didn't know how to think just about herself, although it was time she learned to do that. She'd given enough care—if she had any left, why couldn't she be allowed to just give it to herself?

But then, still hidden in the tense, silent mix room, Maggie turned a little inside herself. What had, for a few minutes, felt tragic began to seem just sort of silly. Her father, Andy Clary, was a Congressional Medal of Honor winner—he had saved his whole outfit on Omaha Beach. Pride in her father was one thing she had always been able to draw on, every minute of her life. Even just remembering her father as he had been during his years in construction made her feel ashamed of her own present behavior. After all, her dad's home life hadn't been perfect, her mother had let the sourdough die and probably had a few adulteries to boot; besides the Congressional Medal her father had two Purple Hearts from having been wounded twice in a terrible war, whereas she had only had a little operation in an excellent hospital, Cedars-Sinai. So now she considered herself so damaged that she couldn't even manage one little loop group? It was pathetic. What was wrong with her? She took her head out of her hands and stood up.

"Come on, folks—let's go check out the burritos de jour," she said, as if nothing at all had happened.

For some reason every person in the mix room immediately cheered, even Cherry, an engineer whom Maggie had never laid eyes on before that day. Lanelda cheered, Karen cheered, Hugh and Christophe cheered, even Jesús cheered, though he wasn't quite sure why. After cheering, Connie and Auberon burst into tears, and Jeremiah Moore gave Maggie his sweetest, sweetest smile.

At the burrito shack everyone sort of laughed too loud. Maggie chatted with Señora Miguela, the old, heavy woman who ran the burrito stand—two of her sons were in prison for life; it was clear that Señora Miguela had not had an easy old age; but she paid attention to her cooking; her nice hot shrimp tacos were really first rate.

The best part of the afternoon was that Johnny Bobcat and his friend the Choctaw, a little barrel-shaped man with friendly eyes, turned out to be really polite. Both of them wore enormous belt buckles they had won riding bulls at various rodeos.

When Karen asked them how much they knew about Comanche music they just sort of shrugged and vowed to do their best. Johnny Bobcat certainly kept his distance from Connie; he never so much as made eye contact with her the whole afternoon. Maggie could tell that this hurt Connie's feelings—no woman liked to be totally ignored by an old boyfriend, but that was Connie's fate on this particular afternoon.

When the last reel of the movie was running and a whole bunch of Comanches came charging down a hill, Johnny Bobcat and his partner stepped up to the mike and whooped and ya-ya-yahed for all they were worth. At times they came pretty close to yodeling, but then they did some wah-wahing and Karen sort of relaxed—to her it did sound somewhat like how real Comanche war songs might have sounded. Still, Native American stuff was dicey.

"I hope I don't get fired—I hope I don't get fired," Karen said, when the long loop day finally ended.

On the way home the loop groupers all seemed a little subdued— they realized there had been a close call of some sort with Maggie that day. For once none of them even asked for a little advance on their pay, to meet an unexpected bill or something; maybe they were all silently facing the fact that Maggie might not be there to look after them forever. The rush hour traffic going east on Pico was really terrible but the I-10 freeway looked even worse: according to the radio an eighteen-wheeler had flipped at one of the interchanges downtown, an accident that could easily put the whole L.A. system into gridlock. What that meant for the Prime Loops team was that they had a little time to think about their lives, and all of them drew the same conclusion, which was that Maggie was a little shaky at the time; probably she needed a little cooperation, which meant not buzzing her for extra money at this delicate stage of life.

As she let each of the men out she reminded them that she'd be by a half hour early tomorrow morning: they were looping a jungle movie involving the Amazon, and there was no telling what traffic challenges they might face getting to the mix studio, which was in Burbank.

The minute Maggie left Jeremiah Moore off at the La Brea and Fourth drop spot, Connie began to complain about the heartless behavior of Johnny Bobcat, the former lover who for some reason had refused all afternoon even to look her in the eye. Maggie had sort of developed the suspicion that big complaints about Johnny were likely to get vented once the guys in the loop group were safely out of hearing.

"He's no more an Indian than I am, the arrogant son of a bitch," Connie said. "If I'd had anything to kill him with, I'd have killed him on the spot."

"That seems a little extreme," Maggie told her. "You're just bitter because he wouldn't look at you. I don't think it means he's not an Indian—how can you be so sure about a thing like that?"

"Because I sucked his cock and it was white," Connie said.

"Forget it, I'm sorry I asked," Maggie said.

14

THE NEXT MORNING Maggie got on her computer real early and did something a little extravagant. She got catalogues from hundreds of retailers—probably everyone in America got pretty much the same catalogues—and one of the retailers was the famous L.L. Bean company of Maine, a company that seemed to emphasize clothes and equipment for outdoorsy people, the kind of people who went about in the wilderness a lot.

Maggie herself had never been the least outdoorsy—it was her daughters who were outdoorsy; they were constantly going skiing or backpacking or hiking or just generally camping out with their families. Even Jeannie took time off from having affairs to go canoeing on Big Bear Lake, the scenic lake not far from where Jeannie's grandparents, Andy and Sally Clary, had been killed in the head-on with the truck.

Maggie had always taken the view that she didn't want to miss her TV shows just to get bitten by a mosquito or something worse—bears, maybe. She considered it fortunate that her daughters had all found husbands as outdoorsy as they were; she herself resolutely continued to fight off efforts to involve her in family camping trips—a picnic in Griffith Park with the grandkids once every year or so was about as much nature as she proposed to accept.

This morning, though, while Connie—still a little raw from her breakup with Billy—slept, Maggie got out the L.L. Bean catalogue and ordered a tent and a sleeping bag to be delivered the next day. The extravagant aspect of the order was that she paid for next-day delivery. Usually paying extra for overnight delivery would not have been Maggie's way; but this morning she felt an overwhelming urge to equip herself with a tent and a sleeping bag immediately, in case she developed a wild urge to hit the road and ended up in a place where all the motels were full.

The one problem with the overnight delivery was that Prime Loops was booked into a mix lab on Sunset to loop a gladiator movie of some kind. If she had the tent and the sleeping bag delivered to the mix studio it would excite suspicion; but if she directed that it be left on her front porch, both items would undoubtedly be stolen long before she got home: some crackhead would get them, or maybe a gang member.

Maggie didn't really want anyone to know about the tent and the sleeping bag, but on the other hand, she wanted them delivered ASAP, in case she cracked up or something and had to leave town in a big hurry.

The obvious solution, of course, was to ask Gwen, her next-door neighbor, if she would mind receiving a delivery from Maine. Gwen, a redhead, was a retired actress of indeterminate age who had worked mainly in the soaps; once she got too old to be in the soaps she made ends meet by giving square dance lessons at some big hillbilly nightclub in the valley. Gwen was from Idaho and had evidently done a lot of square dancing in her youth. Fortunately for Maggie, Gwen was an early riser—Maggie, barefoot and in her pajamas, quickly sneaked down the sidewalk and knocked on Gwen's door. She hoped to make her request and get home before Connie woke up. If there was one thing she hoped to avoid it was trying to explain to Connie why she needed a tent and a sleeping bag.

Gwen was pretty paranoid about the threat from gangs; she had bars on every window and at least five locks on her door.

"It's me, Gwen—Maggie!" Maggie said, in a pretty loud voice.

"Who?" Gwen asked through the thick door with the five locks.

"Maggie, your next-door neighbor!" Maggie said, hoping not to have to yell so loudly that she woke up Connie.

Gwen must have believed her because the five locks began to click. The door opened and there was Gwen, holding her keys in one hand and her false teeth in the other hand. She gave Maggie a big hug anyway—Gwen had always been an outgoing person, an aspect that was probably important in a square dance teacher.

"I just want to ask a little favor, Gwen," Maggie said. "I'm having something delivered tomorrow and I'll be at work when it comes. Would you mind if I had them deliver it here?"

"Where's it coming from?" Gwen asked, obviously a little surprised by the request.

Maggie didn't think where it was coming from was particularly relevant, but she didn't suppose the truth would hurt.

"Maine," she said.

"Maine?" Gwen said. "Maine? Why that's to hell and gone. I thought they mostly had moose in Maine. You didn't order a moose, did you?"

"It's not a moose," Maggie admitted.

"Must be snowshoes, then—you never know when you might need snowshoes out here in snowy Hollywood," Gwen said, and cackled at her own wit.

"Sure, she added. "Have 'em deliver the snowshoes or whatever it is here. I'll handle it for you."

"Thanks, Gwen," Maggie said. "I'll pick it up tomorrow after work."

By a miracle she got home just as Connie was waking up.

15

THE THREE DAUGHTERS of Maggie Clary decided to have a conference call by cell phone in order to decide what their next move ought to be vis-à-vis their mother.

"We blew it when we ganged up on her last Sunday," Jeannie said. She was on the porch of her home, getting ready to pick up her daughter Khristin at soccer practice.

"We know that, Jeannie," Kate said, a little impatiently. Kate was at the marina in Marina del Rey, having a vodka martini in the bar while her husband, Howie, looked at a new boat he was thinking of buying. Howie couldn't bear to ride in the same boat more than about three years.

"I think Jeannie should be the one to go this time," Meagan said. She was jammed up in traffic downtown and needed to get back to Echo Park and get dinner started; her husband ate like a horse and her four kids ate like four horses—Meagan's tentative plan was to make a vast pot of pasta and hope for the best.

"If you're thinking of this weekend you have to count me out," Jeannie informed them.

"Why?" Kate wanted to know—fed up with Jeannie's uncooperative ways, she gestured to the bartender to bring her another vodka martini.

"Because Fred's going to Arizona to bow hunt and I've made plans of my own," Jeannie informed them.

"At least we know what comes first with you, Jeannie," Meagan said. "Your sex life comes first."

"Why shouldn't it?" Jeannie asked—she had no intention of backing down on that score.

There was silence for a minute. Neither Kate nor Meagan had expected Jeannie to be quite so brazen.

"You go, Meagan," Jeannie suggested. "You're her baby—she'll listen to you."

"I could go, but what am I supposed to say?" Meagan asked. "She hasn't actually done anything harmful to herself, exactly."

"Follow your instincts," Kate suggested—she saw Howie and the boat salesman walking back from the far end of the marina, which probably meant they were about to become the owners of a brand-new sloop or cabin cruiser, or whatever kind of boat tickled Howie's fancy. Fortunately, high crane operators made good money, so they could afford it.

"Howie's coming—I'm getting off," Kate said. "Call me once you've seen Mom, Meagan."

"I'll go Sunday but I can't say I'm looking forward to it," Meagan admitted.

"I think we hit her too early last Sunday," Jeannie said. "That stuff about bringing in the paper was stupid. It ticked her off."

"Who can blame her?" Meagan asked. "Sometimes we don't bring in our Sunday paper at all—it just lays there till Wednesday and goes directly into the recycling bin."

"That's irresponsible," Jeannie told her. "You're a citizen—you need to know what's going on in your own city."

Jeannie was the activist of the family—she averaged maybe two protests a week. After fucking, protesting was her next favorite thing.

"Hey, I'm not you," Meagan reminded her. "I don't need to always be getting stirred up about some downtrodden ethnic group or other. As long as they leave the Armenians alone, I can live with the other injustices."

"Why spare the Armenians, may I ask?" Jeannie inquired.

"Because they make the best garlic chicken," Meagan informed her. "My kids would leave home if they couldn't have their Armenian garlic chicken a couple of times a week."

Meagan had just about eased through the big downtown traffic gulch; now her ear was beginning to feel hot from having a cell phone jammed up against it for so long.

"I'm getting off," she said. "I'll see what I can do about Mom. Since you're obviously not going to want to be disturbed during your all-day fuck fest, why don't you call me when you've wrung your boyfriend out?"

"You sound jealous," Jeannie said.

Meagan had to ponder that one. She and her husband, Conrad, did seem to be in a kind of lull in the sex department. It wasn't a total lull; once in a while they did it in a kind of married sort of way—no heights of passion but not total starvation on the sex score, either.

Since Meagan had been married to Conrad seventeen years, the occasional slowdown had to be expected. She had managed to have a boyfriend or two along the way, and she had the sense that Conrad might have managed a girlfriend or two, probably one of the secretaries who worked at the lumberyard. The problem with lovers, from Meagan's point of view, was all the *managing* it took just to go to bed with somebody new for an hour maybe. Her sister Jeannie was a genius when it came to strategies of concealment; old Fred, her husband, was far too slow to catch her, if he even wanted to catch her. Fred seemed to favor his belly rather than his dick: as long as Jeannie kept putting huge meals in front of him, Fred was unlikely to make trouble. Jeannie sort of sedated him with food and kept having lovers.

Meagan, being the youngest, was naturally competitive with her sisters. But she also had four kids, and her sisters just two each. Organizing the after-school lives of four active youngsters took up pretty much all the time that Meagan might have spent having lovers. What with soccer practice, Little League, karate, gymnastics, drama, ballet, and pottery classes, where was the time for boyfriends?

Of course, just at the moment it was summer—all the kids were scheduled into various day camps; Meagan realized she could be looking around. There was a guy or two who had definitely shown some interest—the manager of the big car wash on Ventura for one. But whatever the eventual possibilities, all she wanted was to get home and get the cauldron of pasta started, before everyone raised a clamor. Nobody in her family was the least reluctant to raise a clamor, either, if they felt she wasn't performing as she was supposed to in the wife-and-mother department.

Meagan didn't consider that she was complaining, exactly—after all, she *was* a wife and mother. It was what she had chosen to be, so why complain? It was mainly just jealousy of Jeannie, who always seemed to manage to get more of what she wanted than anybody else.

16

MEAGAN SPENT MOST of Sunday morning wavering. Should she call her mother and mention that she might be dropping by a little later in the day? The worry was that if she called ahead, her mother might take umbrage and scuttle off to a movie somewhere, or even the beach; probably she *would* do that if she was not particularly in the mood to discuss her state—Meagan could well understand how discussions of that sort could become tiresome.

Still, she had promised her sisters that she would at least check on their mother—it might be that she was sinking or something, in which case action would have to be taken.

To postpone the decision, not to mention the visit, Meagan took her kids to the Armenian carryout down on Sunset, where they stocked up on garlic chicken. She got home just in time to see Conrad head off to the archery range in North Hollywood—like Howie, he was becoming obsessed with bow hunting.

Fortunately their daughter, Clarice, sixteen, was at home—she could be trusted to bash the three younger children into submission if they became unruly. Clarice was merciless when it came to disciplining her three younger brothers. Also, she knew how to call an ambulance and which emergency room to head for if blood flowed or something.

When Meagan pulled into her mother's driveway on Las Palmas she immediately felt a little disquieted, though she couldn't have said why. The house just looked sort of closed up or something. What if her mother had run off? Of course, that was a silly fear, because the Prime Loops van was sitting right there at the curb. Maggie never parked the van in the driveway because she was not a very good backer and had once backed into a passing cement truck.

It was only a fender bender—the truck was going real slow—but the mere fact that she had backed into a cement truck destroyed Maggie's confidence in her ability to back out of her own driveway; and the best solution to that problem was just to park at the curb.

Meagan tried the front door, which was locked. She rang the doorbell and waited—the doorbell was tempermental and only worked about half the time. Standing on the porch of her childhood home, Meagan continued to have a vague, bad feeling—totally irrational, as far as she knew, but so strong that she immediately dug out her cell phone and called Kate; but Kate was playing softball in Santa Monica, leaving Meagan the option of speaking to her voice mail, which she declined to do.

Then it occurred to her that her mother might just be in the backyard, dipping leaves out of the tiny swimming pool. The gate that led to the backyard was usually locked, but this time it wasn't— any passing rapist or gang member could have walked right in. Meagan had just begun to prepare a little lecture about how important it was to keep that crucial gate locked, but before she could deliver her lecture she saw a sight that stopped her in her tracks. Maggie Clary, who had never been known to go on the simplest camping trip—not even a simple overnight—was sitting on a sleeping bag in front of a small tent, sipping tea. She had brought the tiny TV from her bedroom and plugged it into the outlet where she usually plugged in the big pool vacuum that she used to suck bad stuff off the bottom of the pool. The TV was off, though—when Maggie looked up and saw Meagan, her face brightened at once.

"Hi, honey—can I get you some tea?" Maggie asked. "I'm having Red Zinger but you can have something different if you'd rather."

"Herbal would be good," Meagan said, struggling to absorb what she was seeing. The *L.A. Times* was in a big heap on the lawn, so her mother was reading the paper at least, and in a timely fashion.

"Mom, why is there a tent in the backyard?" Meagan asked, as she accepted a cup of tea.

"Isn't it nice? It's from L.L. Bean," Maggie told her.

"It's a cute tent, but why is it in the backyard of your home?" Meagan asked—she was not to be deflected.

"Oh, because I'm living in it for the time being—I have a great sleeping bag too," Maggie told her.

"I don't think I believe what I'm seeing," Meagan said. "Maggie Clary, the anticamper, is living in a tent in her own backyard?"

"Sure, why not? People change," Maggie reminded her.

"Nobody's going to believe this, you know," Meagan informed her. "Kate and Jeannie are going to fuckin' freak out. How long has this state of affairs been going on?"

"Since last Wednesday—that's the day the tent came," Maggie said.

Meagan was feeling pretty manic, but she tried hard to just be calm and patient and not fly off the handle. She took some deep breaths, in hopes of avoiding hyperventilation.

"Mom, I just don't know what to say," Meagan admitted. "The last thing I expected to find when I came over here was you living in a tent in your own backyard, where any wayward gang member could prance in and murder you at any time."

"Personally I think all this gang stuff is being overhyped," Maggie said. "I walk around Hollywood a lot and I've never been threatened by a gang member.

"Now, crackheads and panhandlers are a different story, I admit," Maggie went on. "I give crackheads a wide berth."

"I'm not going to argue with you about the gangs," Meagan said. "I'm too freaked out to get into *that*. In fact I'm too freaked out to think straight. I never thought I'd come over here and find you living in a tent beside your pool."

"But don't you think my tent is the perfect size?" Maggie asked. "It just fits perfectly between the pool and our fig tree."

"It may well be the perfect tent," Meagan admitted, "but that doesn't explain why you've suddenly started living in it.

"Why, Mother—why?" she asked again.

Maggie sighed. Her daughters were not the sort of girls to let change happen quietly—much less mysteriously. For them there had to be answers—and the kind of answers that would make sense to sensible women who married working-class guys.

"I couldn't live in the house anymore—it's that simple," Maggie pointed out. "I couldn't live in the house anymore, and what's more, I never want to live in it again."

"Oh, boy—oh boy!" Meagan said.

17

ONE THING MEAGAN had to admit was that her mother was looking better than she had been looking recently. Despite no longer wanting to live in the house where she had lived the whole six decades of her life, Maggie looked good. She was a petite woman, never had a weight problem in her life, had good legs still, trim ankles, and she had had her hair cut shorter than usual—it was definitely an appealing haircut.

"Is Shirley still cutting your hair? I'm glad she got rid of the bangs," Meagan asked.

"Nope—I got tired of Shirley," Maggie told her. "I went to that salon on Melrose Place."

"Mom, that place where all the movie stars go?" Meagan asked. "That place must cost an arm and a leg. Jeannie won't even get pedicures there, it's so expensive."

Maggie shrugged. "It's just a beauty parlor," she said. "Maybe I felt like splurging, for once."

"It's a great haircut—it makes you look foxy," Meagan said. "Now you'll have a million guys hitting on you, but it still doesn't explain why you don't want to live in your house anymore."

"If you ever have a hysterectomy, God forbid, you'll understand it," Maggie suggested. "The house was where I lived when I was the other Maggie. The house belonged to her and she belonged to the house.

"But I'm not that Maggie, anymore," she said. "Now when I'm

inside I feel like a trespasser in somebody else's house—didn't like the feeling, so I moved out into my tent."

Just then Connie stepped out the backdoor in her cotton pajamas.

"Why's Connie here?" Meagan asked, surprised.

"Her ex-boyfriend Billy, the one who dumped her, decided he made a mistake, so now he's stalking her," Maggie explained. "I told her she could stay here until he gives up, which could be anytime."

"Hi, Meagan," Connie said, waving. Mother and daughter seemed to be having a serious conversation and she had no intention of interfering.

"Can I have some of the paper? I want to see if there are any good sales," Connie asked.

"You can have all of the paper—want some tea?" Maggie asked.

"You're a tea person, I'm a coffee person," Connie reminded her. She scooped up a big armful of the *L.A. Times* and strolled back into the house.

"Actually it might be good if you and Connie lived together," Meagan reflected. "You could share expenses and you wouldn't both be so dependent on dubious guys."

Maggie had had the same thought—she and Connie had even discussed it—but so far Connie was just sort of an off-again, on-again roommate—she always had been, really.

"We've talked about it," she confessed. "Sometimes we get on one another's nerves, and sometimes we get along fine."

But Meagan was only half listening. Mainly she was wondering if Jeannie had finished her fuck fest or not—she really wanted to talk to one of her sisters, and Kate didn't seem like a good option. Usually after a softball game she went to a bar with about a dozen of her teammates and drank a lot of beer, as a means of winding down.

"Meagan, please don't worry about me so much—and tell your sisters not to either," Maggie said. "I'm not suicidal. I'm just pursuing a slightly different life path, one that's more suitable to who I feel I am now."

"Hard not to worry a little," Meagan told her. "Today you're living in a tent in your backyard—what'll it be tomorrow?"

"I haven't really made any plans yet but I've been thinking of going on a trip," Maggie said.

"You? A trip? A trip to where, may I ask?"

"That's what I have to figure out," Maggie admitted. "Right now I'm just thinking of it as sort of a trip to America. Maybe I'll go see the Mississippi River or something."

"The Mississippi River? Why?" Meagan asked.

Maggie didn't really know—it had just popped out as a possible destination.

"Maybe because I liked *Show Boat* so much," Maggie told her.

"Knock me over with a feather," Meagan said. "So what happens to your loop group while you go boating on Old Man River?"

"That's the part I haven't figured out," Maggie confessed.

In fact, for the last few days, the fate of the loop group had been constantly on her mind.

"Dr. Tom said that I have a need to create dependencies," Maggie mentioned.

"That may be the smartest thing Dr. Tom has ever told you," Meagan said. "You do create dependencies. Even your shrink's dependent on you—you're his regular Sunday night date."

"I guess, but for the longest time we didn't date at all," Maggie reminded her.

"Date? You're dating him? That old man?"

"I like to think of it that way," Maggie said. "Everybody likes to think there's a little romance left in them, I guess."

"Oh, boy . . . oh boy," Meagan said, again.

"But nothing's happened," Maggie said. "For all I know I'm barking up the wrong tree."

"I have a feeling something will happen—because you'll make it happen," Meagan told her. "If Terry wasn't romance enough for you, what do you expect from this old man?"

"Oh, Terry wasn't a romance, honey," Maggie said. "Terry was something else."

"Maybe it's good that you're thinking of going someplace," Meagan allowed. "After all, what has been worrying us all so much was that you didn't seem to want to do *anything*."

"I do, though," Maggie said. "I'm only sixty. I don't want it all to be over so soon—it's just that right now I haven't felt much like myself."

"Here's my advice," Meagan said. "Forget the loop group and take your trip. Say adios and go. How long do you think you'll be gone?"

"Forever's a possibility," Maggie told her—but the minute she said it, she knew she didn't mean it. Her stay away from Hollywood forever? Not likely.

"You know the movie business," she told her daughter. "There's no shortage of loop groups. All those producers who call me now will forget in a week once I leave.

"Once I drop the ball it'll stay dropped," she added.

"Oh boy, do I ever wish my sisters were here," Meagan said.

18

"ANOTHER THING I MIGHT DO on my trip is visit Aunt Cooney—she's my last living aunt," Maggie told Meagan. "She was the only member of her family that Momma seemed to like."

She had decided to table the question of the loop group for a minute. It was her choice, and sooner or later she'd make it.

Meagan had allowed herself to drift into a harmless little fantasy in which she was a girl again. Her sisters had been picking on her; she was the littlest. Jeannie had stolen her favorite teddy bear and drowned it in the pool, a heartless act. Meagan was sobbing and her mother was holding her tight and explaining that teddy bears were immortal—hers wasn't really drowned: they'd dry him with a hair dryer and he'd be as good as new. Her mom even made cocoa—and she smelled good too.

It was just a little fantasy Meagan sometimes permitted herself. It grew out of the fact that she had been the baby, the youngest girl, and jealous Jeannie would not stop picking on her. Given the chance, she would probably have tried to drown Meagan in the pool, not just her teddy.

"But Grandma's been dead a long time," Meagan pointed out. "Aunt Cooney must be really old."

"Eighty-six, but she doesn't sound it," Maggie said. "I called her on her birthday. She was quite a bit younger than your granny."

"Where does she live?"

"In Texas, in a place called Electric City—she says there's a dam nearby that makes electricity," Maggie told her.

Meagan vaguely remembered that Aunt Cooney had visited when she was about seven. She remembered a tall stringy woman with peroxided hair who took them to the Santa Monica Pier but then refused to let them eat hot dogs—she explained that hot dogs were made from very bad parts of a cow, parts that nobody should be ingesting into their bodies. That had been a letdown—why go all the way to the Santa Monica Pier if you weren't allowed to eat hot dogs? Instead they got cotton candy and got all sticky and behaved badly on the way home. Aunt Cooney threatened to slap Kate if she didn't quiet down, but nothing came of the threat.

"So, Mom, when do you plan to start on your big trip to the Mississippi River?" Meagan asked.

"Prime Loops is booked for the next ten days, so it would have to be sometime after that," Maggie said. "I think I can get most of the guys jobs with other loop groups if I make a few calls. Lavish Loops is usually shorthanded, and Bud Stone is an old friend of mine.

"Jesús may be a problem," she added. "I doubt I can get anyone to take Jesús.

"I may take Connie with me," she suddenly blurted out—she was aware that her daughters were a little ambivalent about Connie.

"After all, she's my best friend," Maggie added. "She's even offered to split the gas."

"Oh, boy—*Thelma and Louise II*," Meagan said.

"She's been my best friend since the sixth grade," Maggie reminded her daughter. "Our lives are just sort of intertwined.

"It'll be fun," she added, sort of tentatively, when Meagan didn't say anything. Or course, she wanted her daughters to know that she knew they loved her and wanted her to be all right.

"You've got a big family to look after, honey," she reminded Meagan. "I'll be fine on my trip, if I go. I'll be fine."

"Okay, Mom," Meagan said, after a long hug. "I guess I just never knew that you liked *Show Boat* that much."

Driving home, Meagan waited too long at a green light—she was thinking about it all—and of course immediately got honked at. In L.A. nobody was willing to wait.

19

MEAGAN HADN'T BEEN GONE two minutes when Connie popped out of the house—as usual, she was dying to know what Maggie and Meagan had talked about. Sometimes Maggie didn't mind Connie's inquisitiveness, but at other times she did mind, and this was one of the other times. It was just one more example of Connie going overboard in her possessiveness of Maggie.

"Connie, she was just checking up on me—it's nothing I want to talk about right now," Maggie said.

"Oh," Connie replied. She sounded hurt, which didn't necessarily mean she was ready to back off.

Fortunately Connie could sometimes be led off the scent—sometimes she even led herself off the scent by assuming that all problems had their root in the unreliability of men.

"I bet Conrad's got a girlfriend," Connie said. "I never trust men who go in for bow hunting—that's a redneck practice if you ask me."

"She didn't ask you, she asked me," Maggie insisted. "Just leave it alone, if you don't mind."

She noticed that Connie was now in full makeup, which meant either that she had a date, or had noticed a sale she wanted to check out. The thought that if it was a date, it might be with Terry Matlock, flitted through her mind, but she dismissed it. She had too much to think about herself to give too much space in her head to Terry and Connie. Anyway, it was not as if Terry had been the love of her life or anything.

But then it occurred to her that she hadn't really had a love of her life. Of course, there had been a lot of guys, some of whom had shown promise in the love-of-her-life area, but somehow they had all drifted away to be the love of somebody else's life. And Rog had been anything but love-of-her-life material—once he had even given her a mop for her birthday. What did that say?

Then it popped into her head that Auberon had once told her that the love of *his* life had been a boy he had kissed once, in chapel, when he was fifteen—a boy who grew up and went on to marry and have a bunch of kids.

So the reckoning—where the love of one's life was concerned—wasn't simple.

"Hey, Nordstrom is having a great sale—why don't you come with me and check it out?" Connie asked. "We could eat Mexican food at that place on Pico."

"Thanks, I don't think so, not today," Maggie said. Somehow the thought that she had never really had a love of her life left her feeling discouraged—too discouraged to just go check out one more sale at Nordstrom.

Connie, though eager to get going, couldn't help noticing that there had been a change in her friend's demeanor. She had been bristly a little earlier, but now she had stopped being bristly and just looked sad.

"You've been luckier than I have," Maggie said, in the defeated-sounding tone that Connie hated to hear.

"How do you figure?"

"You had a love of your life—that's why," Maggie said. She was referring to Nigel Bankes, a propman Connie had been madly in love with for something like fifteen years.

"What are you talking about?" Connie asked—but only to buy time. She knew perfectly well what Maggie was talking about. Connie *had* had a love of her life and it was definitely Nigel Bankes. Maggie, despite many lovers, had somehow never bingoed to quite that extent.

And now she was sixty—what were the odds of it happening now?

"At least you had Nigel," Maggie said, driving home her point.

"Oh sure—I had Nigel—and look how that one ended," Connie said.

How it ended was that Nigel married a young niece of Connie's—a girl named Kimberly—and begot a huge family with her, six kids, whereas he had only given Connie one child, her son, Danny, who was still struggling with drug problems at the age of forty.

"I know—he married Kimberly," Maggie said. "But that's not the point. You and Nigel lasted fifteen years, and Nigel was the love of your life."

"You know what, I'm going to the sale," Connie told her. "It's a pretty day—I'm not going to let you drag me back into a lot of bad memories. Why don't you get up from there and come with me? Do something positive for a change."

Maggie just shook her head.

"There's a mood that goes with buying things and I'm not in it," she told Connie.

"You know, sometimes I just want to shake you till you rattle," Connie said. "I feel like if I shook you hard enough you might turn back into the old Maggie and we could go have some fun."

"Don't you think I'd like to be the old Maggie?" Maggie asked. "Don't you think I'd like to?"

But she was talking to an empty yard, with a few leaves on the surface of the pool. Connie was the sort who would accept only so much frustration. She was gone—but then, a moment later, she reappeared.

"Can I take the van?" she asked. "I forgot my stupid car's not running."

"I still can't believe that stupid Billy wouldn't even replace your fuel pump," Maggie said.

"As to the van," she added, "help yourself. You know where the keys are.

"I hope it's a good sale," she added, as Connie was leaving.

"Even if it isn't, I'll eat some great Mexican food," Connie said.

20

Four hours later Maggie was cleaned up and dressed and ready to go to her session with Dr. Tom, who had called and asked if she would maybe be in the mood for sushi after their session. Maggie wasn't much in a sushi mood—she suggested Italian, though she knew that Dr. Tom was highly critical of Italian restaurants in L.A. The only one he really approved of was an old-fashioned place in Brentwood, which was actually fine with her. It would give the two of them time together, plus it would mean more money for Sam, the driver.

Sunday afternoons did stretch on, though. Once she got cleaned up, Maggie still had nearly two hours to wait—much too long to spend with the CNN crawl, even if she had liked being in her house, which she didn't. For some reason being in her house laid a weight on her spirit, and not a light weight either. If she saw an opening she meant to ask Dr. Tom why she no longer liked being in her house, the place that had seemed like the perfect home for almost sixty years.

Just before it was time to walk over to Highland and try to struggle through the pushers and the pimps, Maggie was suddenly blitzed by a terrible panic attack. For some reason a huge gust of wind suddenly swept through the yard, sending maybe as many as a hundred leaves into her swimming pool. If there was one thing she couldn't tolerate it was leaves in her pool, so she immediately grabbed up her dip net and began scooping out the leaves. She was making good progress, but then, to her horror, a dead squirrel suddenly plunged into her pool—the squirrel had been walking along an electric line over her fence line and had made a mistake, got zapped, and blown into her pool. Thousands of squirrels had walked that electric line with no problem, but this little brown squirrel was unlucky—Maggie smelled burning squirrel just before the poor little critter hit the pool, an event that unnerved Maggie so that she had to sit down, and when she sat down the big panic attack hit—for a minute she felt like she must be losing her mind, going bats for sure. All she could think of to do was crawl into her tent and huddle there, which she immediately did. For some reason water sloshed out of her pool.

Then she heard the fire trucks and the sirens of ambulances and realized that she was having her panic attack as an earthquake was happening. Probably it was the earthquake that had caused the squirrel to get zapped.

Maggie decided that it wasn't *that* major an earthquake—certainly it wasn't the big one. The first thing she needed to do was check on Gwen, her neighbor: she ran next door and there was Gwen, safe and sound, sitting on the curb. In fact everyone on the block was sort of out on the street, which is where they always ran if there was an earthquake.

"*No problema,* it was just a little tremor," Gwen informed her at once. "I'd say maybe two-point-two on the Richter. I don't see any houses falling down."

Gwen had lived in California a long time and was not one to get unduly stressed out just because the ground shook a little.

"I guess I got the earthquake confused with my panic attack," Maggie admitted. "I thought it was inside me but actually it was outside of me."

Gwen was well aware that her neighbor was struggling with depression—and had been ever since her operation—but this was the first time Maggie had mentioned panic attacks. She took a closer look and saw that her neighbor did indeed look shaky—shakier than could be the result of such a modest earthquake.

"Since when have you been having panic attacks?" Gwen asked—it seemed the least she could do since Maggie had been so helpful to her when she misstepped and broke her foot. Maggie had not only taken her to the emergency room, she had stayed with her until the break was properly set.

"A few months," Maggie said—then she happened to glance at her watch and saw that she was due at Dr. Tom's in only fifteen minutes. She could make it well enough but she could not afford to linger.

"Gwen, I've got to go to my shrink appointment," she said. She could tell that Gwen was concerned about her, which was reassuring. It was nice to have a neighbor who was not a heartless person.

"Bye, honey—I'm always here, you know," Gwen said. "Very little takes me off the block. If one of them panic attacks hits you, just knock on the door. We'll play gin rummy or something until it tapers off."

"Thanks, Gwen—I may do that," Maggie told her, although she doubted she could play gin rummy when she was upset. Even *not* upset she had never been good with cards.

21

ON THE WAY TO DR. TOM'S Maggie resorted to her cell phone to call all three of her daughters, just to make sure none of them had been hurt in the earthquake. Maggie was not too keen on cell phones—she had read somewhere that if you had enemies, they could get your cell phone number and blow you up somehow; she didn't suppose she had any enemies who would go to that much trouble—on the other hand, there was Terry, who had a real cold look in his eye when he left. Also he was young, and young people were really good with technology.

Calling her daughters proved to be just another frustration—all she got was their voice mails, which was understandable. It was Sunday—maybe they were doing things with their kids, or even their husbands—Kate and Meagan at least might be. Jeannie was a different story. Anyway Maggie left three voice mails, assuring her family that she was fine, it had just been a tremor, maybe two-point-two on the Richter.

There seemed to be fewer pushers outside Dr. Tom's office when Maggie got there—maybe the little tremor had scattered them. One who was there was a dapper black man named Diego Jones, whom Maggie had known for twenty years at least. In the early days she and Connie had bought pot from him, and once when three pimps beat him up and took all his money Maggie had given him bus fare so he could get home. Diego's curly hair was snow white now—he was really too old a guy to be pursuing such a dangerous profession. She and Diego always gave one another at least a nod when they passed one another.

"It's a bad day at Black Rock," Diego said, when Maggie approached.

"Why, what's wrong?" Maggie asked.

"That cunt bodybuilder beat him up again," Diego informed her.

Actually what Maggie found when Dr. Tom let her into the office wasn't as bad as Diego had led her to expect. Dr. Tom just had a small band Band-Aid on one cheek, and a cast on his left hand. It wasn't as if he were reeling around bleeding or anything. He had on his nice flannel suit and a deep blue scarf around his neck. Of course, he got up and made Maggie a little bow.

"What's the matter with your hand?" Maggie asked. Her feelings for Dr. Tom sort of surged up in a rush.

"My Nini broke it with her hairbrush," Dr. Tom admitted, with a little smile. "She said she hates me now. She hit my hand with the back of her hairbrush.

"I think my little Nini just doesn't realize how strong she is," Dr. Tom added.

That could be true, Maggie supposed. She herself had taken a whack or two at a couple of irritating lovers with her hairbrush. One guy she hit—Ernst—just laughed it off, but the other guy, who was a wrangler on some Western, slapped her so hard her ears rang for the rest of the day. It was what she got for being dumb enough to date a wrangler; the notion that it was wrong to hit women had not trickled down to the wrangler culture at that time. In the course of all her love affairs Maggie had provoked a few slaps and one or two punches, but nobody had ever hit her as hard as Jody, the wrangler whose hand she had whacked with her hairbrush.

"Dr. Tom, I hate to think of you being in danger," Maggie told him—she had not yet stretched out on the couch.

Delightful as he was as a dinner companion, Dr. Tom was pretty strict when it came to psychoanalysis.

"Discipline, please—now it is your turn to talk to me," he told her, with just a touch of severity in his voice. There were times, and this was one of them, when Maggie felt a little impatient with Dr. Tom's strictness. After all, it had been nineteen years—if she wasn't analyzed yet, when would she ever be?

But she didn't complain. That might have shattered their bond, and they did *have* a bond: Connie didn't understand it, her daughters didn't understand it, the guys in the loop group didn't understand it, and to tell the truth, Maggie didn't really understand it; but even so, it was real and she wanted it. So it was onto the couch she went—in no time at all she was babbling around her mother's relationship to Aunt Cooney, her younger sister.

Of course, Dr. Tom had long ago informed her that many of life's difficulties were rooted in sibling rivalry. According to him, sibling rivalries mostly didn't taper off—they festered, or something, which had probably been the case with her mother and Aunt Cooney. Maggie could remember them having some pretty bad fights, when Aunt Cooney lived with them for a while on Las Palmas. All Maggie could remember was a lot of slamming doors, and maybe a plate getting thrown once in a while. Probably Aunt Cooney just wanted to bring her boyfriends home and sleep with them, which probably didn't sit well with her sister Sally, who was trying to bring up a young family in a respectable neighborhood.

Out of respect for Dr. Tom Maggie babbled on for the full one hundred minutes—memories of Aunt Cooney got her through the session, although the fact of skipping lunch was beginning to make itself felt. She was definitely hungry, and meant to put down a lot of pasta once they got to the old-fashioned place in Brentwood, a place with deep leather banquettes where, according to Dr. Tom, a lot of gangsters and union people ate—the higher-ups, that is, not the workingmen, of course, who could never have afforded such a fancy restaurant except maybe on a big anniversary or something.

As the session was beginning to wind down—when Maggie was scraping the bottom of the barrel insofar as memories of Aunt Cooney went—something began to happen that was quite embarrassing. To her shock Maggie realized that she could smell herself—she was lubricating. The smell was faint, but it was definitely a moist smell that came from an intimate place. This wasn't unprecedented, of course; she had often had fantasies of Dr. Tom, lubricating in the process, but these fantasies mostly occurred at home in her bedroom, not on an analyst's couch three feet from Dr. Tom himself.

This was was definitely a shock and a surprise—in the last few years her loins had not exactly been a flowing stream. Sometimes she needed patience and a good deal of stimulation, two things she didn't always get. But be that as it may, Maggie had trouble babbling on about the distant past when anyone with a working smeller could tell that something sexual was brewing, and Maggie was the one brewing it. The rush of feeling that she had felt when she came in and saw the cast on Dr. Tom's hand had now arrived at its real home and there was not much she could do about it: the fact was she was in love with Dr. Tom and she wanted him in the way a woman was supposed to want someone she was in love with. She didn't care that he was old or that being in love with him might be a violation of the doctor-patient relationship—about none of that did she care. The fact was that she was in a state of desire far stronger than anything she had felt in the last few years.

She didn't dare look at Dr. Tom—being such a good shrink, he must have at least some inkling of what was happening: the moment that had been coming a long time was there, and it couldn't wait—even if he kicked her out she had to take the gamble. She cast one look at him—he had a kind of bemused expression on his face; he seemed to be just kind of waiting to see where life took them next, and where it took them was that Maggie rolled off the couch onto her knees. She was a practiced unzipper; in only about five seconds she had Dr. Tom's rapidly hardening dick out of his pants, a little bit larger dick than she had expected, him being such a tiny man; she immediately took him into her mouth—maybe it was true, what the sex books said, that healthy people were capable of sexual activity well into old age. What she was doing was what she had wanted to do for so long that Maggie soon had a whopping orgasm of her own without Dr. Tom even touching her. Wow!

22

NOW THAT THEY WERE LOVERS, Dr. Tom seemed proud as a peacock—he kind of strutted a little when they walked into the restaurant in Brentwood, and he ordered a very good bottle of wine. Maggie had the impression that the wine cost over one hundred dollars. He turned out to be a randy little old guy, too: on the ride back from Brentwood he put her hand inside his pants and put his hand inside her panties—quite a bit of mutual stimulation went on, but Maggie tried to hold it down, mainly because she felt embarrassed for Sam, who was a very dignified man. She didn't want Dr. Tom to get too lathered up with Sam sitting right there.

When Dr. Tom walked her to her door, she finally got to kiss him—his breath smelled sort of like almonds and he had an active little tongue. Of course, she asked him in, but Dr. Tom said he had better go to his house for the night—he didn't have his toiletries. When Maggie offered to run down to the Circle K and buy him a toothbrush and razor, he still demurred; he said he had to use a certain mild kind of shaving soap, something you lathered on with a brush, otherwise his face broke out.

To Maggie it seemed a little odd. Here they were playing with one another on her porch, he was hard as a rock, she was wet as a swamp, and yet he had to go home because he used a certain shaving soap? It occurred to her that probably she was rushing things a little. Ninotchka could still be in the picture, though Dr. Tom might not want to admit it or talk about it.

"I don't want to wait a week to see you again," Maggie told him bluntly. She *really* didn't want to wait a week.

"Oh no, come as soon as you get off work," Dr. Tom said. "Our suite will be ready—then we can pleasure ourselves as much as we want."

"Our suite? Our suite where?" Maggie asked.

"Oh, the Chateau Marmont, of course," he said.

Then he bowed and was gone, leaving a puzzled woman on her porch on Las Palmas Street. Why did he think he had to take a suite at the Chateau just to make love? What was wrong with her house? Of course, Connie would have to be shooed away, which she wouldn't like, but she had unceremoniously shooed Maggie away plenty of times when she had a guy she wanted to go to bed with.

In a way it all felt like a kind of dream. She had gone down on her shrink, after only nineteen years' acquaintance; she got to have a big rippling orgasm and some nice wine—and now what? If it was a dream, where would it take her?

Through the window she could see that Connie was watching Jay Leno—she decided to go in and tell Connie what had happened—they had always been open about such things.

"Where the fuck have you been?" Connie asked, the second

Maggie stepped inside. "All three of your daughters are worried sick about you."

"Brentwood," Maggie told her. "We went to that old-timey restaurant where all the hoods used to eat—I think that guy who was with Lana Turner before her daughter stabbed him used to eat there.

"My daughters know I usually have dinner with Dr. Tom on Sunday nights—what's the big deal?" she asked.

Connie didn't reply—she just looked sulky.

"Hey, Con—guess what? I finally seduced him," Maggie told her. It was not in her to keep a secret from her best friend.

"Big whup!" Connie said, but then she threw a pillow at Jay Leno and began to cry; all her fears of losing Maggie burst to the surface when Maggie got a new boyfriend. It was an old pattern.

Maggie sat on the couch and hugged Connie and whispered to her until she had had her cry and was able to accept the fact that what had happened wasn't the end of the world, exactly.

Under the circumstances Maggie felt it best to omit the part about the suite at the Chateau and the date the next night and all that; she didn't want Connie going off the deep end or anything. And she didn't go out to her tent that night, either. Once she had called her paranoid daughters and calmed them all down, she slept in the bed with Connie—sometimes that was the best way to handle things if Connie happened to be really stressed out. Having a friendly body next to hers helped Connie calm down and go to sleep—Maggie too, for that matter.

23

THE LOOPING IN BURBANK was pretty much a disaster—in fact, Monday was usually the day when the Prime Loopers were at their worst, which was mainly because they had their weekends to recover from. Auberon had food poisoning; he spent the whole morning throwing up. Jeremiah had done meth and had the shakes.

Hugh and Christophe had mainly just played volleyball on the beach—they were okay. And Jesús was absent—nobody at the hospital had seen him all weekend.

Connie looped well enough but she was in a manic state and kept running to the ladies' to call guys on her cell phone—which guy she finally located was revealed late in the day when Johnny Bobcat showed up; as soon as the day's work ended he and Connie headed off for parts unknown.

From Maggie's point of view it was just as well that Connie split—she had not been looking forward to telling Connie about her date, a serious date too.

On the way back to Hollywood Maggie dropped a tiny hint to the guys—just a little hint about future changes that could occur.

"I'm thinking about taking a trip," Maggie explained. "I've only got one aunt left and she's eighty-six years old. I kind of want to go see her before she dies."

"Where does your aunt live?" Auberon asked.

"Texas," Maggie told them, after which a kind of gloomy silence descended upon them.

"When would you go, sweetie?" Christophe asked. He was the one loop grouper who considered that Maggie actually had a right to a life of her own.

"It's the gutter for us then, chaps," Auberon declared, before Maggie could even speculate about her departure date. He said it in his most superior-sounding British voice too.

"Don't you be snotty with me, Auberon," Maggie warned. "How many times have I taken you to the emergency room in the middle of the night to save you from overdosing?"

"Hundreds, you're a saint, but we all have the future to think about," Auberon said. "Am I right, chaps?"

Jeremiah didn't say anything. He would never criticize Maggie, but Hugh was sort of like Auberon in some of his attitudes.

"Come to it, I suppose I could manage you blokes about as well as Mag here does," he said.

"Piss off, you don't even have a driver's license," Christophe reminded hm.

"A telling point—I suppose you would expect us to avail ourselves of public transportation, is that right, Hugh?" Auberon asked.

"It's not an unheard of practice—millions do it every day," Hugh pointed out.

Maggie was pretty shocked—Hugh and Auberon were talking about her as if she already didn't exist.

"Auberon, I wouldn't leave without making arrangements for all of you," Maggie insisted, in her own defense.

"Meaning what?" Auberon asked, still icy.

Maggie was being reminded of something Dr. Tom had told her: people who depended on you might resent the fact that they needed you.

"Look, Jesús is gone and Connie is going with me if I go," Maggie said. "There's just the four of you, and Bud Stone at Lavish Loops will take all four of you in a minute if I call him."

"Bud Stone's a fucking queen, I hate his putrid guts. Please be so kind as to omit me when you hand these boys over to his tender mercies," Auberon said. The way he said it brought Jeremiah out of his stupor.

"Shut up, you fucking little dipshit," Jeremiah told him. "If you don't stop being rude to Maggie I'll beat the crap out of you."

Jeremiah rarely got angry, but it was scary when he did. The sight of him all red in the face with fury sort of brought all of them to their senses. They all looked abashed—even Auberon.

"I'm sorry," he said. "It was just such a shock, you see. Our Mag going away and all."

"I suppose I could live with Bud Stone a few weeks, if I have to," he added—a big concession. Once Auberon got down on someone, he rarely relented.

Although she was going to see everyone the next day—they still had a week of looping to do, after all—the mere fact that Maggie had mentioned leaving made the whole bunch of them real emotional. They all hugged Maggie and kissed her when she dropped them off. Auberon apologized again and looked as if he might cry when Maggie let him out. Underneath the English ice he was a sweet man really. When she pulled away she saw him linger on the sidewalk for a minute, looking lost. It made her feel sad. Why was life so hard?

24

ALL THE WAY to Normandie Avenue, where she dropped off Hugh and Christophe, Maggie was sort of wondering what she would wear to her big date at the Chateau Marmont. Since the whole point of the date was to get naked and make love—at least, that was the point from her angle—getting too dressed up would be sort of silly. Something she could shimmy out of quickly seemed to be what she should aim for.

She was very glad Connie had gone off with Johnny Bobcat— Connie would be sure to have some acid comments if she saw Maggie getting dressed up to go be seduced. So would her daughters—fortunately they knew nothing about it.

When she walked into the Chateau and asked for Dr. Tommaso Balducci's room, the desk clerk just said, "Penthouse A." He was reading the sports page and didn't look up.

"He has a penthouse?" Maggie said, a little surprised. Rumor had it that only the most top-drawer stars—the Greta Garbo level— had penthouses at the Chateau.

"Penthouse A," the guy repeated, so Maggie took the elevator all the way up. She was feeling pretty nervous. She hoped they could get to the sex pretty soon so maybe she could calm down.

Another shock was Dr. Tom himself, who was wearing a burgundy velour running suit when he opened the door.

"Dr. Tom, do you jog?" Maggie asked. Somehow the thought that the doctor might exercise had never occurred to her.

"I do nothing, my Nini does everything," Dr. Tom said, ushering her into a room so large Maggie's whole house would have fit in it. She was flabbergasted by the size of the room, and there were evidently other rooms. From the big picture window she could see to Santa Monica. At first all Maggie could think about was how much a penthouse suite at the Chateau Marmont must cost. There was a huge bouquet of lilies and roses on a table. The furniture was a little bit old-fashioned, maybe it was sort of from the time of Greta Garbo, but it wasn't ugly or anything, it just hailed from an earlier era—and so, she supposed, did Dr. Tom, despite his burgundy velour running suit.

The opulence of it all had the effect of making Maggie feel subdued—if it had just been an ordinary hotel room where two people had gone to fuck they would probably already be doing it by now—but it was not an ordinary hotel room, it was more like an intimidating hotel room, enough so that Maggie lost a little bit of the horny edge she had been feeling all day.

Almost before she could take it all in, the doorbell rang and a waiter came in bringing caviar and vodka. Dr. Tom seemed to know the waiter, who soon had the table set up and the caviar ready to eat.

"*Grazie,* Bertie," Dr. Tom said, handing the waiter a fifty-dollar tip—another shocker to Maggie. Never in her life had she seen a man tip a waiter fifty dollars. So was Dr. Tom actually rich, or was he just showing off for her sake? Which would have been a waste of money—she was already plenty impressed with Dr. Tom.

Dr. Tom poured her some vodka in a little thin glass he called a vodka flute; then, while she helped herself to the caviar, he explained to her that caviar should only be eaten off gold, ivory, or mother-of-pearl; fortunately the service was mother-of-pearl—her activist daughter, Jeannie, would never have spoken to her again if she had eaten caviar or anything else off ivory.

The vodka must have been of some superpowerful kind, because Maggie, who could comfortably down six or seven vodka martinis with only a mild buzz, soon found that she was quite drunk—this vodka really hit her hard.

Dr. Tom didn't talk a lot—he was too busy scooping up beluga caviar, which he said was the best kind. He said the tsar of Russia and the shah of Iran used to drain off most of the beluga, but, of course, they were no more.

Maggie tried to keep from thinking about the expense—she herself would have been just as happy with a nice room at the Ambassador or maybe the Beverly Wilshire.

Dr. Tom—after all, he was a shrink—figured out what she was thinking and sat beside her to reassure her.

"Don't worry, I have private means," he said. "Did you know that we Sicilians invented cunnilingus?"

And then he nipped her earlobe, which startled her. It had been a while since a guy had nipped her earlobe, and as for cunnilingus, she had always supposed that Adam and Eve invented it—or else an ape—but it was soon evident that it was a big interest of Dr. Tom's. He peeled out of his burgundy velour running suit and helped Maggie get naked. She had not worn a bra, she had known too many guys who sort of lost it while trying to get a bra off a woman—why take a chance?

Cunnilingus would not have been Maggie's preferred way to start a romance; she saw nothing wrong with the good old missionary position, but Dr. Tom was of a different opinion; he was right down there between her legs, licking and diddling. It was not what she wanted—she wanted him close, where she could hold him and kiss him. As it was, he just seemed so far away—guys always seemed sort of far away when they happened to be eating her. But Dr. Tom did have a real delicate touch; he knew what he was doing—pretty soon she did have a little orgasm.

She was hoping that meant that Dr. Tom was finally going to let her bring him inside her—she even reached for his cock to encourage him, but he evaded her and turned her on her stomach, which was a surprise. Was he the dog-fucking sort, or what? But then she felt him pushing at her asshole.

"Uh-uh, Dr. Tom," she said, flipping back over. It had been

maybe thirty years or so since she had let anybody butt-fuck her; only a few times when she had been madly in love had she indulged a guy in that particular way.

"I don't want that. Can't we just fuck?" she asked, feeling that she already knew the answer.

"Oh no, I can't do that, my Nini would kill me," Dr. Tom explained. He seemed surprised that Maggie seemed not to know that straight-A sexual intercourse was something one did with one's wife; more advanced activities were what mistresses were for.

"I thought you wanted to be my mistress," he said, looking a little hurt.

"I did—I do," Maggie said. "I love you. I love you. It's just that I never did like anal sex."

Dr. Tom, full of surprises, got a twinkle in his eye. Maggie was still holding his cock, maybe there was still hope, but then he pulled away.

"Excuse me for a minute, I know something we can do," he said—then he trotted off into another room. Maggie felt an immediate pang of loneliness—she was alone and naked on a bed, and the man she wanted had just told her he only had sexual intercourse with his wife. Of course, it wasn't the first time she had been with a married man—if there was a wife in the picture anywhere, things were apt to get sticky.

Then Dr. Tom came trotting back into the room, his erection sort of at half-mast, looking extremely pleased with himself; he was carrying a proper black-and-white maid's uniform in one hand and a whip and a paddle in the other.

"I have been a bad boy," he said. "I want you to put on this maid's uniform and punish me. First the paddle, then the whip, if you don't mind."

Maggie just stared at him, stunned. The attempt on her ass she could forgive—guys did things like that when they were in the process of getting their rocks off. But a maid's uniform and a paddle and a whip? Maggie Clary, paddle her own analyst? Of course, she knew there were people who liked to be spanked—she had seen lots

of such equipment in the sex shops along Hollywood Boulevard—
but the S&M stuff and the leather outfits had never interested her in
the least. She didn't condemn it—people could do what they wanted
to do—but it was just not for her.

"I don't do that, Dr. Tom—I think I better just go home," Maggie said.

"But my dear, it's only a little game," he said. He saw that he had
upset her and spoke in a kindly voice; that much was nice, at least.

"I didn't come here for a game—I came here because I'm in love
with you," Maggie told him. "I didn't know you were determined to
save it for your wife. I made a mistake and I think I better just go
home."

Dr. Tom looked saddened. His erection drooped until it wasn't
an erection anymore. Maggie stood up and began to get dressed—
she felt a very low low coming.

Dr. Tom sighed and picked up the telephone.

"Let me call Sam for you, at least," he said.

"No, please don't—I live in walking distance," Maggie reminded
him, as she put on her shirt.

"I've disappointed you, I see," Dr. Tom said. He looked small
and sad.

"Yes, you did," she said. "You've been my analyst for nineteen
years—what could have made you think I'd want to come here and
spank you?"

Dr. Tom pulled on the pants of his running suit. He shrugged, a
sad shrug.

"Some people like to," he said, sitting down by her, on the bed.
She had meant to slip on her panties but hadn't got that far—to her
surprise Dr. Tom began to fondle her. Maggie was half of a mind to
sock him, but she couldn't work up the old socking spirit. Instead
she sank into a sort of passive state and let manual sex happen.
While it was happening Dr. Tom kissed her, and he was such a good
kisser that, despite herself, hopes began to rise. He was a good
fondler, too—he knew what to touch and how to touch it. As much

from the kissing as anything she got off again, a sort of soft orgasm. It didn't shake the rafters but it was still nice of Dr. Tom to try and ease her out of her low mood.

He even kept fondling her while they waited for the elevator—the guy was still pretty active, that much she knew.

"Maybe sushi on Sunday night?" he suggested.

"Maybe—I can't predict a food mood that far ahead," she said, a little elated. At least he wanted something to continue.

Right up until the moment the elevator door opened he kept rubbing her pussy. He hadn't had enough and neither had she—so maybe, just maybe, there'd be a brighter day tomorrow.

25

THE MINUTE MAGGIE stepped out onto the sidewalk the brighter-day-tomorrow mood passed and the vodka suddenly hit her. Far west of the Chateau, at the end of Sunset Boulevard, the sun was just setting: the whole basin was filled with golden sunset light. For about two seconds Maggie thought how beautiful it was, and then, desperately drunk, she began to wobble. She had to grab a parking meter and hang on to keep from falling on her face. Worse yet, even as she clung to the parking meter, the world kept swirling and swirling until Maggie sort of slid down on the sidewalk, drunk as an owl, just as a police car pulled up at the curb and a nice officer, black, with a very large face, looked down at her in a quizzical way.

"Ma'am, are you all right?" the officer asked. He had a deep baritone voice, sort of like the voice of James Earl Jones when he was singing "Ol' Man River." It was a comforting voice.

"I am totally drunk," Maggie confessed. Why try to hide what was obvious?

"What happened was my boyfriend gave me some vodka of a kind I wasn't used to—and I drank too much of it," Maggie told the officer. She wondered if she was going to be read her Miranda rights, or what.

"I just live a few blocks from here," she told the officer. "I think if I just sit here my head will clear in a moment and I can walk home."

Just as she said it, who should come walking up the street but Diego Jones, wearing a nice fedora. He looked as if he might have been to church, only it wasn't Sunday. Somehow the arrival of Diego made Maggie feel better.

Better still, Diego seemed to know the officer with the big face.

"Hey, Tub," he said. "Don't you be harassing Maggie now. Maggie's a fine lady, just temporarily a tiny bit intoxicated."

"Nobody's harassing nobody," the officer pointed out. "The lady seemed a little wobbly, that's all."

In her mind Maggie kind of drifted away from the scene—she was remembering that she had mentioned her boyfriend, who would be Dr. Tom. Who else? Was he her boyfriend? They had, after all, done intimate things. He had already invited her out for Sunday dinner, but would he ever invite her up to Penthouse A again? After all, she had declined to spank him. She had just wanted to consummate things normally, and yet here she was, sitting by a parking meter on Sunset Boulevard, being scrutinized by a large nice cop and a small dapper drug dealer.

A moment later she noticed that she was only being scrutinized by Diego Jones. The cop had gone on this way.

"Diego, would you walk me home, in case I get wobbly again?" Maggie asked, once Diego had helped her up.

"No need to walk, here's Sam," Diego told her. "Old Doc Tom, he seen you had a little too much."

Sam held the door for her; Diego helped her in and got in with her, which was nice of him.

"Diego, would you like to come for tea?" Maggie asked. "I have herbal if you don't use caffeine."

"Would-I-like-to-come-for-tea?" Diego repeated. It was clear that the invitation had taken him by surprise.

"I believe I'll take you up on that," Diego said. "Nothing I'd like more right now than some nice herbal tea."

"Sam, thanks for coming, I don't think I've ever been this drunk," Maggie said.

Sam chuckled—he had a nice, reassuring chuckle. Maggie felt that at least she was in the company of friends.

"Old Doc Tom, he serve that communist booze," Sam said. "Hits like a sledgehammer, don't it?"

Connie seemed surprised when Maggie walked in with Diego, but it was obvious at once that she was pie-faced drunk and needed a guiding hand. Connie had once bought a good deal of pot from Diego—she adapted quickly to his reappearance. She also happened to notice that Maggie wasn't wearing a bra and that her panties were about to fall out of her handbag, which meant that hanky-panky of some sort had probably occurred, somewhere up the line—probably with the Sicilian charmer Dr. Tom, Connie suspected.

Maggie was glad that Connie was being nice to Diego—often she was rude to pushers and might not notice that Diego was just being a good shepherd on this occasion.

Then Maggie felt her stomach coming up. She stumbled off to the bathroom—Connie and Diego would just have to sort out the social niceties for themselves.

26

"I KNEW HE WAS AN M the minute I saw him," Connie said, speaking of Dr. Tom's desire to have Maggie spank him. Connie believed that she could immediately determine the sexual tendencies of anyone she happened to meet; she could be real arrogant about it. Sometimes this brash assumption on Connie's part irritated Maggie no end, but just then she was smoking a joint; mainly she was trying to recover from the violent upheaval her stomach had just made. Diego had sold Connie a little pot before he vanished into the night.

"That's M for masochist," Connie added.

"I know what M stands for—I wasn't born yesterday," Maggie said. "It's better than being an S, in my opinion."

She felt weak and weary and didn't want to be harassed on the subject of Dr. Tom or any other subject—she wanted to feel better, in her body first and then in her emotions. The marijuana definitely helped.

"What about Johnny Bobcat?" she asked—she and Connie always immediately discussed their sexual adventures with one another—even in the sixth grade they were having little harmless sexual adventures and revealing them to one another; it was nice to have a best friend you could be that open with. Once in a while, of course, Connie cheated, if it happened to be a case of overlapping boyfriends—Maggie had to admit that she had cheated a few times herself, but in general the two of them were open about their involvements. Sex also happened to be something they enjoyed talking about. Neither of them cared about politics, which annoyed Jeannie no end—she was always lecturing them about being bad citizens, but they went their merry ways despite her.

At the mention of Johnny Bobcat, Connie made a little face.

"He just had a prostate operation," she revealed. "We had falafel together instead of sex."

"Uh-oh," Maggie said. "I guess neither of us had much of an evening."

"Well, like I said, I just had falafel—*you* had caviar," Connie pointed out. There was no equivalency in her opinion.

"So what? I threw it up," Maggie pointed out. But then she lost all interest in conversation and scooted over by Connie, hoping Connie would hold her for a bit, which Connie did—she was usually helpful when her friend needed comforting. Wrestling was on, with the sound muted. Sometimes Connie liked to see hefty guys throwing themselves around.

"If we go to Texas, will you really split the gas?" Maggie asked. She was trying to find some positive things to think about.

"I'll split the gas. When's the earliest we can leave?" Connie asked—failure to get it on with Johnny Bobcat seemed to have made her restless.

"Monday—we can leave next Monday—it's one week," Maggie said.

"Why not Saturday? The loop group's through on Friday," Connie asked.

Maggie didn't answer. She didn't want to reveal the real reason, which was that waiting until Monday gave her one more shot at Dr. Tom.

"You're going to give him one more chance, aren't you?" Connie asked, as if reading Maggie's mind. She didn't say it meanly, though—Maggie was too low and vulnerable at the moment for her to need to go on the attack. But still, why not be honest about the lay of the land?

"Yes, please don't criticize me," Maggie begged. "It's hard to give up on the only real thing that you have."

"Don't I know it? If I had anything real on the horizon, you couldn't drag me to Texas," Connie said.

They switched from wrestling to Comedy Central but the change sort of misfired. Nothing seemed funny to either of them. Connie found a bottle of chardonnay in the fridge and began to drink it. Then the two of them sat by the pool and smoked another joint.

"Why is it so hard to get anything right with men?" Maggie asked, when they were finishing the second joint.

Connie took a pass on the question. It was a pretty night, airplanes were going over, and somewhere there had been a car wreck, probably on the Hollywood Freeway. Two or three ambulances were in the hunt.

"Hadn't we better phone your aunt—what if she doesn't want us to come?" Connie asked.

"I'll call her tomorrow," Maggie promised.

For the second night in a row she abandoned her fine new tent and slept with Connie.

"Why do you think men become M's?" she asked at some point, but Connie was sound asleep.

27

"I TELL YOU, we have to do something," Kate insisted.

"Then you do it—I tried and failed," Meagan said, over the sound of revelry. They were at a park in Playa del Rey, celebrating Howie's forty-second birthday. Guys were guzzling beer and kids were screaming and swinging and being kids. It was the Fourth of July—there would be fireworks a little later, when it was darker. Everything was fine, it was a normal American birthday party in a park. Howie's real birthday was two days later but they had decided to take advantage of the Fourth of July and have it a little early this year—the only fly in the ointment was Maggie, who, for the first time in history, wasn't there. And what's more, she hadn't even bothered to pretend to have an excuse.

"Please excuse me, I don't feel like a party at this time," Maggie said, in a rather formal tone.

When Jeannie called to apply just a tiny bit of pressure—she just sort of mentioned how disappointed the grandkids would be if their grandma didn't come to the party—Maggie simply hung up.

"She never hung up on me before, not in my *life!*" Jeannie said. The experience left her a little stunned, in fact.

"That's the second time you've upset her by mentioning the kids—don't you ever learn?" Kate said.

Privately all three of the daughters had taken it upon themselves to quiz Connie quietly, via cell phone, about their mother's state. Connie, as usual, took a what-business-is-it-of-yours tone, but she did let slip to Jeannie the bit about the maid's uniform and the paddle and the whip. Jeannie instantly relayed this news to her sisters, more evidence, if more was needed, that their mother was in a seriously deteriorated emotional state. But how to deal with it? Would it be better, or worse, if she really did run off to Texas with crazy Connie?

"I can't believe that little Sicilian prick wanted her to spank him," Kate said. She was the most indignant of the three. Irregularity of that sort didn't fit with her life picture at all.

"If he wanted to spank *her*, maybe I could see it," Jeannie said. "That might have a certain appeal."

"It does *not!*" Meagan shouted. The thought of behavior of that sort horrified her. Conrad might not be the most exciting male in the world but at least he didn't try to spank her.

Jeannie saw no point in trying to persuade her square sisters that a little variety in one's sex life might be good. Her husband, Fred, was doing the barbecuing for the big birthday party; Fred had grown up in Lockhart, Texas, which he claimed produced the best barbecue in the world. Fred wasn't vain about much—he was always admitting to people that he wasn't the sharpest knife in the drawer, an admission that irritated Jeannie no end; in her view that was the kind of thing you should let people figure out for themselves. The fact was, there were people even less sharp than Fred, and she had slept with some of them; intelligence wasn't the only human quality to be prized, not in Jeannie's opinion. Fred happened to be steady, a pretty important quality in a husband. At the moment steady Freddy was basting some pork ribs with his own special homemade barbecue sauce, the recipe for which was probably Fred's only closely guarded secret. He had been taught the recipe by an old black man in Lockhart, Texas, and had never even shared it with his own wife—not that Jeannie minded. Barbecue was not among her favorite foods.

"Freddikins, have you ever felt like spanking me before we have sex?" she asked. "You know? just to spice things up a little?"

"Whut?" Fred asked—his first thought was that he had mis-heard—Jeannie probably wanted him to spank one of the kids for some infraction. Maybe they were burying one of their little cousins in the sandbox or something.

Mainly he was attending to his sauce, applying it carefully, like Rembrandt or somebody might apply paint to a canvas.

"Who did what?" he asked, reluctantly. The ribs were almost done—he really needed to pay close attention at this stage.

Not for the first time, Jeannie found herself getting irritated with steady Freddy. She tried again.

"Don't you ever feel like whacking my naked butt with a paddle when we're getting ready to fuck?" she asked, trying to be a little more direct.

Fred had no trouble answering that question.

"No," he said, dipping his little basting brush in the barbecue sauce again.

Jeannie began to get a kind of wild feeling, of the sort that was likely to come over her when she spent too much time in the company of her foursquare family. Nothing could possibly be more foursquare and normal than her family. Here they were having a perfect American birthday party on America's birthday itself. The younger kids were on the jungle gym, the older kids were listening to weird rock bands on their Walkmen. It was so completely normal that Jeannie had a sudden wild urge to take off all her clothes and have an orgy, if she could only find a few outcast swingers to have the orgy with. Of course, swingers were pretty unlikely to be in a park in Playa del Rey, waiting to watch fireworks on the Fourth of July. Glendale, where her boyfriend lived, was a little too far away to dart off to for some nice pounding action—the only easily available source of sex was her husband, the devotee of Lockhart, Texas, style barbecue.

"Hey, Freddikins, finish those ribs and let's go fuck in the van," Jeannie said.

"Do what?" Fred asked, his mind still mainly on his culinary task.

"Fuck in the van, fuck in the van, fuck in the van!" Jeannie said. "Do I need to draw you a picture?"

The F-word sort of floated through the park; both her sisters turned their heads, but only briefly.

Fred Keller realized his wife was issuing a challenge of sorts—big family gatherings seemed to affect Jeannie strangely, making her want to do sexual things that weren't likely to turn out any too well. Having sex in the van would be fine if the kids were one hundred miles away, but they weren't one hundred miles away, they were within the picnic area, meaning that the minute he and Jeannie got in the van and attempted to do something sexual, both of them would immediately show up wanting their Rollerblades, or a particular CD or something. Didn't it make more sense to wait until they got home? Then they could have nice comfortable sex in their big, king-size bed.

Jeannie was serious, though. She began to run her hand up and down the crack in his ass, activity that was not easy to ignore.

"Aren't you even going to answer me?" Jeannie asked. "Doesn't doing your conjugal duty in a little different setting appeal to you at all?"

"'Fraid the kids might see us," Fred told her. It was a reasonable possibility, Fred considered.

Jeannie stopped running her hand up and down the crack in his ass. It seemed steady Freddy would rather baste than fuck.

"Just give me the car keys," Jeannie demanded.

"Why?" Fred asked—it was clear that Jeannie was getting into one of her wild moods. Why these moods came on her he didn't know, but now and then they did—sometimes she'd jump in the car and be gone for hours. Where she went he didn't know. But if he gave her the car keys and she was gone for hours, she'd miss the fireworks for sure.

Nonetheless it was her van—he himself just drove a pickup—so he handed Jeannie the keys and she left.

"I thought I heard the F-word. Are you guys having a fight?" Meagan asked, when Jeannie came striding by.

"The fact is we're not having much of anything," Jeannie said. "If I'm not back by the time the fireworks are over, would you mind taking my family home?"

"Well, no—not if the grill will fit," Meagan said. "Are you pissed at Fred or something?"

"Yep," Jeannie said—she did not elaborate.

Then, as she was nearly to the van, she happened to notice Howie, the birthday boy, sitting all by himself with a beer in his hand. He looked at her wistfully, as he often did. Jeannie supposed Kate and Howie were happy enough—on the other hand it could be that they weren't—but it could be a mistake to read too much into Howie's wistful look; wistful was just sort of the way Howie looked at life. Even if he and Kate were deliriously happy, Howie would probably still look wistfully at whatever woman happened to be passing.

On impulse, though, spurred on by the wistful look, Jeannie reversed her course and went back and gave Howie a big sister-in-law's kiss—she thought he deserved a kiss for putting up with Kate, if nothing else. Katie was pretty hard-driving. Howie smelled of aftershave—to Jeannie's shock and surprise Howie opened his mouth and stuck his tongue deep into her mouth.

Jeannie jerked back as if Howie's tongue was a hot iron—the last thing she had meant to do was exchange saliva with Kate's husband, even if he was a birthday boy.

"Hey, don't I get a real kiss?" Howie asked, still looking at her wistfully.

"You need to change your aftershave, Howie," Jeannie said—it was the only retort that popped into her mind before she got out of there ASAP.

28

CONNIE HAD DRIVEN over to her house to pick up her mail and pay a few bills, so Maggie was alone when Jeannie rang her doorbell. It was just about full dark; soon Fourth of July fireworks would be lighting up the sky, from various parks here and there in the city. Jeannie had an angry look on her face—Maggie saw that much immediately.

"Howie French-kissed me!" Jeannie told her, getting the problem right off her chest.

"It was his birthday party," Jeannie went on. "I thought I'd be a nice sister-in-law and give him a hug and a smooch, and the next thing I knew he's sticking his big slobbery tongue in my mouth."

"Oh my, let's smoke a joint," Maggie said—in the past few days, since her shocking experience at the Chateau Marmont, she and Connie had sort of renewed their old pot-smoking ways—Diego had started dropping by to be sure they were supplied.

Jeannie was amenable to the marijuana so they went into the backyard and sat by the pool; soon the pop and crackle of fireworks could be heard from distant parts of the city.

"Maybe he was just drunk," Maggie suggested. Men were always likely to behave in a coarse fashion when they had had too much to drink.

"Nope, he knew exactly what he was doing," Jeannie said, still fuming. "Kate says Howie's always nursing little plots—so the son of a bitch nursed a little plot and stuck his tongue in my mouth."

Maggie knew that being French-kissed by a brother-in-law must be an unpleasant experience, but if you weighed it in the scale of the world's woes, it just didn't loom very large—a reflection she didn't share with her daughter. But even unpleasant surprises could sometimes yield nice consequences—in this case, the consequence was that she got to spend a little time with Jeannie, her favorite daughter. Mothers weren't supposed to play favorites, but of course they did. Having boyfriends while married was one of the habits she and Jeannie shared. The whole time she was married to Rog she had only been without a lover a few times, for a few months. Long before Kate was born Maggie had realized that holy matrimony was going to need supplementing. She took her first lover while five months pregnant with Kate and never gave much thought to monogamy again.

"I hear your shrink wanted you to spank him," Jeannie said. It was time to put Howie's kiss behind her, and the marijuana helped in that regard.

"Blabbermouth Connie," Maggie said mildly. She knew Connie would soon have spread *that* news. You couldn't expect normal human beings to keep secrets of that nature.

"Now that I've had a few days to think about it, I guess the real surprise is that Dr. Tom is so rich," she said. "He *owns* that penthouse at the Chateau. He tipped the waiter fifty bucks and yet he keeps that ratty little office on Highland where he could be robbed or beaten half to death every time he goes to work."

"Well, if he's a masochist, maybe that's *why* he keeps that office," Jeannie suggested.

That aspect had not occurred to Maggie—once she thought about it, it made a certain sense. Maybe the bruises Dr. Tom sometimes sported weren't made by Ninotchka after all.

"Connie and I are going to Texas on Monday," Maggie said—she wanted to forestall questions about Dr. Tom if she could.

"You're in love with Dr. Tom, aren't you?" Jeannie asked.

"Half in love at least," Maggie admitted. "I'm not a whole person so I don't know that I can be wholly in love."

Jeannie had a deep love for her mother—she wanted to understand why she felt incomplete, if possible.

"I don't know, Jeannie—I can't really explain it," Maggie said. "I ought to be perfectly okay, and yet I'm not."

Jeannie gave her mother a hug. They passed the joint back and forth. She had calmed down and felt she ought to be getting back to the park, to help Fred load the grill in the van. It was nice, though, to sit with her mother for a bit—or at least it was until the back door slammed and Connie popped into the yard. Jeannie and Connie had a bristly relationship; each was jealous of the other's place in Maggie's life.

"I'm broke, I'm broke, I'll soon be in the poorhouse," Connie said. She was prone to little financial panics every time she paid her bills.

"As to the problem with Howie, just try and forget it," Maggie advised—she knew her daughter would be going. Jeannie and Connie just weren't comfortable together.

Connie knew that here there had probably been a secret or two passed between mother and daughter, but for once she took the wise course and held her peace.

By the time Jeannie got back to the park in Playa del Rey, fireworks had died out of the violet sky and the only trace of the birthday party that had been was Kate, who was sitting around with a couple of girls from her office softball team. The ice chest only had a few beers floating in it, one of which Jeannie appropriated.

"Where's our grill?" she asked.

"Conrad was in a helpful mood for once—he gave the grill a ride to your house, along with your husband and children," Kate informed her.

It annoyed Kate slightly that Jeannie had just casually waltzed off from Howie's birthday party—she hadn't even bothered to stick around to help sing him Happy Birthday. Kate put great store by traditions like Happy Birthday but obviously they meant nothing to her little sister.

"I went to see Mom, she's leaving for Texas on Monday," Jeannie said.

"It hurt Howie's feelings that you didn't hang around to sing 'Happy Birthday' or watch him blow out the candles," Kate said— she saw no reason to let Jeannie off the hook on that score.

If you knew what I know about Howie, Jeannie thought, but she didn't say it.

"Sorry—I'll sing it twice next year," Jeannie said. Then she split for home.

29

After Jeannie left, Maggie revealed the business of Howie's French kiss to Connie, who had two sisters herself and more experience of brothers-in-law than Maggie. Connie took a dark view, as usual—in her opinion brothers-in-law could rarely be trusted. Often they were apt to get a little grabby, under the guise of family feeling.

"Remember Nick, that thug my sister Chloe married?" Connie asked. "The minute Chloe turned her back, the little dickhead was all over me—Nick was the main reason I stopped having Thanksgiving dinner with my family."

"Wow, that's major," Maggie said.

"He had his comeuppance though, the little shit," Connie reflected.

"What was his comeuppance?"

"Impotence—I guess I should have called it his comedownance," Connie said, giggling at her own wit.

"After the fourth baby, Nick got a vasectomy," Connie went on. "They must have snipped the wrong cord or something because Nick was no good after that. It's why Chloe finally divorced him."

"It just goes to show that people shouldn't let themselves be cut on unless it's absolutely necessary," Maggie said.

"Oh shut up—I'm not in the mood for any more of your womb-less bullshit," Connie snapped. "I need to know if this Texas trip is on or off. When are you going to bite the bullet and call your aunt?"

"Right now, if you're going to be rude about it!" Maggie told her. She got up and marched inside.

"Hey, remember the time zones!" Connie called after her. "It's way after midnight in Texas."

"Aunt Cooney's a night person—she won't care," Maggie said, hoping she was right.

"Just call her in the morning," Connie said, mildly appalled by the chain of events she had set in motion.

"No, I'm calling her now!" Maggie insisted. Connie's rudeness wasn't really what motivated her, though. The real reason was that Maggie felt herself losing her impetus where the Texas trip was concerned. It was something that had been exciting to think about for a few days, but did she really want to do it? Connie's unexpected offer to split the gas had made it look even better. Maggie had had impetus enough to disband her loop group and get her performers placed with a decent outfit. But now that all that had been done, and her daughters duly informed of her intention to leave, Maggie felt her confidence slowly slipping away. She had never been particularly good with maps and directions; several times she had got lost just try-ing to find Antelope Valley. What if she got lost and missed Texas?

"Mom, it's a vast state," Kate assured her, when she voiced her doubts to her oldest daughter.

"A lot of roads go to it," Kate insisted, trying to reassure her.

Maggie, once she grew doubtful, began to blame the whole thing on Paolo—even if he was a headwaiter and even if he had the hots for her, why couldn't he just have minded his own fucking business? Was her life really so empty that she had to drive to Texas, looking for adventure?

Besides, that very day, she had got a good job offer from an old producer friend named Marcus Choate—he had had a big success with a movie about Koreatown and wanted to set up a production company in Santa Monica. He also wanted Maggie to be his assistant. He asked if she was interested and Maggie said sure. Then he explained that he had to go to Europe for two weeks to see some distributors, but when he got back, the minute he had his finances together, he would call her and they'd have lunch.

Of course, that meant that there was really no reason why she shouldn't go to Texas. And she had sort of promised herself that she'd see America at last—if Beavis and Butt-head could manage it, why not Maggie and Connie? And even her daughters had come round to the notion that a trip might be just what she needed.

"It will restore your perspective," Meagan reasoned. Maggie took it as a compliment; someone thought she had once had perspective. Jeannie and Kate came round to the same opinion—if she backed out now and just moped along in her old routine, all her daughters would be mad at her.

In her kitchen, which Maggie rarely entered now, she began to feel kind of whirly. Maybe she was at some kind of turning point—it was hard to tell. There was a half bottle of gin in her liquor cabinet—she poured herself a generous splash, over three ice cubes. What she asked herself about her Hollywood routine was whether she was really making any progress. Dr. Tom had eaten her pussy—was that progress?

Next thing she knew she had gulped down the gin and was dialing her Aunt Cooney, an old woman she had not seen in fifteen years.

Somehow a decision had been made.

30

"Wake me up? Shucks, no!" Aunt Cooney bawled, when Maggie sort of timidly asked if she had maybe called too late.

"A good night's sleep is anathema to an inquiring mind, but my hens ain't got inquiring minds and you did wake up a few of them—I been living in the henhouse lately. It's a good thing you called my cell."

"Do you remember me, Aunt Cooney?" Maggie asked.

"Honey, I knew who you were the minute I heard your sweet voice," her aunt assured her. "You sound just like your mother, bless her heart."

"Why would you live in the henhouse? Just curious," Maggie asked, trying to imagine her aunt's environment.

"There's an aggravating old bull snake who keeps slipping in and stealing my free-range eggs—so I'm plotting an ambush," Aunt Cooney said.

"I see," Maggie said. "How many hens do you have?"

"Two million," Aunt Cooney told her. "Plus about two hundred that are free-range."

"Two million?" Maggie said, shocked—the thought of any one person owning two million chickens was a pretty startling thought.

"Honey, in this day and time it's big agribusiness or no agribusiness—that's the nature of the beast."

"I'm between jobs and I thought I might come to see you—would that be something you'd like?" Maggie asked. Why not cut to the chase?

"And I have a friend who might come with me—Connie. I think you met her the last time you were in Los Angeles," Maggie went on. "We could just stay in a motel or something—we don't want to be any trouble."

Aunt Cooney cackled at the thought of her niece being any trouble.

"My house has thirty-two bedrooms," she said. "It's the biggest house between Amarillo and Kansas City. You won't be any trouble—are you driving, or flying?"

"We thought we'd drive—see America, you know," Maggie said.

"Now be truthful, Aunt Cooney. Is it really okay if we come? We don't want to impose."

"It's hard to impose on a person with two million chickens and thirty-two bedrooms," Aunt Cooney pointed out. "All you have to do is show up and you'll be welcome."

"We thought we'd try to leave Monday," Maggie told her.

"Fine—Electric City's a snap to locate," Aunt Cooney assured her. "You just hit the old I-40 and keep on keeping on until you come to Conway, Texas, which is a town named for Conway Twitty. At Conway turn left—we're up north between Borger and Dial. You can't miss the house—it's nearly bigger than the town."

"I hope we don't have car trouble," Maggie mentioned. She had actually bought a road atlas at a Circle K and had been peeping in it from time to time. To her, Texas seemed far away, but on the 40 freeway maybe they could make good time.

"The I-40's thick with killers—don't venture off without a firearm," Aunt Cooney advised.

The advice sort of set Maggie back. She could not remember ever having held a gun, much less shooting one.

"Just buy a .38 special and avoid automatics," Aunt Cooney told her. "A .38 will stop most serial killers, and the ammunition is readily available."

Maggie could actually hear chicken noises in the background while she had her aunt on the phone. It occurred to her that maybe she could discuss the gun problem with one of her sons-in-law, all of whom were hunters.

"Hey, I gotta go, sugar—I believe I hear Mr. Bull Snake rustling around," Aunt Cooney said. "You and Connie hustle on over here. I'll wake up the cook and we'll have a ball."

31

"I DON'T KNOW THAT I OUGHT TO let you have this gun—you're so emotional," Kate said, showing Maggie a .38 special Howie had kindly agreed to lend his mother-in-law. Howie owned over forty guns. The .38 special was an old police model he had carried during his brief stint with the LAPD, a stint that had convinced him that being a crane operator, even on the highest crane, was safer than patrolling the streets for the LAPD.

"It was Aunt Cooney's idea, not mine," Maggie pointed out. "I'll never shoot it but Connie says she can shoot if she has to—she played Annie Oakley in a school play once."

"Oh, good training I'm sure," Kate said. "Just be careful with this gun, and now tell me about that weird business with your shrink."

Maggie felt a little resentful of Kate's tone, which was, as usual, a bullying tone. Kate, the oldest daughter, seemed to be the one who had difficulty with the notion that Maggie might want to make her own decisions and live her own life.

"I guess Dr. Tom's a little bit of a masochist—he wanted me to spank him," Maggie said.

They were in the backyard and Maggie was smoking a joint— her mother's resumption of marijuana use was another thing Kate wasn't too pleased about.

"I hope you just take the gun on the road and not the pot," Kate said. "The last thing I need is to have to take off work in order to come get you and Connie out of jail for possession in some hick town."

"You won't have to do that, Kate—you're the last person I'd look to for help if I got arrested," Maggie said, going a little overboard maybe.

Kate's face immediately got red—she had always been quick to flare.

"I suppose you'd rather ask Jeannie," Kate said, "even though she's so self-centered she didn't even wait around to sing 'Happy Birthday' at Howie's birthday party."

Then Kate stopped looking angry and began to look sad.

"That didn't come out the way I meant it to," Maggie admitted. "What I meant to say is that you're more focused on your family than either Jeannie or Meagan. You're the best mother of the three."

Kate looked weary at the thought of what a good mother she

was—that very afternoon she had to take her older daughter, Melanie, to Nordstrom or somewhere to help her pick out a bridesmaid's dress for a wedding she was going to be in. Ordinarily Maggie would be happy to go along on such an excursion, but now, because of an operation that had taken place over a year ago, she seemed unable to be a responsible grandparent. Kate herself had never been much interested in clothes and was not necessarily the best person to deal with an issue as serious as Melanie's bridesmaid's dress.

"I'm sorry I said it, I'm sorry!" Maggie said—she couldn't bear to see such weariness in her daughter's eyes; she immediately hugged Kate, who was stiff at first, but then she cried a little and let herself be hugged. Kate had noticeable B.O. She was a large woman who sweated easily. Also, she did have a tendency to become resigned. Nudging Kate up from the tar pits of resignation was a task that took patience.

"Couldn't you just help Mel pick out her bridesmaid's dress?" Kate asked. "It'd make me feel a whole lot better if you would just do that one thing."

The plea touched Maggie—she agreed. Kate had never been good with clothes—of course Melanie would want to look her best at the wedding. Melanie was tall and skinny and, so far, flat-chested, an esteem-lowering factor in a town as tit-obsessed as L.A.

Kate was stunned that her mother would actually agree to be a grandmother for an hour. She raced off and got Mel. Maggie met them at Nordstrom, where she advised Mel that for a bridesmaid simplicity was best. Not only did they choose a charming pink dress but Maggie actually paid for it, four hundred dollars in fact, which was a huge relief to Kate, who had been quietly worrying what Howie would do when he saw a four-hundred-dollar charge on their Visa. Of course, he would think nothing of it if he had made the charge, which would either be for another gun or maybe deep-sea fishing tackle for the boat.

"Mom, please be careful on your trip," Kate urged, as Melanie was giving her granny a big tight hug.

Driving home, Maggie passed several garage sales but she wasn't in the right frame of mind to stop and look. Making an effort for Melanie, a sweet girl who had braces at the moment as well as flat-chestedness, had been the right thing to do, but it had also required a huge effort at reconnection; and mainly it had failed, not in regard to Melanie so much as in regard to the big glamorous stores with all the expensive stuff in them. The whole world of high-end shopping, which Connie loved so much and which Maggie herself had once loved too, now just disgusted her. All those fancy stores—Saks, Dillard's, Bullock's, Neiman's, Barneys, Nordstrom, and the rest— were so crammed with goods that the thought made Maggie almost nauseous. She needed bras in the worst way and yet she had walked right past the lingerie department at Nordstrom without even stop-ping to look. It might be that she was about to be a top assistant at Marcus Choate's new company, which meant that she'd mainly be on the phone all day—dressing up to be on the phone would just be silly. Buying her shy grandaughter a four-hundred-dollar dress was appropriate but she was thinking that for her own needs Penney's or Sears would probably be fine.

When she got home she found a note from Connie saying she had gone over to East Whittier to tell Johnny Bobcat good-bye, but would be back in time to help Maggie pack the van—they had been hoping to leave real early Monday morning—maybe they could get out of town before the rush hour started.

Just then Dr. Tom called to discuss dining possibilities—he sug-gested a fish restaurant in Santa Monica, which was even farther away than the Italian place in Brentwood.

"Okay, fine," Maggie said—he was paying for dinner, let him pick. All week she had been sort of hoping Dr. Tom would call. They had had their big date on Monday, why not another big date on Tuesday or Wednesday? She had even been thinking that she might try spanking him—Connie had made it seem like a harmless diversion. What could it hurt?

But Dr. Tom had waited until the usual time to call, leaving Maggie without much to do for several hours except smoke pot and

wonder what travel in America would be like. Another thing she
thought about was how far she was prepared to go with Dr. Tom,
assuming he still wanted her to have sex with him in some form.

On that question it was hard to decide in the abstract. Maggie sat
by her pool and smoked joint after joint while indulging in all sorts
of fantasies, the best of which involved just making love to Dr. Tom
in the basic normal way. Over the years Maggie had indulged in lots
of fantasies involving lots of guys; she knew perfectly well that real-
ity seldom matched up to a good fantasy. In real life the guy would
come too soon, or wouldn't be good at foreplay, or she would be having the curse, which freaked quite a few guys out. Fantasies could be
sort of seamless and perfect, whereas the actual act was a good deal
more chancy. One thing that could definitely be said for marijuana
was that it eased the passage of time. Maggie was kind of floating,
floating pleasantly, by the time she pulled herself together and pro-
ceeded over to Highland Avenue.

32

"THIS IS NOT CORRECT PROCEDURE," Dr. Tom said. "There'll be no
charge for this session—you are so beautiful I got carried away."

They had just made love, fully clothed, on Dr. Tom's analyst's
couch. For her part Maggie felt more rumpled than beautiful—but
Dr. Tom was still giving her kisses with his active little tongue. She
wished they had taken a minute to dispense with at least some of
their clothes. What she really wanted to do was get naked and try
again—but Dr. Tom was slipping out, there was no Kleenex handy,
there would soon be a good-sized puddle on his couch. That his first
thought after making love was not to charge her for the session
seemed a little unromantic too.

"I'm hot, can't we undress?" Maggie asked, and they did—Dr.
Tom carefully hung up his nice flannel suit.

At last Maggie got to hold him in her arms, as she had wanted, but the fervor that had caused them to fall on the couch in a big clinch did not come back.

"I don't really have to go to Texas—Aunt Cooney will understand," Maggie told him. Now that she finally had him for a lover, it seemed absurd to go driving away. Instead of answering, Dr. Tom gave a little demonstration of his manual skills. Maggie played with him a little but was relieved when he gave it a rest and just lay quietly in her arms.

"Your aunt is older than I am and I am not young," Dr. Tom said, in a reasonable voice. "She could die any day. You should go and see her before that happens."

"I know—but I love you and I want to be with you a lot," Maggie told him.

Dr. Tom sighed. There I go, coming on too strong again. Watch me run this man off.

But it turned out that Dr. Tom had no intention of running off— he just had some complicated thoughts about where Maggie was in her life and what she needed to do next. After all, he was her shrink, as well as her lover. His body was sort of tough and rubbery—probably his bodybuilding wife saw to it that he kept in good shape.

After a bit, when it seemed that no more sex was in the offing, they got dressed and had Sam drive them to the Italian restaurant in Santa Monica that Dr. Tom had chosen.

On the way, after only nineteen years, Dr. Tom suddenly started drawing some shrinklike conclusions.

"I think you always distrusted your womb because your son died," he said. "When we made love you seemed different. You seemed to have become your real self."

Whoa! Maggie thought. Dr. Tom had made what seemed like a complicated statement. But there was one part of it she agreed with: she *had* felt like her old self while they were making love.

"When you first came to me your son was all you talked about, remember?" he asked.

That she did remember. Billy had died on the third day of his life because of a hole in his heart—in those days doctors didn't know how to fix such a flaw. Billy had flown through life like a tiny sparrow, here two days, gone on the third.

"It wasn't only because of your son that you came to distrust your womb," Dr. Tom went on. "The other reason was your husband's secret family."

Maggie certainly remembered Rog's secret family, which consisted of a well-to-do woman named Ethel and three illegitimate sons. Ethel owned an olive plantation in Azusa—Maggie had not the slightest inkling about Ethel and the three boys until the day Rog dropped dead, which he did while trimming an olive tree on Ethel's plantation. When Ethel called to tell Maggie that Rog was dead and that she had been involved with him for fifteen years and had three sons to prove it, Maggie assumed the woman on the phone was crazy. How could Rog, who was lazy by nature, have a whole family in Azusa? She assumed it was some kind of weird joke; but soon enough Rog's embalmed body arrived in a hearse which Maggie was expected to pay for—so the fact that he was dead was no joke. Ethel came to the funeral with her three sons; the minute Maggie saw the boys she realized the secret family was no joke either. The boys were the spitting image of Rog. The loss of Billy was the deepest grief of her life, but the discovery that Rog had three children by another woman was the biggest shock. All she ever knew about the origins of the secret family was that Rog and Ethel met at a bowling tournament. The discovery knocked Maggie for a loop and she stayed knocked for several years. She would not have thought it possible for dull old Rog to deceive her to that extent, but then she had never been particularly interested in what Rog did in his spare time. Probably her indifference made it easy for Rog to set up a separate family on an olive plantation.

"You mean you think I distrusted my womb because of *that*?" Maggie asked.

"Your womb gave you a damaged son and three daughters, while your husband was giving his mistress healthy sons," he said—but then he quietly dropped his whole theory about Maggie's distrust of her womb and concentrated on his sea bass.

Maggie did likewise, only hers was swordfish, until she happened to glance up and notice that Dr. Tom's eyes were filled with tears—when he took his wallet out to pay for the meal, tears splashed out and got his money wet. Not once, in her company, had he ever used a credit card.

"Uh-oh, did I do something wrong?" Maggie asked.

Dr. Tom shook his head.

"My Nini is leaving me," he said. "I am too old. She no longer finds it worthwhile to love me."

The man had a hopeless look in his eye.

"How old is Ninotchka?" Maggie asked—up to then she had been afraid to ask.

"Twenty-six," he said.

"It's none of my business, but is there a boyfriend in the picture?" she asked. If Ninotchka was only twenty-six, then Dr. Tom was about fifty-five years older than his wife—but only about twenty years older than Maggie. The thought cheered her up. Twenty years was nothing. Even Rog had been fourteen years older than she was.

"Her boyfriend throws the javelin—he's the third best in the world," Dr. Tom said—and then he sighed again.

"What chance does an old man have?" he asked.

"Oh, she'll probably change her mind," Maggie said—she said it partly to restrain her own wild hopes, so that maybe she wouldn't have to endure a big hit to the heart. Many women left their husbands and then changed their minds.

Dr. Tom left the waiter a hundred-dollar tip.

In Sam's car she took his hand.

"I feel as if I'm going away just when you might need me most," she said.

"No, it will be better if you leave for two weeks," he said. "I don't want my Nini to find out about you. She might beat you up."

"If she's leaving you, why would she care so much about me?" she asked—a second later she realized what a stupid question it was. Moving out rarely ended possessiveness—some women never stopped being possessive of their ex-husbands or boyfriends.

"You're better off out of harm's way for a few weeks," he said. "When you come back, Nini will be gone with her javelin man."

The drive back from Santa Monica was an example of how easy it was for well-meaning people, even people in love, to act at cross-purposes. Maggie considered that her new love affair with Dr. Tom took precedence over going to see her Aunt Cooney; but Dr. Tom was obviously at a different place in his life—his twenty-six-year-old wife was moving to Oakland with a javelin thrower. Maggie was prepared to be filled with joy because she had just seduced the man she wanted; but Dr. Tom was losing his wife and was definitely *not* filled with joy.

And yet, when he walked her to her door at Las Palmas Street, he couldn't quite seem to let Maggie go. The closer they got to the threshold of her house, the more unwilling he was to let her cross it. He started kissing and caressing—it embarrassed Maggie for Sam, who sat not far away. When the caresses grew more intense, Maggie insisted that they slip around to the side of the house so Sam wouldn't have to watch them necking, which went on for some time, with Dr. Tom employing his manual skills again.

"I gotta ask once more—are you *sure* you want me to go off to Texas?" she said. She was drifting back to the car with him—they were just holding hands.

There was really nothing she felt less like doing than packing up a van and going to see an aunt who owned two million chickens, and doing it at a moment when a major love affair was finally starting to groove.

"You must go," Dr. Tom insisted. "This is not a good time for you to be here."

Then he gave her one more kiss—it smelled a little of clams—and got in the car.

Maggie could tell that he was one of those men who had a really hard time getting over a woman. Despite all their heavy petting in the walkway beside her house, once he got in the car he looked like a sad little old man, who still had a faraway, hopeless look in his eye.

33

"BULLSHIT, IF HE'S RICH ENOUGH to leave a hundred-dollar tip, why should he be so hopeless?" Connie wanted to know, when she breezed in around 3 A.M. Johnny Bobcat, despite the prostate operation, had been mighty reluctant to let Connie leave.

"Riches don't prevent hopelessness," Maggie pointed out.

Another thing she went on to point out was that they had yet to load a single item in the van, though they had meant to leave at five A.M., an hour that was fast approaching.

"Be practical, honey," Connie told her. "We can't be loading stuff in the van at three A.M. We'd be sitting ducks for some rapists or something."

Maggie had to admit that the five A.M. deadline no longer seemed realistic. Dr. Tom and Johnny Bobcat between them had sort of wrecked that plan.

"I could eat a blueberry waffle if I had one, what about you?" she asked Connie, who agreed that a waffle might hit the spot. Why rush off to Texas when they were both tired, hungry, and on the threshold of complex love affairs? Instead they tootled up to the big pancake house on Sunset, the place Connie referred to as the battered wives' co-op because so many of the waitresses had clearly been the target of violence at some time in their lives.

Once she was occupying herself with a nice stack of blueberry waffles Maggie realized that she had no idea what kind of clothes might be appropriate in Electric City, Texas.

"The first thing we need to get is a snakebite kit," Connie informed her.

Maggie remembered that her aunt had mentioned a bull snake.

"Not every snake is poisonous," Maggie pointed out.

"So what? The ones that aren't poisonous squeeze you to death," Connie retorted.

"Okay, besides the snakebite kit, what do you think we ought to take?" Maggie asked. "I'm serious. If we're going, we need to get started pretty soon."

"Well, cowboy boots in case we go country dancing," Connie said. "And black bras."

"Why black bras?"

"Because cowboys think they're sexy," Connie said. "We might seduce a cowboy or two along the way."

"Connie, I'm in love with Dr. Tom," Maggie reminded her.

"So? Just don't be a spoilsport," Connie warned.

Back home on Las Palmas, both of them stuffed with waffles, they fell victim to fatigue. Maggie smoked a joint and fell asleep in her tent for five hours. When she stumbled back into the house Connie was sound asleep and snoring loudly.

Whatever they were doing, they weren't making a fast getaway.

Maggie took a long shower and washed her hair, in the process discovering that her shampoo was low. She got dressed, dashed up to Walgreens, and stocked up on shampoo—who knew what kind of toiletries were available in Texas?

As she was walking up the aisle to pay up, what did she see but a snakebite kit. To be on the safe side, she took three. When she expressed surprise that a drugstore in L.A. would stock snakebite kits, the old cashier looked at her as if she were crazy.

"Where have you been living? L.A. is full of rattlesnakes," the cranky old lady checker assured her.

"I've lived here sixty years and the only snakes I've seen were in the snake house at the zoo," Maggie maintained.

"Then I guess we have to agree to disagree," the old checker said.

When Maggie got home with her supplies Connie was talking on the phone to Johnny Bobcat, which she did five or six times while the two of them attempted to load the van. Of course they had to make a run to Connie's apartment, so she could pack her sexy lingerie. What with one thing and another the day slowly passed and the van even more slowly filled up with this and that. Listening to Connie talk to Johnny every hour or so made Maggie wish she could call Dr. Tom—it would be reassuring just to hear his voice—but Dr. Tom, as he had once explained, was telephone intolerant. The few times when she had called him at desperate moments he had been pretty brusque. If she called and he was brusque it would just make her feel worse, so she held off—but it wasn't easy.

Then the predictable happened: Connie began to defect, which is what she usually did when it actually became time for the two of them to go someplace they had planned to go.

"I can't go because Johnny needs me," Connie announced. "He thinks he might be getting an infection down there."

"So all that talk about splitting the gas was just idle talk, right, Con?" Maggie asked. "Now I find that the one person I thought I could count on I can't count on."

Connie got a surly look on her face—she did not like to be accused of being a bad friend.

"I might go, I can't decide," she said, and ran off into the bedroom to have another long conversation with Johnny, who seemed to have become a towering presence in Connie's life in the last few days. When she emerged she looked more cheerful.

"Johnny had a good idea," she told Maggie. "He suggested we flip a coin, heads we go, tails we stay."

"Connie, I don't need to flip a coin—I'm going," Maggie said— but she didn't say it with much conviction, because she had begun to wonder if she really had the energy to cast off routine and drive thousands of miles across America. Part of her just wanted to stay where she was and smoke pot for a few weeks.

In the end she gave in and got a quarter out of her purse. Let the quarter decide their fate, she thought.

"Heads we go, tails we stay—correct? Is that a firm decision?"

"Oh yeah, you bet it's firm," Connie assured her. Connie was usually lucky in casinos—she had won several pretty good jackpots playing the slots.

Maggie flipped the coin and it came up heads.

"Oh shit!" Connie said. "Do it again, just one more time."

"Nope, that's cheating," Maggie said.

"So cheat—just one more time," Connie insisted. In certain situations she couldn't bear to lose.

"You shouldn't tempt fate," Maggie pointed out. "It could bring on a curse of some kind, you know."

"Just once more, please, sweetie?" Connie begged—nobody hated to lose a coin flip worse than she did.

"A deal is a deal," Maggie said, putting the quarter back in her purse.

"I hate you, you won't ever give me a chance!" Connie raged.

Maggie assumed, at that point, that she would be traveling alone, but when the sun began to set at the distant end of Sunset Boulevard, Connie, who looked as if she had been crying for a week, came out with her big canvas bag and got in the van.

"If you'd really rather stay, stay," Maggie conceded.

She realized it could be hard to leave a guy who might have an infection down there.

"Just drive," Connie told her.

Maggie had already entrusted her house keys to Gwen. She was thinking that one disadvantage to growing old in the place where she had been young was that memories came floating up—which could make you really want to do it all over again, live life a second time. The tree where Jeff Brent had kissed her for the first time—she had only been twelve—was just three streets over, near where Connie lived. The tree was still there but Jeff Brent she had lost track of; but just for a moment, she felt a huge urge to be back at that tree, accepting that first kiss, with all her lovely adventures in the kissing line still to come.

"Connie, do you ever wish you could be young again?" Maggie asked.

"Maggie, just start the car—just start the car, before I lose my fucking mind," Connie said.

Book Two

THE HIGHWAY

1

MAGGIE AND CONNIE had each indulged in a little hasty map study over the past few days, the result of which was an immediate disagreement about their exit strategy vis-à-vis L.A.

"Go through downtown—I want to see the tall buildings one more time, they're so romantic," Connie demanded.

"No way, José," Maggie told her. Far too many major freeways converged downtown—the Harbor and the Santa Monica, for example, not to mention the Pasadena Freeway and the I-5. So many big roads coming together held rich prospects for disaster, in the way of mammoth traffic jams.

"In no time we can be up on the 210 and we're gone," Maggie said. "There are several tall buildings in Pasadena that you can look at."

"Not as tall as the ones downtown," Connie pointed out—but she had lost the argument. Once behind the wheel, Maggie got adrenalized; wasn't it exciting to be part of the great river of cars that were forever flowing in and out of Los Angeles? Pretty soon Burbank slid behind them; Pasadena loomed and then fell behind, just as Burbank had. Soon the river of traffic thinned a little—it became more like a rushing creek.

"Ever been to Rancho Cucamonga?" Maggie asked. Connie was being a little too quiet.

"Never! Why would I go to a dumb place like Rancho Cucamonga?" Connie replied.

"Well, there's a famous vineyard there," Maggie pointed out. "My parents used to go on outings there."

This bit of history left Connie unmoved, but she perked up immediately when they saw the lights of seven or eight police cars ahead.

"Look, I bet they caught some drug lord, let's pull over and check it out," Connie said. She had never been able to resist crime scenes.

"Connie, we're on the freeway, we can't just stop and check it out," Maggie protested.

"Eight cop cars," Connie said, counting rapidly. "It must be a major drug lord. I don't know why you won't stop."

"Because the cops will just yell at us, that's why," Maggie said. All she saw was three scared teenagers, standing by a beat-up Toyota. It was not the first time Connie had let her imagination run away with her. Two of the cops were searching the Toyota, trying to find something to nail the teenagers on. Cops busting teenagers was a common sight, but this particular sight caused Maggie to remember something: she had forgotten to bring Howie's gun, the gun he had so graciously lent her.

"Oh my God, I forgot the gun," Maggie said. "Did you remember it, by any chance?"

"I didn't remember it—why would I?" Connie asked. But then she remembered something that immediately caused her to cheer up.

"Hey, Johnny's got guns," she said. "East Whittier isn't far out of our way."

For once Connie's sense of geography was accurate. East Whittier was only a small detour, and they had already agreed to stop for the night in Victorville, which wasn't that far away either.

"Call him, he might not be home," Maggie suggested, so Connie dug her cell phone out of her big bag and called Johnny Bobcat.

"Yeah," a voice said. Even from where Maggie sat it sounded like a female voice, and a not particularly friendly female voice at that.

"Excuse me, is Johnny home?" Connie asked—it was clear she had not been expecting to have a female answer Johnny's phone.

"He's in the shower, what do you want?" the voice asked.

"Excuse me, who are you?" Connie asked—she was struggling to get a grip on the situation.

"I'm his girlfriend, who else would I be?" the voice said. "Are you that old blonde slut who's been pestering him? If I catch you over here I'm gonna beat the living crap out of you, I can guarantee you that."

Connie clicked the cell phone off. Then she threw the cell phone out the window. Then she burst into tears and cried as hard as she could cry for seven exits, by Maggie's count. Maggie tried to rub her neck but Connie shrugged off her hand.

"And two hours ago the man was trying to get you not to leave," Maggie reminded her.

"Now I wish we did have the gun—I'd go shoot that ugly fat whore," Connie said.

"You've never seen her, how do you know she's fat?"

"She had a fat voice," Connie said.

"What about Johnny?"

Connie pondered the question for another exit or two.

"I couldn't shoot him, the son of a bitch," Connie concluded. "He's not himself right now. It's because of his infection down there."

"I see," Maggie said, and let the matter drop.

2

THE NEXT MORNING, at a big Wal-Mart in Victorville, Connie bought a new cell phone and Maggie bought a .38 special and a box of bullets. Somehow the bullets seemed more scary than the gun. The salesman demonstrated the safety features of the gun—namely a safety catch—while Connie wandered around the vast store buying miscellaneous articles of apparel, including string panties.

"Aren't you a little old for string panties?" Maggie asked—her query went unanswered. The sun was very bright in Victorville, so that both of them had to put on their dark glasses.

"What do people do here—it takes hours just to get across the parking lot?" Connie asked, gesturing in the general direction of Victorville.

"Just live, I guess," Maggie said.

"This sun is much too fucking bright," Connie went on. "I'm going to get a sick headache if I have to travel very far in this bright light. I prefer hazy weather, like we have in L.A."

Maggie had the same worry—a worry so strong that Connie went racing back into the store to buy scarves they would wrap around their heads. The van was burning hot, from having been locked up. Maggie drove it around and around the vast parking lot, playing the air conditioner for all it was worth. The air conditioner began to rattle, which was an ominous sign, but fortunately, after a bit, it stopped rattling.

Just as they were pulling back on the freeway, Connie happened to spot a sign advertising the Roy Rogers and Dale Evans Museum, which, it seemed, was right there in Victorville. Naturally Connie wanted to go have a look.

"Maybe on the way back," Maggie told her.

"You never want to do cultural things!" Connie accused. "Why the big hurry to get to Texas anyway?

"I think Trigger's in that museum, stuffed," she added.

"So, who wants to see a stuffed horse?" Maggie asked.

"It isn't just any horse, it's *Trigger!*" Connie insisted, at which point Maggie gave in. When they entered the museum, sure enough there was Trigger, after which they spent most of their time looking at Dale Evans's many outfits.

"Being a cowgirl might not be such a bad life," Connie remarked.

"She wasn't a cowgirl—she was an actress," Maggie pointed out.

"She must have had a nice little butt when she was young," Connie said. "Those cowgirl outfits don't work unless you have a nice little butt. A butt sort of like yours."

Connie had always been envious of Maggie's trim butt.

"You could have a butt just as good if you exercised more," Maggie said, a comment Connie didn't challenge.

"It's my turn to drive," Connie said, when they got back to the van.

"Drive, just stay in the right lane unless you really need to pass," Maggie advised.

"What's wrong with the fast lane?"

"This van won't run fast enough to qualify for *this* fast lane," Maggie said. "This is the freeway to Las Vegas—we'll just be a smear on the highway if we get in the way of a high roller who's in a hurry."

Connie, a cautious, both-hands-on-the-wheel driver, soon saw the wisdom of not getting in the way of high rollers or big trucks, many of which went whizzing by them as if they weren't moving.

Ahead, as far as the eye could see, was nothing but bare desert and a white-hot sky.

"I didn't know it would be this hot. Why didn't you tell me?" Connie asked.

"It's July, which is normally a hot month," Maggie pointed out.

"If we break down we'll die of dehydration before anyone can come to our rescue," Connie said.

"When we get to Barstow we'll stock up on water," Maggie promised.

"How far is it across this stupid desert anyway?" Connie asked.

"I have no idea."

"You could get out the road atlas and add up the distances between towns, then you'd have an idea," Connie pressed.

"No, then I'd have a headache from squinting," Maggie mentioned. "It's obviously a very long way but if you just keep driving we'll be across in a day or two, maybe."

"I'll go mad with boredom," Connie predicted. "Why didn't we just fly?"

Maggie began to remember how skillful Connie was at finding fault. There was almost no human activity, including sex, that she couldn't find fault with. She had many good qualities, of course—it's just that patience wasn't one of them.

In fact, the desert did look daunting. She did so little traveling that she had forgotten how long and lonesome-looking some roads could be. When she rolled down the window even for a second the desert air was really hot—hot enough to crack the skin, at least. Giant trucks went whizzing by, going very fast. Maggie decided that her main hope was just that the air-conditioning didn't start rattling again. The huge emptiness could be crossed successfully if they could just stay cool.

"This trip was Paolo's idea," Maggie remembered. "He said a trip would make me feel better—I wonder if it will."

"How can it, unless the scenery improves?" Connie said. "How dumb do you have to be to take a trip just because a waiter suggests it?"

Maggie didn't rise to that bait. The trip had just started—it was too soon for bickering to start.

"Paolo never told me that *I* needed to take a trip," Connie mentioned.

"You're not the one in despair," Maggie reminded her.

"No, it's because he has the hots for brunettes," Connie told her. "Besides, you're not really in despair. You've got okay tits and a nice butt—why despair?"

With nothing to do but think for quite a few miles, Maggie realized Connie had said something true. She *wasn't* in despair anymore, a surprising realization. She tried to trace back to when despair had left her, and her best guess was that it happened when Dr. Tom took down his pants and made love to her on his analyst's couch. Until that moment she had lived with the fear that there might be no more real love for her.

"You're too quiet," Connie complained.

"I'm just thinking about something," Maggie said.

3

IN BARSTOW THEY BOUGHT a whole case of Evian water, as a hedge against the dangers of dehydration. Connie wanted to buy a five-gallon container of gasoline, just to be on the safe side, but Maggie nixed that notion.

"If we had an accident we might be burned alive," she pointed out.

"No, we could douse it with the Evian," Connie said, but she wasn't that serious about the gasoline.

Maggie took over the driving again, while Connie immersed herself in the *Mobil Travel Guide*. Their visit to the Roy Rogers and Dale Evans Museum had been a nice diversion—she wanted to see what other cultural wonders lay ahead.

"Hey, we could see London Bridge," she informed Maggie. "It's at Lake Havasu City—there's a road you go down after we get to Needles, if we ever do."

A road sign had just informed them that it was one hundred and thirty-two miles to Needles.

"I've never been in a place where it's hundreds of miles between towns," Connie allowed. "What's the point of putting big highways in remote places like this?

"This is the road that used to be Route 66," Connie reminded her. "The beatniks traveled on it, and probably the Okies too."

Sure enough, every now and then, there would be an exit sign to some short fragment of old 66, but the only tourists who seemed to show any interest in this famous road were Japanese, all of them clicking away with cameras.

"What if they're building up to another Pearl Harbor?" Connie asked.

Maggie let that one float by.

Bored with the endless gray desert, Connie dug her new cell phone out of her bag and dialed Johnny Bobcat's house.

"I'm hanging up if the whore answers," she said, moments before she discovered that they were so far out in the desert that her cell phone wouldn't work. Connie's cell phones were always in constant use. To discover that she couldn't immediately call back to the civilized parts of the country came as a big shock.

"This is terrible—it's worse than having the batteries run down," Connie complained.

"If you don't mind my saying so, you shouldn't be calling that man anyway—not after the way he treated you," Maggie told her.

"Beside the point—he's not the only person I might want to call," Connie insisted.

"It's temporary," Maggie assured her. "We just need to get closer to Needles—then it will work again."

"What if there's an emergency and we can't even call nine-eleven?" Connie asked, just as seven huge semis came whooshing by.

"A trucker would rescue us—a nice trucker," Maggie said.

At the truck stop in Barstow Connie had made a little study of the truckers as they came and went, and her conclusion had been that most truckers were not good-looking enough to bother about. Also, they all smoked, a vice she had finally given up. The thought of being rescued by heavy smokers did not appeal.

"It's hard to break the L.A. habit, isn't it?" she said. "There's no reason to ever be bored if you live in L.A."

"True," Maggie agreed.

"We *could* just turn around and go back," Connie pointed out.

Maggie could understand the feelings that were tugging at Connie—the same feelings were tugging at her too. It seemed odd that the two of them were traveling thousands of miles in a van to see an aunt she could barely remember. Paolo had thought a trip might cheer her up, but falling in love with Dr. Tom had already cheered her up.

Still, taking a trip was a normal thing. She and Connie had planned many trips: to Hawaii, to a ski lodge, to Chicago, where Connie had cousins, to Lake Louise, and so on; but none of the trips had ever happened. Money had something to do with it. Connie's son, Danny, would get arrested, so that whatever money Connie had to spare would get spent on lawyers or rehab; or if it wasn't Danny in trouble, one of Maggie's daughters would need a little loan—or it might be an emergency with Auberon or Jeremiah or someone else in the loop group. The trips finally came to be fantasies they projected to convince themselves that they weren't in a rut, whereas in fact they *were* stuck in a rut.

Now, though, they had actually made a move. They were actually traveling. The desert itself looked pretty bleak, but there were still exciting prospects ahead: they *could* see London Bridge, or even make a huge detour up to the Grand Canyon. Going back to L.A. without ever having even got out of California would seem like a huge defeat.

"Try and look on the bright side," Maggie urged. "Seventy-five more miles and we'll be in Needles."

"Big whup!" Connie replied, in a tone that suggested she didn't think there was likely to be anything so great about Needles.

"At least your cell phone ought to start working again," Maggie said. It was the one thing she could think of that might be nice about Needles.

4

"Hey, bingo!" Connie said. They were still twenty miles from Needles but her cell phone had come back to life. But when she called Johnny Bobcat his phone just rang and rang. After twenty rings Connie gave up.

"He *had* a perfectly good message machine," Connie declared. "Probably that fat whore turned it off."

While Connie was trying to think of someone who might know where Johnny could be, Maggie's cell phone rang.

"Who could that be?" she asked, before noticing from the call window that it was her daughter Meagan.

"Hi, sweetie, what's up?" she asked.

"Kate left Howie," Meagan said.

"Kate left Howie," Maggie said to Connie, but Connie was preoccupied with her own problems and didn't even shrug.

"Surely Jeannie didn't tell her about the French kiss, did she?"

There was silence on the line. During the silence Maggie remembered that it was Meagan who was the family snitch. Jeannie had the most to conceal, and she concealed it, but Meagan couldn't keep a secret much more than five minutes.

"I told her, but it wasn't just about the kiss," Meagan explained. "He did something worse to me that same evening."

"What?"

"He grabbed my hand and put it on his dick," Meagan told her. "And he squeezed my tit. He said he just did it to see if my breast was real. Why would my breast not be real?"

"A lot of guys try that hand-on-the-dick number," Maggie mentioned. "A very famous actor has done that to me not once but twice."

At the mention of "dick" Connie stopped cruising her address book, looking for people who might know Johnny. She looked at Maggie, waiting for more about whoever's dick it was that Maggie and Meagan were talking about.

"You *would* leave just as everything falls apart," Meagan complained.

"Where's Kate staying?" Maggie asked.

"With us—she's devastated," Meagan said. "But she's at work. Kate wouldn't miss a day of work unless somebody died."

"That's a good point, honey—nobody's died," Maggie said. "It's a mess but it's not a tragedy."

"If Kate's marriage is over, it's a tragedy," Meagan insisted. "Think of the kids—they love Howie."

"Let's not overdramatize, please," Maggie said. "Kate's had a shock, but she needs to consider the context. Her husband was drunk at his own birthday party and he wasn't perfectly behaved when it came to his own attractive sisters-in-law. I don't think it's the end of the world, or even the end of Kate's marriage.

"Maybe Howie just needs counseling," she added.

"Counseling, when the asshole came on to both his sisters-in-law?" Meagan said.

"It wouldn't hurt," Maggie replied. "Howie's just a typical guy—that's his virtue and also his defect. He's a good provider and a good father and not the worst husband in the world."

Meagan rushed right past her mother's comments—she was in

no mood to hear about Howie Tucker's good points, although obviously he wasn't Hitler or some other terrible dictator.

"If my husband ever comes on to either of my sisters he's gonna get something worse than counseling," she declared. "I'll bust his fucking head.

"And I still wish you hadn't gone away just when things were falling apart," she added.

"Well, Connie and I were between jobs—it just seemed a good time to go somewhere," Maggie told her. "I'll call Kate when she gets home from work and try to cheer her up."

"Thanks a lot," Meagan said, but not in a grateful voice—as the baby of the family, she needed more comforting than the others.

"I guess you never get a break from being a mother," Maggie said, after she filled Connie in on the substance of the situation.

"At least your daughters have normal heterosexual problems," Connie remarked. "I'd trade Danny's problems for their problems any day.

"I don't think Danny's had ten real dates in his life," she added.

Maggie could only squeeze Connie's hand as a gesture of sympathy. Drugs had caught Danny early, before his sex drive really kicked in. He had his mother's good looks and could have had plenty of dates if he hadn't been more interested in getting high.

"Did you tell him we were leaving?"

"No, because I was afraid he'd tell me he's back on meth," Connie said. "Or he might tell me he got fired from the library—then I would have felt too guilty to go off and leave him."

Danny had worked at the Hollywood Public Library for years, shelving books. Despite his problems he was said to be extremely good at shelving and alphabetizing, skills that went far in library work.

"I don't think they'll fire him," Maggie said—but who knew, really?

"We should have bought some vodka in Barstow," Connie said.

"Danny's more stable than most addicts, and besides, he's *nice*," Maggie reminded her.

"Brag on him all you want to—I still feel guilty and I still feel like getting drunk," Connie replied.

"All parents feel guilty," Maggie remarked. Contemplating their mutual failings as parents was no way to have a fun trip.

"Do you think if I'd just gone to PTA meetings it would have changed anything?" Connie asked.

"I went to PTA meetings, hundreds," Maggie told her. "Did it change anything? No."

Both were glad when the highway slanted down a long hill, with a beautiful green river visible in the distance. A lot of gas stations and truck stops loomed between them and the river.

"We made it to Needles," Maggie said in triumph.

"So what does that make you, Columbus?" Connie retorted. To her it didn't count as much of an achievement. After all, untold thousands of Americans and uncountable numbers of Japanese made it to Needles.

"Now we have to decide about London Bridge," Maggie told her.

"We might as well go see it—why not?" Connie said. "But first I want to stop at a liquor store."

"I don't know that you ought to be getting drunk, in your present mood," Maggie ventured.

It was an opinion Connie felt free to ignore.

5

IN NEEDLES THEY bought many necessities, including a Styrofoam cooler and two big bags of ice. They bought some limes, some canned iced tea, plenty of V8 juice, and two fifths of vodka. Just having the vodka handy made Connie feel better, but she couldn't immediately get drunk because it was her turn to drive.

"Oh my God, look!" Maggie said—on the road ahead, nicely spaced along the shoulder, were more hitchhikers than she had ever seen in one place before—maybe twenty in all. Most of them were young men but there were two little families, husband, wife, and young child; there were even three hitchhikers with dogs. All of them, as Maggie and Connie sped by, appeared to be trying not to look hopeless—and yet, to Maggie's mind, few things could be more hopeless than to hitchhike with your dog or your little family out of a hot, mean little desert town where the competition for rides was especially fierce.

There was even one old-timey hobo, an old man with a white beard down to his waist. He was the last hitchhiker and he managed to make eye contact with Maggie as the van sped by; the old hobo actually waved at her, but Connie, of course, had not slowed down and he was soon left behind.

"He looks like Father Time," Connie remarked. "It'd be awful having to hitch when you're that old."

"I think it would be worse to have to hitch with a little baby," Maggie said. "What if the baby got sick?"

"What if your *dog* got sick?" Connie wondered. "I doubt if there are many good vets in these little towns."

They had agreed to see London Bridge—why not?—and took the turnoff to Lake Havasu City.

"That old guy waved to me," Maggie said. "I wonder if I knew him from somewhere."

"We're not picking him up," Connie said firmly. "Even if he didn't murder us, he might be smelly—most hitchhikers smell, and you know how sensitive my smeller is."

"Okay," Maggie agreed.

Unfortunately, after they took the trouble to find London Bridge, it didn't really impress them all that much. It was just a short stone bridge over a kind of backwater of Lake Havasu, surrounded by hundreds of nice little suburban houses, of the sort that housed well-off retirees by the millions in southern California.

"Is this all?" Connie asked—pictures she had seen of London Bridge made it seem a lot different, perhaps because then it had been in London and hadn't been surrounded by all those thousands of subdivision houses.

"Big whup!" Connie concluded. "We came all this way to see a subdivision."

"Still, Shakespeare might have walked across that bridge—for all we know," Maggie pointed out. "It's historic, at least."

"To me it's just creepy," Connie insisted. "I never was into antiques."

6

JUST AS THEY PULLED BACK onto I-40 they saw the same old Father Time hitchhiker again. He was waiting just past the entry ramp, and he looked right at them as if he had been expecting them to come along.

"Don't make eye contact!" Connie warned, but too late. Maggie had already made eye contact: the old hobo looked at her sternly as they whipped by. It was almost as if he thought he had a place in their lives. It only took a fraction of a second to sweep by him, but the fraction of a second was long enough to make Maggie nervous.

"I think he's stalking us—I wish you hadn't looked him in the eye," Connie said, accusingly.

"I didn't mean to—it just happened," Maggie assured her. "There's not much he can do—he's on foot—there's no way he can catch us."

Before they could ponder the threat of the old hitchhiker at further length, the cell phone rang and rang. It was Kate.

"Hi, honey—are you at Meagan's?" Maggie asked.

"Of course I'm at Meagan's—I wish you hadn't left," Kate said.

"We're in Arizona now," Maggie told her, feeling unapologetic. "Has Howie apologized yet?"

"Oh sure, maybe a thousand times, for what that's worth," Kate said.

"Did he send you flowers?"

"Yes, roses—for what that's worth," Kate admitted.

"So do you want my advice?"

"I already heard it—counseling," Kate said. "I doubt Howie would go for it. He equates stuff like that with mental illness."

"Well, his marriage is ill—why not try?"

"I don't think I would have minded so much if he had just made a pass at some random woman," Kate said. "It's the fact that it was my *sisters*—my younger sisters—that hurts the most."

"I'm sure," Maggie said. "And yet a lot of widowers turn around and marry their deceased wife's sister."

"Is that supposed to console me?" Kate asked. "If I die, do you think I want Howie marrying Jeannie?"

"I'm sorry, I guess I misspoke."

In fact, Maggie found that she had trouble connecting with Kate's distress—even though she could plainly hear the distress in Kate's voice. But Kate was forty-two, old enough to negotiate life's little speed bumps for herself. Maggie wanted to be left alone to enjoy her lovely ride into Arizona with Connie. It seemed as if the farther she got from L.A., the harder it was for her to really connect with family issues. For the first time in her life she felt as if she really were on vacation, with family discords left behind. It was a good feeling, but one that rendered her a little unsympathetic.

"You're not even listening," Kate protested.

"We're getting into the mountains—the cell phone is cutting out," Maggie said, and it was true.

"If I were you I'd go home and freeze Howie out for a couple of weeks and see what happens."

"A week or two—if Howie had to go two weeks without sex he'd lose his mind," Kate said, at which point Maggie switched off the phone—she thought she could blame the disconnect on mountainous conditions. Kate did not call back.

"You're a cool one," Connie said. "If I was in trouble and you took that cool tone with me, I'd crack you one."

"I just want to enjoy our vacation—don't you?"

"I am enjoying it, except for that old tramp," Connie said. "I think he's sinister."

It was tending toward evening, but it would be a long fade from sunset to dusk, thanks to the long days. As they gained altitude the air outside didn't seem quite so searing.

"Let's stop at a grocery store and buy some grapefruit," Maggie suggested. "Then we can get a motel in Kingman and drink vodka and grapefruit juice."

"Now you're talking—I'm sorry I criticized," Connie said.

7

"Do you think Mom and Connie ever get it on?" Jeannie asked. The three sisters were sitting on the big back porch of Meagan's house; and the kids, inside, were watching *South Park,* which, normally, they wouldn't have been allowed to do—just at the moment, standards had been relaxed so the sisters could have a nice peaceful visit on the porch.

"Are you crazy, of course not!" Meagan burst out.

"Of course not," Kate seconded. "What made you ask a question like that?"

"They're together practically twenty-four hours a day, and half the time they sleep in the same bed," Jeannie pointed out. "I just wondered if maybe they kind of slipped into a little sex, once in a while."

"Everybody isn't sex obsessed like you, Jeannie," Meagan said. "Our mother is not a dyke, and neither is Connie."

"Look at how many boyfriends they've had," Kate offered.

"Forget it—be square if you want to," Jeannie said. "It was just a thought that popped into my head."

There was a lengthy silence. Kate was on her fourth beer and Meagan was sipping a nice chardonnay. It was a peaceful summer evening but Jeannie, as usual, had a restless look.

"It wouldn't be the end of the world if they had sex once in a while," Jeannie suggested. Both her sisters got stiff looks—they would never agree that their mother and Connie making love could be anything but an immoral perversion.

"She's our *mother,* after all," Meagan reminded her.

"You guys are paleos, I'm going home," Jeannie said. She grabbed her kids and left.

8

THE MOTEL THEY CHOSE in Kingman was a vast improvement over the dump they had stayed in in Victorville. The room cost seventy-two dollars—far too much to be spending on a motel at the beginning of their trip, Maggie thought, but Connie had other priorities.

"We've been in the desert—I may take several showers and I need good towels," Connie pointed out. "And I want a room with real glasses in it, not those crappy little plastic glasses. Who wants to drink vodka and grapefruit juice out of plastic glasses?"

The complaint signified a reversal of roles—usually it was Connie who was the cheap one. Maggie didn't bother to argue; she liked plenty of towels herself, when she stayed in a motel.

The motel had a lounge and a kind of mini casino they thought they might visit, but after a long shower apiece and liberal amounts of vodka and grapefruit juice, they decided they would rather just lie on the bed and watch *Everybody Loves Raymond,* which they did.

"Ray Romano is so cute," Connie volunteered. "Patricia Heaton's lucky she gets such a cute leading man to play opposite."

"It's hard work, though, episodic TV," Maggie reminded her. "I worked on *I Dream of Jeannie.* I was young and bouncy then, but it still wore me out. Long days, long days."

By then Connie had faded out, and was snoring more loudly than usual. Being on vacation had really sapped her strength. Maggie switched over to the Weather Channel and turned the volume up a little; the most soothing channel on TV, in her opinion. While the weather was being explained Maggie studied the road atlas, hoping to find a less trafficky route from Kingman to Electric

City. She wanted to avoid the old hitchhiker, for one thing; but the atlas revealed no promising alternative routes. I-40 went straight to Amarillo, and then a little road pretty soon shot up to Electric City. Maggie quickly gave up the project—she was too tired for serious map study, so she finished off her vodka and grapefruit juice and let the soothing sounds of the Weather Channel lull her to sleep. Unfortunately she was too tired to stay asleep very long—just as she was dozing off for about the third time, Connie nudged her awake.

"Wake up, *The Honeymooners* is on," Connie told her. Connie was probably the world's biggest fan of *The Honeymooners*. She had probably seen every single episode five or six times.

"I'm not in the mood for *The Honeymooners,*" Maggie informed her.

"Why not? I am," Connie said.

"I was having a bad dream—our kitten drowned," Maggie told her. "My daughters were all crying in the dream."

"That's not Jackie Gleason's fault," Connie pointed out.

"I didn't say it was—the minute this episode's over, can we please go back to the Weather Channel?"

"Since I'm splitting the gas you'd think I'd at least get to have some say about our choice of TV programs," Connie said, sounding mildly pissed.

"It's three A.M.—do we have to argue right now?" Maggie asked. "We have a long drive ahead of us tomorrow, remember?"

"How could I forget, with that old serial killer showing up every time we pull onto the freeway?" Connie said.

But out of consideration for Maggie she did turn the TV way down—fortunately she knew most of the *Honeymooners* dialogue by heart.

"I must feel guilty about leaving my daughters," Maggie said. "Otherwise why would I dream our kitten drowned? We haven't had a kitten in twenty years."

"Your daughters will be fine," Connie assured her. She held

Maggie's hand for a bit, and once her favorite show ended, switched the TV back to the Weather Channel.

"Thanks. I don't know what I'd do without the Weather Channel."

9

WITH NO LOOP GROUP to round up, neither Maggie nor Connie set any speed records when it came to getting off in the morning. Overnight, it seemed, they had become world-class dawdlers. It was nine-thirty before Connie concluded that it would be a good time to brush her teeth. Maggie was an Angels fan and browsed the sports channels for whatever intelligence she could pick up.

The two of them packed up, loaded the van, and then sauntered over to the coffee shop; they were discussing whether to risk huevos rancheros in an alien environment when they ran right into the one person they were hoping not to see: the tramp with the long white beard. He was sitting in a booth eating toast with ketchup on it; before they could flee he stood up and greeted both of them by name.

"Maggie Clary and Connie Bruckner," he said—he had a kind of syrupy D.J.'s voice. It was soon obvious that he wasn't as old as his beard made him look.

"Excuse me, have we met?" Maggie asked.

"Sure we've met—remember *The Wrath of God*?" he said.

"*Wrath of God, Wrath of God* . . . I guess I don't," Maggie had to admit.

"I remember it," Connie said. "You held script and I was Rita Hayworth's assistant—it was her last movie."

"I'm Jethro Jordan, I was a wrangler on that show," the man said. "Remember us going to Carpinteria? I took you gals to the rodeo there the day after we wrapped."

"Good Lord, I don't remember that picture or the rodeo or anything," Maggie admitted.

"I never saw anyone eat ketchup on toast before," Connie remarked. Only a few minutes ago Connie had considered Jethro a dangerous serial killer, but now she was beginning to flirt with him.

"It's cheap, that's why—I got to get all the way to Arkadelphia, Arkansas, where my boys live . . . I need to nurse my pennies."

Maggie began to call up a few vague memories of *The Wrath of God*.

"Wasn't it filmed near Altadena?" she asked. In those distant days Altadena hardly seemed like a part of L.A. at all. She remembered that there had even been some trouble with a mountain lion. There were goats in the picture and a mountain lion had eaten a couple of them.

"That's right—we hired a trapper but the cat got clean away," Jethro told her.

It all seemed a little funky, but Jethro at the moment didn't seem all that dangerous, so they bought him huevos rancheros.

"It's like a miracle you spotted us after all these years," Connie remarked, but Jethro didn't think it was a miracle at all.

"The old I-40's a good road," he said. "I never hitch it without meeting someone I knew thirty or forty years ago. I recognized the two of you when you eased out of Needles, and I was sure of it when you came up that on-ramp from Lake Havasu City. I thought then that if I could just locate you, we'd have a nice reunion. I'm a professional hitchhiker, after all. When you're hitchhiking from L.A. to Arkadelphia, it pays to watch close, particularly by the on-ramps. You're not the first old friends who have picked me up."

"But we didn't pick you up," Maggie reminded him—she felt just the faint beginnings of uneasiness.

"We passed you twice *without* picking you up," she reminded him.

"Hey, don't be rude to Jethro," Connie said.

"I wasn't being rude—I was just correcting the record," Maggie said, and just then she happened to look Jethro Jordan in the eye—the look she got was icy cold, as cold and disdainful as the look Terry Matlock gave her the day she kicked him out. In fact, a tension was developing—Jethro was obviously going to ask them for a ride; Maggie's fear was that if Jethro did ask them, Connie's impulse would be to let him join them.

Besides that, for some reason, the waitresses had begun to glare at them. Apparently it didn't sit well with them that Jethro Jordan was breakfasting with two foxy women.

Another thing that had come back to Maggie about the filming of *The Wrath of God* was how sad Rita Hayworth looked.

The same memory hit Connie at the same time.

"Miss Hayworth was dying then," Connie said. "I used to cry every morning at how sad she was—she had been such a looker once."

Maggie knew Connie was right. Rita Hayworth had been a great movie star—so how degrading could it be to end your career in Altadena on a ranch where mountain lions ate goats? Terminally degrading it had been, in the tragic case of Rita Hayworth.

But sad memories of a once-great star did nothing to solve the problem of Jethro Jordan. Connie seemed to be leaning toward asking him along, a move which Maggie adamantly opposed.

Jethro Jordan, professional hitchhiker that he was, read the tension accurately enough not to press his point. What he did was ask if the two of them had already checked out—when they said no, he asked if he could use their room long enough to grab a quick shower.

"A man can get mighty dusty, hitching on the old I-40," Jethro said, being superpolite. "If I could grab a quick shower and wash some of this grit off, I'd be much obliged."

I don't know why I'm doing this, Maggie thought, but she handed Jethro their room key anyway.

10

"JUST YESTERDAY YOU THOUGHT he was a serial killer," Maggie reminded Connie. They were in the van, waiting uneasily for Jethro to emerge from their room, so they could check out. Maggie was behind the wheel.

"I didn't know we knew him then," Connie said. "He's just trying to rejoin his family in Arkansas. What's wrong with that?"

"Nothing, unless it's a lie," Maggie said. "What if he *is* a killer? What if he's just setting us up?"

Connie, convinced for a few minutes that they should offer Jethro Jordan a ride, was wavering. If her life in L.A. had taught her anything, it was how hard it could be to get rid of a guy once he turned out to be the wrong guy.

"He's got a cold eye," Maggie pointed out. "A very cold eye. We fed him breakfast and let him shower in our room—I don't think we need to give him a ride too."

Suddenly she began to feel very, very anxious—she could not have said exactly why.

"I'm getting afraid," she admitted. "Dr. Tom always told me to trust my fear instinct, and right now what I'm feeling is a lot of fear."

"Me too," Connie said. "This is weird, and I don't like weird when I'm on vacation."

"This is *our* vacation, besides," Maggie said. "Why complicate it with a hitchhiker, even if we did work on a picture together forty years ago?"

"You've convinced me, let's leave him," Connie said. "Lock the doors."

The minute he heard the van start up, Jethro Jordan opened the door to their room and glared at them. He was naked. His beard reached almost down to his pubic hair—he was not happy to discover that his prey was escaping him. When Maggie put the van in gear, Jethro made a wild run at them.

"Hurry, hurry!" Connie pleaded, so scared her teeth were chattering.

Maggie accelerated just in time. All Jethro could do was pound once on the door before they sped away.

"Cunts!" he yelled. "Cunts!"

But he was barefooted, the parking lot was gravelly, and he was soon forced to give up the chase. Various couples getting ready to depart stared at him, but Jethro just flipped them off and went walking back toward the room where Connie and Maggie had spent the night.

"But we didn't check out?" Connie remembered.

Maggie was too scared to worry about that technicality—she wanted to get on the freeway and hide amid the trucks. She felt shaky and a little sick. Probably Jethro would just have murdered them—their bodies might never have been found. Her girls would have to wonder forever about the disappearance of their mother.

But Connie could not get her mind off the checkout problem. They had used her Visa when they checked in—what if Jethro ran up some huge bill? After all, he was still in possession of their room. What if he stole the television set or got some crony to come in and haul off all the furniture or something? Her Visa might go straight to the max, where it had been headed anyway.

"Where would he get a crony?" Maggie asked, once she had calmed down a little.

"In the coffee shop—didn't you see those slut waitresses glaring at us?" Connie asked. "They were practically salivating over that fucker."

Connie had always taken a dark view of waitresses in coffee shops.

"Get on the cell phone and call the motel office," Maggie instructed. "Tell them a bum was harassing us, so we left without checking out.

"Tell them the key's in the room," she went on. The old lady who checked them in specifically cautioned them not to lose the key.

"We spend half our profits making new keys," the old lady had informed them. "You'd be surprised how many dumbbells can't keep up with a key for one night."

And now the two of them had done worse; they'd left the key in the possession of a cold-eyed hitchhiker.

Connie did as she was instructed but the lady at the desk didn't seem to be particularly persuaded. It was just one more of the millions of excuses guests made when they discovered that they had lost their room key.

"I sure hope he doesn't steal the television," Connie said.

The morning traffic on the I-40 was heavy, mostly trucks. It was so heavy that Maggie concentrated on not having a traffic accident. She didn't give too much thought to Connie's paranoia about the television but she gave plenty of thought to the fact that Jethro had found them in Kingman, a town on I-40. If he found them once, what would stop him from finding them again? He knew what their van looked like. If they stayed on I-40 he might find them a second time.

"That's an awful thought," Connie agreed. "Now I won't be able to sleep no matter where we stop."

"The point is, we don't have to stay on the 40 freeway," Maggie reasoned. "It may be the shortest way to Aunt Cooney's but it's not the safest way. I think we should get off this road."

"Okay, but what if he planted a homing device in the van?" Connie asked.

"He was never in the van, honey," Maggie reminded her. Once Connie's paranoia kicked in, she could be pretty inventive.

"Underneath it, I meant—next time we stop at a gas station, let's check; she even suggested on splurging on an oil check so as to have a really good look under the van.

They had the oil change and Connie took the wheel, somewhat relieved. Maggie studied the road atlas. They had just passed Flagstaff and were coming up on a Highway 89, which seemed to go to a place called Tuba City.

"Take this exit," Maggie commanded. "There's no way Jethro would suspect us of being in a place called Tuba City."

"I wonder if it's where tubas were invented," Connie said. Just turning off I-40 made her feel a good bit safer.

Soon they went through some forests and some low mountains and then came to a very unusual desert where the land was all ochers and yellows. Once again the space around them got very large—hundreds of miles of air and sky lay around them.

"Oh boy, I wouldn't want to be lost out here," Connie muttered—the empty landscape made her feel insecure.

Maggie thought the weird ocher hills looked kind of interesting but agreed that being lost in such a place would not be ideal.

"Connie, can you remember every guy you ever slept with?" she asked.

"Why would you want to know?" Connie wondered, bristling a little.

"You don't have to bristle—it's just that I'm drawing some blanks when it comes to guys I may have slept with maybe a time or two—not one-night stands, exactly, but maybe a one-week stand or something?"

"I've always had a better memory than you," Connie said blithely. "I'd say I can remember at least ninety percent of my lovers—how about you?"

"Not that much—maybe half, although I get hazy if I try to remember some of the guys from the sixties."

"Then why'd you bring it up?"

"Jethro," Maggie told her. "I don't think I slept with him, because I have no memory of him at all—but you know, I can't be sure."

Connie considered the question for a while, as they drifted through the weird, many-colored desert, where some of the soil was blue and some yellow and some even pink.

"As for Jethro, I think I remember dancing with him after a rodeo or something," Connie conceded. "So maybe he was in our lives a little bit, once."

"Maybe you're not supposed to remember long-ago sex," Maggie suggested. "If you could remember it well enough, then maybe you wouldn't need to go looking for it so hard."

"I don't want to talk about stuff like this," Connie protested. "Not at a time when I have no prospects. I might get an over-the-hill feeling and I don't want to be over the hill."

Maggie shut up. She didn't want to distract Connie while she was driving, but she could not get the strange difficulty of remembering the sex act out of her mind. There seemed to be important questions to ask about the matter, but maybe the middle of the Arizona desert wasn't the place to ask them.

11

"TUBA CITY MUST BE the world capital of turquoise," Connie remarked. They were having a bite at a big, crowded café, and most of the people in the café, male *and* female, sported turquoise of some sort about their persons: belt buckles, bolo ties, rings, necklaces, earrings, even tie clips on the few people who wore ties.

After they ate they gassed up and spent several minutes carefully studying their road atlas. From Tuba City there seemed to be only two options: northeast to some place called Kayenta, or east into the Hopi Indian Reservation. The gas station attendant, who was from Baltimore, urged them by all means to go to Hopi.

"The Hopi are a very spiritual people," he assured them. "They're not big talkers but it's better than having to deal with a bunch of Navahos."

"What's wrong with Navahos?" Connie wanted to know, but the young man just smiled and checked their power steering fluid, which was low.

"If we go to Kayenta we can see Monument Valley," Connie pointed out. "You know, the place where they made the Honda commercials."

"What would we do when we got there? We're not mountain climbers," Maggie reminded her. "It might be better to find some spiritual people."

The road they traveled, east from Tuba City, turned out to be by far the longest and loneliest of any road either of them had ever traveled. It seemed to stretch on forever, into a vast emptiness—a space that had no boundaries.

"I feel like an astronaut," Connie said. "I feel like we're in space."

"It's just a road—it'll take us to a town eventually," Maggie assured her, although she herself didn't feel wholly confident on that score. Maybe they were on the one road in America that didn't actually lead to a town. But in time they did finally come to some poor little villages, all of them perched right on the edge of the mesa, looking off into even vaster space. They began to see Indian people walking beside the narrow roads—kids, young men, old men, old women, teenagers.

"I think these must be the spiritual people that kid was talking about," Maggie said. "They're so spiritual they don't even have cars."

Connie's response to the spirituality around was to dig out the .38 special Maggie had bought and load it.

"What do you think you're doing?" Maggie asked.

"Loading your gun," Connie told her. "If it had been loaded we could have shot Jethro."

"I didn't like Jethro but that doesn't mean I'd shoot him," Maggie informed her.

The road they were proceeding on curved around the edge of the mesa, with the endless and timeless space stretching way to the south. None of the Hopi people walking along the road even so much as looked up when Maggie and Connie drove by.

"These spiritual people seemed kind of introverted," Maggie commented. "They don't seem to be saying much to one another."

Connie registered no opinion about the Hopi, but when, in one of the villages, they came to a tribal crafts center, she was loud in her opinion that they ought to stop and have a look. This was an opinion Maggie was eager to go along with, and the Hopi craft center was a happy surprise. Maggie, who had not been able to get into a real shopping groove, suddenly dropped back into her shopping groove and spent eleven hundred dollars on some black onyx jewelry—two sets of earrings, a bracelet, and a ring, not to mention three elegant pieces of Hopi pottery.

Connie was more cautious but she liked the onyx jewelry too and dropped over seven hundred dollars.

About an hour after this shopping spree, when they were still tiny dots in the huge space of the Hopi Reservation, it suddenly dawned on them that they had just dropped eighteen hundred dollars in one little Indian store, and this at a time when no paychecks were coming in

"Who would have thought there'd be a store that good, way out here?" Connie said. "I could shop for a week in Santa Monica and not spend seven hundred dollars."

Maggie felt no guilt, although she knew her Visa could not be too far from being maxed out. Buying the jewelry and the pottery had been sort of liberating; it had made her feel buoyant for the first time in months.

Just as she was enjoying her buoyant feeling they came to a town that was a good deal larger than the Hopi villages. The first thing they saw was a sign for a big trading post.

"Feeling reckless—should we check it out?" Maggie asked.

"Sure. It's better than driving through space feeling like we're in orbit," Connie said.

The trading post proved to be a large one—the first room they wandered through was filled with rugs and blankets, most of them very appealing rugs and blankets. Maggie picked up a smallish rug whose colors particularly appealed to her. It seemed like the perfect rug for her front hall. She was hoping, since it was small, that its price might be around seventy-five dollars, or maybe one hundred, but when she looked at the price tag it read nineteen thousand dollars.

Assuming there must be some mistake, she showed the price tag to Connie.

"Nineteen thousand, that can't be right," Connie said. "Maybe it's priced in yen."

But when Maggie showed the rug to the small, serious man who seemed to be in charge of the rug and blanket room, he didn't smile or even change expression.

"That's correct, it's nineteen thousand," he told Maggie. "It's a Ruth Little Bird rug."

Maggie must have looked shocked, because the small salesman merely took the rug and returned it to the pile where Maggie had spotted it.

Meanwhile Connie had been snooping around, examining price tags, and getting more and more freaked out in the process.

"They're all in the thousands," she informed Maggie. "One of the big ones is thirty-five thousand. It's worth nearly as much as my condo."

"Gosh, I didn't know Hopi stuff got *that* expensive," said Maggie, only to be immediately set right by the small, serious proprietor.

"This isn't Hopi," he said. "You're on the Navaho Reservation now, and we represent some of the finest weavers alive today. Collectors come from the world over to buy from us."

As if to prove his point, a group of Germans began to pour into the trading post—the men had expensive cameras around their necks and the women, mostly blonde, wore big floppy straw hats. In no time the Germans were exclaiming over the rugs and pots, undeterred by any consideration of price. They had all come off a big tour bus, which was idling outside.

"Let's go, we can't even afford to breathe in this place," Maggie said. "We should have got that kid in Tuba City to explain the difference between Hopis and Navahos a little more clearly."

"The price tags are the difference—let's get out of here," Connie said.

Once again the road atlas offered few options. If they went south they'd soon be back on I-40, where Jethro Jordan lurked.

Unwilling to face that prospect, they went north toward a town called Chinle—but thanks to their late start and their stops for shopping, the day was waning—there was no way they were going to make Chinle before darkness fell. Maggie focused on not taking a wrong turn, while Connie occupied herself with being nervous. There was a beautiful sunset and afterglow, which Maggie appreciated; but once Connie reached a certain level of apprehension, the beauties of nature meant little to her.

"I hate this road, I hate this desert, I hate America, and I miss L.A.," Connie said. Fortunately, before Connie came completely apart, evidence that Chinle was at least a part of civilization began to appear in the form of billboards. First there was a sign for Kentucky Fried Chicken, then a sign for a Holiday Inn, and then signs for a Motel 6 and a Comfort Inn and a Wendy's and even a Western Sizzlin. Somehow just seeing these long-familiar signs made them both feel a good deal more secure.

"Do you think this is a Navaho town, or a Hopi town?" Connie asked. "If it's a Navaho town, I suppose rooms at the Holiday Inn will cost at least a thousand a night."

Fortunately Connie's fears were groundless. Their room at the Holiday Inn only cost eighty-two dollars for double occupancy, which was still a little high in Maggie's opinion, but they were so glad to be in the familiar surroundings of a Holiday Inn that neither of them bothered to haggle—anyhow, the large Navaho woman who ran Maggie's Visa didn't smile at them once. She clearly would not have welcomed any discussion of discounts.

Once they were in their room they were hit by a tsunami of fatigue. It was all they could do to drag their overnight bags inside. They had stopped for a minute at the Kentucky Fried Chicken and bought an eight-piece dinner, but both of them were too tired even to nibble on a chicken wing.

"Maybe it's from being scared all day," Maggie surmised.

"No, it's all this open space—it sort of grinds you down," Connie said. She headed for the shower, changed her mind, flopped on the bed, and was soon snoring.

Maggie didn't blame her—who would have supposed that travel would be so tiring?

12

ABOUT THE TIME Conan O'Brien was finishing his late, late talk show, Maggie woke up, feeling vaguely guilty. Connie, wide awake, was digging into their eight-piece dinner.

"Don't worry, I left you a breast and two drumsticks—also two biscuits," Connie informed her.

"I wanted a wing," Maggie said, but without heat. One piece of Kentucky Fried Chicken was much like another.

"I meant to check with my daughters when we got here, but I was just too tired," she admitted.

"They're grown women, you don't have to check on them—they should be checking on you," Connie reminded her.

Dr. Tom had often made the same point when discussing her need to create dependencies. He, like Connie, was firmly of the opinion that she ought to let her daughters manage their own lives.

"I don't want to meddle, I just want to know what's going on," Maggie said.

Once Conan O'Brien was through for the night, Connie began to channel-surf, CNN, ESPN, and Maggie's personal favorite, the Weather Channel. She even tried the menu, to see what kind of movie fare might be available—then, by accident, she surfed into a porn movie—a skinny blonde was going down on a stocky, heavy-breathing male.

"Turn it off!" Maggie demanded—Connie, as horrified as Maggie if not more so, turned it off, surfing desperately until she got back to the safety of the Weather Channel.

Despite the fact that the porn movie had only flashed into their lives for a few seconds, it managed to trigger sinking spells in both Maggie and Connie.

"I used to love to think about sex, but now I don't," Connie said, getting her complaint in first. "I even liked to watch porn movies, but now I don't. I wish I knew what was wrong with me."

"Whatever it is, the same thing's wrong with me," Maggie mumbled—she felt too depressed even to articulate clearly.

"I just wish I'd had a little more sack time with Dr. Tom," she said.

But Connie's mood was plummeting faster than Maggie's.

"I never want to see a dick again as long as I live," she said.

"Oh, baloney," Maggie said. "You'll change your mind about that, I bet."

Even so, she felt much the same. The one thing evident in the few seconds that they had watched the skinny blonde and the stocky male was that they both had good, hard, young bodies, bodies of the sort that neither she nor Connie would ever possess again.

Connie often relieved her bad feelings by throwing things. While the Weather Channel continued, she threw the box of fried chicken at the TV. Then she threw a pillow and an old copy of *Elle* magazine that she had been carrying around as bedtime reading. Then she sobbed for a while.

Maggie had learned to be patient with Connie's need to throw things: once she had thrown everything she had to throw, she'd cry herself out and calm down, which was exactly what occurred. She even got up and began to retrieve the things she had thrown, which included three pieces of chicken and two biscuits.

"I hope I didn't ruin your dinner," she remarked.

"I don't want it, I'm not a bit hungry," Maggie said, in a tone that suggested that she didn't expect ever to be hungry again.

"I hate it when you lose your appetite," Connie said. "You need to eat."

"I'm sure I'll be hungry tomorrow," Maggie said—she said it mainly to give Connie hope. In fact, she wasn't sure that she'd ever really be hungry again, though it stood to reason that she might, someday. She had brought their road atlas in—traveling in remote places seemed to require frequent map study, but in this case intense map study did nothing to lift her out of her discouraged state. If they kept to their resolution not to use the I-40, then it seemed to be nearly impossible to get from Chinle, Arizona, to Electric City, Texas. Several possible roads seemed to just peter out, blocked by impassable mountain ranges.

"I wish you took more interest in the road atlas," she said to Connie. "It's a big responsibility, having to figure how to get there all by myself."

Connie didn't reply. Exhausted by her emotional fit, she had gone back to sleep. One of Connie's skills that Maggie had often envied was her ability to go right to sleep, no matter what terrible dilemma confronted them. In present circumstances it would have been hard even to decide what their problem was, but Maggie was convinced they faced one. It was just past one A.M. in California, which meant that the only one of her daughters who was sure to be up was Jeannie, a young woman not given to sleeping long hours.

In fact, as Maggie had hoped, Jeannie picked up on the first ring. She didn't sound at all sleepy.

"Where are you by now?" she asked pleasantly.

"Arizona, someplace," Maggie said. "Did Kate go back to Howie?"

"Of course, sucker that she is," Jeannie informed her. "Kate and Meagan had a big fight. Meagan runs a neat ship and Kate's a messy sailor."

That answered the only question Maggie had to ask where family arrangements were concerned, leaving her somewhat at a loss for words. A bit of a silence developed.

"So are you guys having fun yet?" Jeannie inquired.

"Not yet—not much," Maggie admitted. "It's kind of lonely-making out here."

"Aren't you on the 40—what about all those truck stops?" Jeannie asked. "If you're lonesome, pull off and flirt with some cute truckers."

"We had to leave the 40," Maggie admitted, quickly filling Jeannie in on the problem of Jethro Jordan. Jeannie was not too sympathetic—she seemed to consider the episode a hoot.

"Some old naked guy chased you in a parking lot? That's wild," Jeannie said.

Maggie realized that from the safety of a house in Silver Lake, the whole Jethro episode probably *did* sound like a hoot. When Maggie hung up she had a kind of what's-the-use feeling. Instead of making her feel more connected to her family, it had made her feel less connected. Here they were on an adventure that was supposed to lift their spirits, and the adventure was having the opposite effect. Her spirits were sinking so fast that she did the one thing she had vowed never to do: she dialed Dr. Tom's emergency number. It seemed to her that a few words from her shrink might help her level out. But instead of Dr. Tom himself a robot voice came on from the message machine, and all it did was give her the number of a suicide hotline.

In fact there was no immediate help to be had, just the soothing sound of the Weather Channel and Connie's rhythmic snoring. Maggie wanted to sleep but she knew sleep wasn't going to come. In casting about for someone she might call who would talk to her for a while she thought of Aunt Cooney—maybe she would still be up; and, in fact, she was up.

"Chinle, Arizona, lucky you!" Aunt Cooney said. "I wish I was there with you, looking down into that beautiful canyon."

"What canyon?" Maggie asked.

"Why, the Canyon de Chelly, the most beautiful spot in the whole West," Aunt Cooney insisted. "I been there eight times. Be sure when you go to it you go all the way to Spider Rock—it's the last lookout post."

Maggie didn't grasp many of the particulars Aunt Cooney was spewing out—stuff about Kit Carson and the Navahos—but she was so relieved to have a friendly person to talk to that when she finally hung up, she dropped right off to sleep.

She had meant to ask Aunt Cooney for directions from Chinle to Electric City but drowsiness overtook her and anyway, the road atlas was in the van.

To Connie's relief, Maggie, the starveling, actually woke up hungry—she polished off a healthy stack of blue corn pancakes, while the two of them looked at colorful brochures of the big canyon Maggie had promised her aunt they would inspect.

13

"YOUR AUNT MAY have her nutsy side, but she was right about this place," Connie said, in an awed voice, the kind of voice she would normally only use if she had just had the best sex of her life or something.

They were standing at the first lookout place above the Canyon de Chelly. Across the canyon, way down, was a little white ruin tucked beneath a huge cliff of reddish striated rock. The cliff kind of swooped up above the ruin. Far below they could see a field, but no people.

At the motel they had been offered a trip up the canyon floor by muleback, but at that point in time the thought of mules did not excite them—of course, they had no idea what a fabulous scenic wonder awaited them.

"It's just amazing how much space there is in Arizona," Maggie told her friend, who, for once, was not behaving impatiently when asked to appreciate a natural wonder.

As they inched their way along, from lookout point to lookout point, they both became quiet and thoughtful. For once it was enough just to look. The sky above the canyon was perfectly blue—down there, somewhere, there might be people riding mules or growing blue corn, but they didn't see them. They only saw the blue sky, the sheer rock cliffs, and the floor of the canyon, far below.

Connie moved around the lookout points very carefully.

"If I start to fall over, please catch me," she asked.

The last lookout point, the one above Spider Rock, the place Aunt Cooney had particularly wanted them to see, required a bit of a hike through the woods. The woods seemed peaceful enough to

Maggie but Connie's lifelong bear phobia surfaced. There were little patches of unmelted snow under some of the trees.

"Anytime there's this kind of tree there could be bears—I know that much," Connie insisted. But they reached the lookout point safely and stood for a long time, gazing at the tall freestanding spire known as Spider Rock.

"Who do you think put it there?" Connie inquired.

"It seems as if it just grew there, only rocks don't grow," Maggie said.

"I guess God put it there, if he exists and if he's a he," Connie decided. "I'm glad we came and saw this place, but now I want to leave before I get vertigo."

Maggie would have liked to take a few snapshots of Spider Rock to show the grandkids, but they had used up all their film at the first few lookout sites. Neither of them had ever got around to acquiring the fancy digital cameras that were so popular in Hollywood—their photographic equipment had just consisted of two cheap throwaways.

As they were hurrying out of the woods, Connie keeping a close watch for bears, they saw a very small Indian man standing by their van. He carried a little cardboard suitcase and wore a black cowboy hat.

"Look at the cute little man," Connie exclaimed.

"I just promised my girls I wouldn't pick up hitchhikers," Maggie reminded her.

"Who says he's hitchhiking?" Connie asked. "Anyway, I'm not one to tattle."

"You are too one to tattle," Maggie pointed out. "It took you no time to tell Jeannie Dr. Tom wanted me to spank him."

Nevertheless she was not totally opposed to giving the small Indian man a ride—even though he had not yet asked for one.

"Hi, sir," Connie said, when they reached the van. "Need a ride to town?"

"No, but if you have a jack I'll help you change this tire," the man said. He didn't smile but he had a pleasant demeanor. He pointed to their right rear tire, which was indeed totally flat.

"No, no!" Maggie said. "We *don't* have a jack. I loaned mine to Auberon when he was selling the tires off his old Chevy. I forgot to get it back.

"I'm Maggie and she's Connie," she added, thinking they ought to be introduced.

The old man drew back a bit. He seemed to feel that Maggie was rushing things a little, by asking his name. Her brash inquiry might seem like bad manners to him.

"Jiminy," he said, after a bit. "You are young women . . . you may not remember Jiminy Cricket, but that is who I am named for."

Connie drew a total blank on the name but Maggie thought she remembered that there had once been a cartoon character named Jiminy Cricket, way back in the days when all cartoons were in black and white.

"I'm quick, you see, like Jiminy," he said. Now that he had revealed his name he seemed to feel that he should explain it.

"I guess we better get on the cell phone and call a garage," Maggie said, but Jiminy shook his head.

"Here come some of those stout Navaho boys now," he said, pointing to a pickup that was coming their way along the dirt road, throwing up huge clouds of dust.

When Jiminy held up his hand the pickup at once began to slow down. It held six Navaho teenagers and an excellent jack. In no time the flat was changed and the boys went on their way.

"Jiminy, are you Navaho?" Connie asked. She could not seem to rein in her impetuousness when it came to asking questions.

"No," Jiminy replied. "My son made a mistake and married a Navaho woman. I meant to stay with them all summer, up here where it's cool, but my daughter-in-law's a hellion. She cussed me out once too often, so I left.

"I am too old to put up with spiteful females," he added.

Then he gave the two of them a stern look.

"I hope neither of you are spiteful," he said. "If you are, I don't want to ride with you."

"Oh, we're feeling pretty cheerful today, don't ask me why," Maggie said. "We'd be happy to have you ride with us, if you want to."

"Okay, then," Jiminy said. "As you can see, I travel light."

"I guess we better go into Chinle and get that tire fixed, otherwise we won't have a spare," Maggie said, once they were in the van—but old Jiminy threw ice water on that plan.

"That's a bad idea, unless you just want to be cheated by these thieving Navahos," Jiminy warned them. "I know a man in Teec Nos Pos who will fix your flat for one dollar. These greedy Navahos will just treat you like roadkill."

"Roadkill? Us?" Connie asked.

"Roadkill," the old man insisted. "First they'll charge you ten dollars to fix a simple flat, and then they'll probably stick a screwdriver in your radiator or something. Then they'll sell you a new radiator and maybe a transmission too."

Old Jiminy's voice had risen. It was obvious that he didn't like doing business with Navahos—but what did that mean for them? So far he had not even asked where they were going, and they had no idea where he was going either.

"How far is the place where the man can fix our flat?" Maggie inquired. Now that she realized she didn't have a jack she was feeling a little paranoid about the possibility of more flats.

"Oh, it's not even two hundred miles," old Jiminy said. "I know a shortcut. The man who owns the garage is an old army buddy of mine—we were in the Philippines together in World War II."

The prospect of heading into the wild with neither a jack nor a spare made Maggie a little uneasy, but then she remembered how easily old Jiminy flagged down the pickup full of Navaho kids— probably he could do it again if he had too, so she went where he told her to go, and pretty soon they were in country so vast and empty that it seemed as if no human beings were in it at all.

"This is all just too empty—too empty," Connie kept saying. "It's so empty it makes me nostalgic for traffic jams. If we were home I'd go get in the first traffic jam I could find. It would just be nice to have a lot of people around."

"I worked in San Pedro for five years," old Jiminy volunteered. "One of my daughters married a Vietnamese fellow. They had a nice little house."

Then he revealed that he was actually Apache and was on his way to Oklahoma to stay with yet another daughter, who had married a Comanche.

"Her husband fell off an oil derrick and was killed, so there won't be anybody around to cuss me out except my own flesh and blood," old Jiminy said.

"Gosh, you seem so sweet, why are people always cussing you out?" Connie wondered. It was another question she probably should have suppressed; but then again Jiminy was somebody new to talk to. Why not ask questions? He didn't have to answer if he didn't want to.

"Oh, I've been known to lose my temper," Jiminy admitted.

"We all lose our tempers—why should you be the only exception?" Connie asked.

"I ain't got no neutral gear," the old man informed them. "I'm either sweet as pie or I'm a terror."

"You're just like Maggie, then," Connie told him. "She's either sweet as pie or she's in a rage."

But old Jiminy rejected the comparison.

"When I get mad I'm something to see," he told them, smiling at the memory of his own terrible rages.

"I caught my second wife in bed with a copper miner—that was in Bisbee, Arizona," he told them. "Left our kids going hungry and went to bed with this big longhaired copper miner. Made me so mad I shot her four times."

"Uh-oh," Maggie said. "Did she die?"

"You bet she died," old Jiminy said. It seemed to be a happy memory. "It was ruled a crime of passion but I was cool as a cucumber when I shot that low-life bitch. I got six years but they let me out after two and a half—said I was too old to be dangerous.

"Shows how dumb prison officials can be," he added, grinning.

"I wish I were someplace where there were people," Connie said.

"Actually this country is crawling with Navahos," he told them. "You'll see plenty of them in Teec Nos Pos."

Maggie looked over at Connie, who seemed to be paralyzed by the discovery that they were traveling with a wife murderer. Maggie herself was pretty much in the same oh-no state. After strictly promising her daughters not to pick up hitchhikers, she had immediately picked up a murderer.

"Don't tattle," she mouthed to Connie.

"I won't," Connie mouthed back.

14

JIMINY'S FRIEND FROM World War II turned out to be a tall, unfriendly Indian called Big Lewis. He patched Maggie's tire for her, but didn't address a word to either woman.

"Tell her that'll be a dollar," he told old Jiminy—the old man delivered the message and Maggie handed over the dollar.

While the tire was being patched, Maggie and Connie huddled in a filthy little ladies' room, trying to figure out a smooth and foolproof way to get rid of old Jiminy.

"It's a good thing he didn't know there was a pistol in the glove compartment," Connie pointed out.

"Surely he wouldn't have shot *us*—all we did was give him a ride," Maggie pointed out.

What was depressing, though, was how hard it was to judge the character of people one might meet along the road. Their record so far was two strikes, and they had only been on the road about three days.

"Let's just tell him we want to be alone," Connie suggested. They had walked over to a little convenience store to buy a few more throwaway cameras. The woman who took their money was as silent as Big Lewis—she didn't say a word.

"I wonder what you have to do to get speech of some sort, around here," Connie asked, as they walked back to Big Lewis's garage. They had bought six throwaway cameras—in most quick stops that would get you a thank-you, at least, but not in Teec Nos Pos.

The hot July sun was shining on them as they walked back to the garage—Connie wore dark glasses but Maggie had left hers in the van—the sun at that hour was kind of white-bright, which is why it took the two of them a minute or two to react to the fact that something seemed to be missing from the environs of Big Lewis's garage: what was missing was their van! It was nowhere to be seen—nor were Big Lewis or old Jiminy.

"Maybe they're doing an oil change," Maggie suggested. It was the one hopeful thought she could summon. But when they stumbled up to the garage there was no sign of anyone doing anything, and Big Lewis's garage was closed. Worse still, a big rottweiler was growling from somewhere inside the garage.

And their van was gone.

"Oh my God! Oh my God!" Connie repeated, a few times.

"Maybe they're just driving around trying out the spare," Maggie offered—but she knew that there was about one chance in a trillion that something that innocent could be happening.

"Look where we are," Connie said. "I've been seduced and abandoned before, but never in a place like this. There's *nothing* here!"

Actually there *was* a motel of sorts, but its appearance was so awful that Maggie didn't even want to look at it—the likelihood was that the towel quality in such a motel would be the lowest yet.

"Call nine-eleven—hurry, before it's too late," Connie begged.

"My cell phone's in the van," Maggie admitted. "You call nine-eleven."

"Shit, mine's in the the van too," Connie confessed. "Isn't that a pay phone on the wall of the convenience store?" There was a pay phone, but when they got closer they saw that the receiver was dangling from its cord and nothing they could do would raise a dial tone.

"I'll go inside—surely they've got a phone," Maggie said.

The large Indian woman who ran the little convenience store was restocking the peanut butter jars when Maggie raced in with a request to borrow their phone just to call 911.

"It's an emergency—our van's been stolen with all our possessions in it," Maggie pled, but her plea met with complete indifference. The large woman went right on stacking jars of peanut butter on the shelf, her main concern being not to mix the smooth with the crunchy.

"We don't let nobody use this phone," she said, finally. "Big Lewis got a phone, go try him.

"We did, he's *closed!*" Maggie cried, but the large woman did not look up again.

Maggie was about to race across the street and make a similar plea at the ratty motel, but before she had to resort to that, a miracle occurred. The one thing in the universe that she most wanted to see—a state trooper—happened to be coming into town in his patrol car.

She and Connie ran out of the store and both began to wave at the trooper as if they were the last survivors on a life raft or something, but it soon developed that they could have saved themselves the trouble, because they were the very people the trooper was looking for.

The trooper was thin, grizzled, and not very middle-aged. He sported a certain amount of gray stubble.

"Howdy, ladies," he said, with a tired grin. "Is this place hell on earth, or what?"

"It's hell on earth," Maggie agreed. "Have you seen a white van with California plates?"

"Oh sure, we have the van, and we're holding the thief," the trooper said. "I'm Officer Sheffield. You wouldn't have given Old Pinto permission to go joyriding, would you?"

"Excuse me, who's Old Pinto?" Connie asked. "We gave a lift to an old Indian man but he told us his name was Jiminy."

Officer Sheffield smiled.

"His name's not Jiminy," he assured them. "Around here he's Old Pinto. He's a car thief and now he's broken his parole yet again."

"Oh my God, it's just a miracle you caught him so quick," Maggie said.

Officer Sheffield chuckled.

"Oh, we catch Old Pinto every few days," he told them. "His daughter-in-law called to let us know he was missing. That little suitcase he carries has nothing in it but tools for breaking into cars. Usually he just goes down to one of the lookout spots on the canyon and steals a car while the owners are taking pictures. He can't get through Chinle without being picked up, so usually he shows up here."

As they were talking their van came rapidly back toward them, with Big Lewis driving. He parked where it had been parked and reopened his garage. He said not a word to anybody.

"People aren't very friendly, up in these parts," Maggie said. "I've never been anyplace where people are *this* unfriendly."

"They've got good memories," Officer Sheffield observed. "They haven't forgotten what white people have done to them. You know? Coronado, or Governor Albuquerque, or even old Kit Carson."

Maggie and Connie knew that white people had done a lot of bad things to Indians over the years—she didn't know which white people had been bad to which Indians.

Just then another state trooper's car pulled up, with Old Pinto in the backseat. A big Navaho trooper was driving the car. As for Jiminy, or Old Pinto, or whoever he was, he seemed to be in a sulk. He didn't look at anybody.

"His daughter-in-law is on her way to pick him up," Officer Sheffield said. "We could send him back to the pen but they don't want him. Unless you ladies want to press charges, I think the best thing to do is just send him home."

"We don't want to press anything," Maggie said. "All we want is to get to a safe place to spend the night."

"That would be Farmington. It's not friendly, but you won't get murdered."

"We're on our way to Texas—how far do we have to go before people get friendly again?"

"Albuquerque," Officer Sheffield said, without a moment's hesitation. "Once you get to Albuquerque you'll run into a few friendly people, but even then you have to be careful about hitchhikers."

"Thanks a whole bunch for getting our van back so quick," Maggie said. "I don't know what we would have done if you hadn't come along."

"You'd have been fine—my wife runs a nice little motel here," the officer assured them. He nodded toward the depressing, paint-flaking-off cabins that they had already decided they never wanted to see the inside of—the Bad Towel Motel, they had jokingly named it.

Both of them waved at the old man in the backseat of the police car. The old man, Jiminy or Pinto, did not wave back, but he did look at them as he drew one finger across his throat.

"Uh-oh, do you think that means what I think it means?" Maggie asked.

"It means he wants to cut our throats," Connie said. "I still can't help liking him a little. He didn't do anything bad to us. Why hold a grudge?"

"Who's holding a grudge? I just want to get out of here," Maggie told her.

Twenty-five miles up the road she remembered that they still didn't have a jack, but by then Connie was fast asleep.

15

HAVING ESCAPED BIG TROUBLE with Old Pinto, Maggie and Connie, once the latter had taken a nap, both felt giddy with relief—giddy enough to start doing touristy things like taking photographs of natural wonders. They used up two whole throwaway cameras taking pictures of Shiprock, the massive bluff that came in view once they were in New Mexico. Both of them had visited a real ship, the *Queen Mary,* once it had retired from the seas and come to live in Long Beach, where tourists could even spend the night in it if they wanted to. Shiprock didn't really seem much like a ship—no ship could be *that* big—but it was so impressive in its own way that they used up two cameras photographing it. Neither of them were very good with a camera, but at least they'd have some documentation to take back to L.A.

They got a nice enough motel room in the town of Farmington; Connie was even gracious enough to let Maggie take the first shower, once they were checked in. They were both thinking it might be a good night to eat steak—quite a few cowboys were present on the street, making it likely that decent steaks could be obtained somewhere in town.

Maggie went into her shower in a happy mood, and Connie seemed to be in a happy mood, but when Maggie came out of the shower, Connie was in tears. She had been planning to give her son a call—Maggie began to fear that there was new bad news about Danny. After all, most news about Danny was bad.

"No, it's the opposite, these are tears of joy," Connie told her. "I just had the best news of my whole life."

"What, did you win the lottery?"

"Better—Danny's getting married," Connie said, sounding proud all of a sudden. "And that's not all: he's marrying the head librarian."

"Oh my God, congratulations—let me buy the steaks," Maggie exclaimed.

"I guess my son turned out to be normal after all," Connie said. "I always hoped he would. I always did."

And then she sobbed and sobbed.

Maggie knew that was true—all those years when her own three daughters were growing up normal, having boyfriends, getting married, producing healthy children, Connie had suffered and suffered through Danny's setbacks: addiction, no girlfriend, barely scraping by on his little salary from the library. Somehow she kept on hoping, as mothers will, but there had been, more or less, a million disappointments. When it came to rearing normal offspring, Maggie seemed to have all the good luck and Connie had all the bad luck. And yet there was a sweetness in Danny that Maggie had always sensed: how nice that the head librarian had finally sensed it too.

"There's even a better part—I guess his bride-to-be has finally straightened him out," Connie said. "It's my birthday. Danny's birthday present, besides the engagement, is to tell me that he's been off drugs for a year."

"Oh my God, is that sweet or what?" Maggie told her, feeling a stab of guilt. She and Connie had always been very observant of one another's birthday—ever since the sixth grade the two of them had gone out and tried to do something special on their birthdays.

"I guess with all this traveling I got my days scrambled," Maggie admitted. "Hurry and shower and we'll do the town—and you know that little pot I snatched out from under your hand at the Hopi store? That's your birthday present."

Actually she had meant to keep the nice little pot for herself, but she had to have something to give Connie for a birthday present. The Hopi pot would have to fill the bill.

The waitresses were not real friendly at the steak house they chose for Connie's birthday dinner, but there was a nice loud country band and the cowboys at the bar were certainly no sticks in the mud. Maggie and Connie both got asked to dance nearly every dance, and would probably have been invited to do other things had they both not fallen victim to another tsunami of fatigue. Maggie was so tired she could barely drive back to the motel, and the motel was only six blocks away.

"I guess being kidnapped by a murderer wears you out," Connie said.

Maggie was so out of it she didn't even turn on the Weather Channel.

"Happy Birthday," Maggie said to Connie, who seemed a little discontent. But Maggie was just too tired to talk—in no time she slid right into sleep.

16

"You didn't really buy this nice pot for me," Connie said. "I know you didn't. You just felt guilty for forgetting my birthday, so you gave me the pot."

It was not unusual for Connie to wake up in a persnickety mood—Maggie had known it to happen at least a few thousand times; the best thing to do was just to ignore her until her coffee kicked in, or she got over her snit, whichever came first.

"Connie," Maggie said, but then she gave up and finished zipping her suitcase. They were both pretty hungover, which did nothing to reduce Connie's persnicketiness factor. Maggie herself didn't have the energy for a real fight, though a real one could easily have developed.

"Here I am in the middle of nowhere with you when I ought to be home helping my son plan his wedding," Connie complained. By then they were rolling across a vast plain. As far ahead as she could see there was not even the glimmer of a town.

"Did you hear me?" Connie asked.

"I heard you—what do you want me to do about it. This is where we happen to be, and I'm hurrying as fast as I can. With any luck we might make Aunt Cooney's tonight."

"That is if we don't fall prey to Jethro or some other bad person," Connie said.

"At least we have a jack now," Maggie pointed out—they had bought one at an auto parts store in Farmington.

"Big whup!" Connie said. "If there was an airport nearby I'd leave you to your own devices and fly right home to L.A."

Fifty miles passed with no further comment and gradually Connie's mood began to improve.

"I was just mad that you waited all day to wish me Happy Birthday," Connie said. "Usually on my birthday you wish me Happy Birthday first thing in the morning."

"I guess the sight of the Canyon de Chelly drove it out of my mind," Maggie said, being cautious. Part of her wanted to tell Connie to get fucked—why pout for a hundred miles about a birthday? Fortunately, before she could say it, giving Connie material for a lasting grudge, her cell phone rang.

"It looks like Melanie's pregnant, how about that?" Kate said, over the crackly cell phone.

"Maybe it's a false alarm," Maggie suggested—the thought of little Melanie being a mother already was a little disturbing.

"What's wrong now?" Connie asked. She had seen Maggie's expression change.

"Naturally this would happen when you're out of pocket," Kate said, in her usual accusatory tone.

"Stop it, Kate—why is everyone trying to make me feel guilty for leaving on my one trip? Do I leave often? Do I shirk my responsibilities?"

Kate didn't answer.

"If it's Kate, can I tell her the good news about Danny?" Connie asked. "It's time everybody knows that my son is as normal as anybody else."

So Maggie told Kate that Danny Bruckner was getting married to a head librarian—probably the news would have made more of an impression on Kate had she not been so preoccupied with her young daughter's problems.

"That's wonderful, tell Connie I'm really happy for her," Kate said, in a sort of dutiful tone. It wasn't an insincere tone, exactly—it's just that Kate was totally focused, for better or worse, on her own household and the crisis in it.

"If she's pregnant, then she's pregnant by Claudie, right?" Maggie asked. Claudie, a tall shy boy, had been Melanie's boyfriend for at least two years—a long time as teenage romances went in Marina del Rey.

"Presumably," Kate said, in a hesitant voice. "But things haven't been too smooth with Claudie and Melanie lately. There's a Mexican kid who's been hanging around a lot. You can imagine how mad Howie's gonna be if his darling little daughter turns out to be pregnant by a Hispanic."

"I know—Howie's a racist," Maggie replied. "It's always bothered me about him."

"He's a typical working-class male of his time and place," Kate responded. That was what she always said if her mother or one of her sisters happened to point out that her husband was a total racist—maybe not quite at the Aryan Brotherhood level, but he definitely was likely to have a major fit if it turned out that his daughter was pregnant by a person of any color other than white.

"Has she just missed a period, or what?"

"Two periods," Kate said, in a flat tone. "When are you thinking of coming home?"

"Well, we should get to Aunt Cooney's tonight, if we're lucky," Maggie said. "I suppose we'll probably stay maybe two days, and then drive home. That means we'll be home within a week."

"We've got a few things to thrash out," Kate mentioned, cautiously.

"Well, of course," Maggie said. Kate was stridently pro-life, Jeannie just as as stridently pro-choice, and Meagan more or less on the fence.

"There's not going to be any abortions, not in my family," Kate said emphatically—it was as if she had been listening to her mother think.

"No, no—I know," Maggie assured her. "But do you think Mel will want to keep it, or give it up for adoption?"

"Of course she wants to keep the baby, if there is a baby," Kate assured her. "I'm all right with that. I think Mel would be a good little mother, but she *is* pretty young."

"The problem is Howie," she went on. "If the baby comes out brown, he's not going to want it in the house. No way, José."

"I wish Howie were a little more live-and-let-live," Maggie said.

"Maybe when he actually sees the adorable little thing, he'll decide to live and let live."

"I wouldn't bet on it," Kate said. "Howie has never once changed his mind about anything."

Maggie knew that Connie was getting a little restive, as she always did when Maggie spent too much time chatting with one of her daughters. Her restiveness hadn't reached the danger point yet, but the danger point was fast approaching.

"Maybe Mel could live with one of your sisters for a while, if it comes to that," Maggie said. "But Mel is just barely pregnant, if she even is pregnant—we've got several months in which to figure this out."

Fortunately the quality of the cell phone reception deteriorated and Kate went blank. Maggie's feeling was that Kate had really been angling to get her to offer to take the baby—but Maggie was in no shape to make that offer.

The minute the phone died, Maggie stopped the car.

"You drive—I'm upset—I might have an accident," Maggie said.

Connie looked around at the empty plain.

"How could you have an accident out here?" she wondered. "There's nothing to hit."

But she took the wheel and had soon absorbed the news about Melanie's pregnancy and the possibility of a slightly Hispanic child arriving in Kate's household.

"You know the bad thing about cell phones? You can never get away from your life," Maggie said. "I could just be enjoying the scenery, but am I allowed to? No. Now I have to think of my granddaughter, who is thin as a stick and too young to be going through childbirth."

"She'll do fine," Connie said. "I forgot to ask Danny how old his fiancée is. I wonder if *they'll* want children."

"Let's hope they do," Maggie put in. "If I have to be a great-grandmother at my young age, I hope you at least have to be a grandmother."

"Even if Danny has children, I won't have to be a great grand-mother until I'm at least ninety," Connie said smugly.

These thoughts put her in such a good mood that she drove hap-pily and rapidly—sooner than either of them had expected, they were confronted with their old nemesis, the 40 freeway, which, according to the map, would bear them east almost to the town where Aunt Cooney lived. It was also the preferred freeway of Jethro Jordan, but both of them had sort of put that episode in per-spective: it was by no means the only time one or another of them had been threatened by a naked, angry man.

"He's probably thousands of miles from here by now," Connie reasoned. "And if he should show up, I bet the two of us could beat the crap out of him—that is, if he tries anything."

"Or we could shoot him—we have a gun, remember?"

"That's right, we'll shoot the fucker," Connie said. "Check and see if our gun's still loaded."

"Of course it's still loaded," Maggie said, opening the glove com-partment. She expected to see the nice little .38, but all that was in the glove compartment was the manual that told them how to work the car.

"Oh my God, Old Pinto took it," Maggie exclaimed. "He proba-bly put in it in that little suitcase with his car thief tools. What if he shoots his daughter-in-law with our gun?"

Connie, having just negotiated the big interchange in Albu-querque successfully, was not in the mood for any worst-case sce-narios.

"Just shut up, don't think about bad things of that nature, please," she said.

"But our gun was stolen by a known murderer," Maggie pointed out.

"You don't know that—the man who sold us the jack could have stolen it," Connie said. "And as for Jethro, if he shows up we'll just run over him and plead self-defense."

Maggie could not entirely free her mind from bad possibilities that might result from Old Pinto having their gun—but there wasn't much she could do about it other than hope that the old man's daughter-in-law was on her toes.

Connie was wild to get to Texas, so, under a blazing sun, on they went.

Book Three

THE
CHICKEN
GULAG

1

"My God, it's like the house in *Giant,* remember?" Connie said.

She was referring to a huge, multistoried house that suddenly loomed ahead of them on the prairie. It looked more like a castle than a house.

"Of course I remember *Giant,*" Maggie said. "Don't you remember my crush on Rock Hudson? I had it for years. It's just my luck that he was gay."

"Look at the top—look at the top!" Connie insisted, as they got closer to the house.

"Is that a neon flag?" Maggie asked. "A neon flag?"

"Do you think it's legal?" Connie asked.

"Legal or not, it's the first thing I've seen in Texas that I like," Connie said.

It was midmorning; it was hot. They had not managed to make it all the way from Farmington to Electric City in one day. Forced by fatigue to give up, they spent the night in a big motel in Amarillo, a motel just off the 40 freeway. All night huge trucks roared by, only yards from their heads; they had to leave the Weather Channel turned on lower than usual just to get a few hours' sleep. But at least they were up and rolling early. Now, according to a road sign, they were only seven miles from Electric City. In the distance Maggie spotted a water tower; the town was probably somewhere beneath the water tower; but the big weird house was between them and it.

And not the house only: on both sides of the road, as they approached the house, they began to pass long rows of low build-

ings, each about as long as a football field. Someone had hand-
lettered big signs in front of each of the long buildings: the signs said
Chicken Gulag #1, Chicken Gulag #2, and so on up to twelve.

"It's a concentration camp for chickens," Connie said. "I guess
your aunt wasn't lying when she said she had millions of chickens."

"I wonder what inspired Aunt Cooney to get so many chickens,"
Maggie asked, as she drove slowly past the chicken gulags. She happened to glance in her rearview mirror just in time to see a large
fire-truck red pickup with huge oversized tires of the sort that usually showed up in demolition derbies. The pickup was coming so
fast that Maggie instinctively jerked the van to the right, into the
shallow ditch that ran beside the roadway. A second later the big
pickup swooshed by.

"What did you do that for?" Connie asked; she was attempting to
do her makeup at the time.

"Because I didn't want to be rear-ended," Maggie told her.

"Good move, I guess," Connie said. She was pretty impressed
with the way people in Texas just blazed along whatever road they
happened to be on. In her opinion there couldn't be much wrong
with people who drove so fast.

Maggie eased the van back onto the narrow paved road, but in
fact, their eastward journey was over. The fire-engine red pickup
bounced over a cattle guard of some kind and came to a stop right in
front of the huge, castlelike house. Immediately a tall skinny woman
jumped out of the pickup and began to wave her arms in welcome.
For a second Maggie felt a pang, for Aunt Cooney walked exactly
like her sister Sally, Maggie's mother, had walked. She was striding
out to meet them at the moment, wearing an old mashed-up cowboy
hat, a cowgirl shirt, jeans, and boots. As they drew close, to their
immense surprise, Aunt Cooney yanked a pistol out of her hip
pocket and fired it into the air three times—she was grinning a big
grin, and even at a distance, it was clear that she favored a lot of
rouge.

"Good Lord, your aunt is packing heat," Connie said.

"I guess she's shooting off her gun because she's glad to see us," Maggie ventured.

"Maybe she has to have a gun to protect her chickens," Connie suggested.

The minute she stopped the van and stepped out, her tall, skinny aunt enveloped Maggie in a close embrace.

"Oh darling . . . oh darling . . . ," Aunt Cooney said, and happy tears began to trickle down her red cheeks. It was a much more emotional reunion than Maggie had expected—in a moment she began to cry too, and even Connie, who also got a big hug from Aunt Cooney, cried a little too.

"I thought you two would never get here," Aunt Cooney said.

"We almost didn't, we were kidnapped by a murderer," Maggie commented. "He was an old Indian man and he stole our pistol."

"Probably just as well—very few people are competent to shoot handguns," Aunt Cooney said. "I bet you two are hungry. Let's go in and wake up the cook—I'll have him whip up some huevos with a few chilis and whatever else he wants to throw in."

There was a big fenced yard around the huge house, a yard filled with poultry of every description: Maggie spotted little gray chickens and big red chickens and feathery guinea hens and big bossy turkeys and peacocks and geese and even two emus—at least she thought they must be emus.

"Why do you have so many birds?" Connie asked. "I don't think I've ever seen this many birds in one yard."

"Technically most of these are fowls, if you'll pardon the distinction," Aunt Cooney told her. "I've always been partial to fowls. They're brainless little things but I like to hear them babble. Of course the bottom's dropped out of the emu market—I'm down to two, which it would be a good idea to avoid close contact with. Emus kick worse than mules."

Then she took a close look at Maggie.

"You little darling, you look like you've had a rough passage," she said. "A rough passage inside."

"She has—it all started with her hysterectomy," Connie said at once. It surprised her that Maggie's aunt had been so quick to zero in on Maggie's "condition," as the girls called it.

"That's right—that's when it started," Maggie agreed.

Aunt Cooney didn't answer, but she put her arm around both their shoulders and led them through her chattering, pecking flocks, across a long porch, and into her huge, many-turreted house.

2

"IF YOU THINK I OPERATE a floating garage sale, you wouldn't be far wrong," Aunt Cooney admitted, leading them through piles of clutter into a huge dining room. Most of the clutter seemed to be objects of the sort that would only be of use to cowboys. They passed a whole room filled with saddles and saddle blankets; in the hallways were stacks of lariat ropes and piles of spurs. One whole wall was lined with gun racks filled with rifles and shotguns. Photographs were tacked onto the wall willy-nilly, their edges curling up. Most of the photographs seemed to be of cowboys too, although there were a few of Aunt Cooney holding up prize chickens at county fairs and chicken shows and such. There was a huge fireplace in the big dining room, with three giant stuffed roosters looming over them from the mantelpiece.

"I don't stuff just any old roosters, I just stuff the ones who have enough personality to keep me entertained," Aunt Cooney explained. "Those three naughty boys kept me entertained pretty good."

A long table that looked as if it might seat forty or fifty people was in the center of a huge room, which had stained glass windows.

"Hey, it's Elvis," Connie said, nudging Maggie—sure enough, the central panel of the stained glass window depicted Elvis Presley playing his guitar.

"Yep, the King, there'll never be his equal, not in my lifetime," Aunt Cooney said, looking as if she might shed a few tears.

"Excuse me, is someone sleeping on the table?" Maggie inquired. A figure was rolled up in a blanket of some sort on the dining room table—whether the figure was alive or stuffed she could not immediately tell.

"Oh, that's the cook," Aunt Cooney said. She walked over and vigorously shook the foot of the person sleeping on the table.

"His name's Mickey and he's my grandson," Aunt Cooney said proudly.

She had plenty of reasons to be proud, in Maggie's opinion and Connie's too, because the young man who threw off the blanket and looked at them sleepily and sheepishly was about as handsome as a youth could be. He had very black hair, coppery skin, and a smile that would rapidly melt any female heart.

"How about fixing us a little light lunch, sweetie?" Aunt Cooney said. "These ladies have driven all the way from California just to visit us hicks."

"If they come from California they're probably used to fusion cooking. I could make them crayfish dumplings and a quail's egg omelet," Mickey said.

Then Mickey smiled his smile again and sort of loped off toward the kitchen.

Connie, meanwhile, feeling nostalgic for her own garage sale days, wandered into a room heaped with Indian pots and blankets.

"I'm not a collector—I'm an accumulator," Aunt Cooney admitted. "Old Gene Autry used to pester me to give all my Western stuff to his museum, but I resisted his blandishments and the old fart finally died off."

"Neither of you ever met my Adele—come upstairs for a minute," Aunt Cooney said. The two of them followed her up a wide staircase.

"I've got interested in astronomy lately," she added, with a wave of her hand at one of the various balconies on the second floor. "I may build me an observatory out on one of these worthless balconies."

She opened the door into a large room whose walls were completely covered with large colored pictures of a beautiful young woman riding very fast on horseback. By the fireplace were some fancy saddles, not heaped up like the saddles in the front room; these saddles each rested on a nice saddle stand—on big shelves along one wall were what looked like dozens of shiny trophies and huge belt buckles. Over the mantel was a life-size picture of a young woman standing by Aunt Cooney. The young woman held a big trophy and Aunt Cooney was helping her lift it.

"My Adele—the best barrel racer of her era," Aunt Cooney said in a proud voice. "Won the barrel racing at the National Finals Rodeo six times, which no one else in history has ever come close to—my Adele was the gold standard when it came to running those barrels."

Maggie and Connie were both a little stunned at the sight of the huge photographs and the many trophies.

"So Adele was Mickey's mother?" Maggie asked. She knew that the trophy room was a kind of shrine to Adele—the gold standard when it came to barrel racing in her era. The fact that it was a shrine probably meant that Adele wasn't among the living anymore.

"Oh, my, my!" Connie said—she had a feeling something sad was about to come out.

"If ever a human being could be said to have rodeoing in her blood, it was Adele Miller," Aunt Cooney said. "Won her first barrel race when she was six, and that little thing just never looked back. She won those six championship saddles and one hundred and eighty-five trophies of various kinds.

"And then she met her Waterloo," she added, and sighed.

"Wouldn't you know, it happened at a little podunk rodeo over in Broken Arrow, Oklahoma," she related. "She grazed a barrel that hadn't been set right—it popped under her horse, a thing that won't happen once in a million rides. That little thing was dead before the arena hands could even get to her. She never opened her pretty blue eyes on this sad life again."

Maggie and Connie immediately burst into tears—Aunt Cooney just let them cry.

On the way back along the upstairs hall Aunt Cooney opened the door to her own bedroom. A little gray hen immediately jumped off a large bed and followed them down the hall.

"This is Minnie, she's my beauty," Aunt Cooney explained. "She's also my fly-catching hen. I've yet to meet the fly that could get past Minnie, or the mosquito either."

When they passed a window that looked off to the west, where the twelve chicken gulags were, Aunt Cooney stopped. Lots of small brown men were scurrying around the gulags, some on tractors, others in tiny pickups, some afoot.

"I just raise fryers now," Aunt Cooney explained. "I had half a million layers once, but the goddam egg business is too labor intensive."

Maggie was thinking how different Aunt Cooney was from Sally, her mother.

"You must be a good businesswoman," Maggie said. "I wonder what my mother would think, if she could see all this."

"Oh, this wouldn't interest sweet Sally at all," Aunt Cooney said.

Maggie hoped she would elaborate, but she didn't.

3

"THESE LITTLE SPICY dumplings are delicious," Maggie reported.

"They are, and so is the omelet," Connie chimed in.

Mickey, the cook who slept on the table, just smiled his heart-melting smile. It was clear he was used to getting compliments on his cooking.

"Mickey, how come you sleep on the table?" Maggie asked, hoping he wouldn't think she was being rude.

"I got him started sleeping on the table when he was just a tyke," Aunt Cooney said. "He was just a year old when Adele got killed. The last thing I wanted to do after that was go to bed and dream sad dreams—mostly I'd call up my poker-playing cronies and drink and gamble and raise hell all night. We'd argue politics and cuss the government for going socialist. Mickey never liked to be left out, so we started making him a pallet down at one end of the big table. I guess the habit just stuck. Mickey got so he could sleep through anything.

"Someday I'll be gone and Mickey will own all this—and every goddam clod of it is free and clear."

"But that won't happen for a long time," Mickey said nervously. It was clear that he loved his grandmother and didn't like to think of her being gone. Aunt Cooney put Minnie, the little gray hen, on the table, and Minnie modestly tipped around, eating a few tiny scraps of quail's egg omelet that the diners had left.

"I might have a decade left, I guess," Aunt Connie said, as if considering the question of her own longevity for the first time.

Despite the novelty of Aunt Cooney's vast house and the excellence of Mickey's cooking, both Maggie and Connie began to fade a little. The mere fact that they had come to the end of their long journey made them feel a little confused, in a what-next way. How long were they going to stay, for example, and how many days would it take them to get home?

Aunt Cooney was not slow to pick up on their fatigue and their confusion.

"It's nap time for you wanderers," she said. "Would you like separate rooms, or what?"

"The bedrooms are so big we might get lonely if we had separate rooms," Maggie said. On the trip she had sort of got used to sharing a bed with Connie—the thought of being all alone in this vast house in Texas was for some reason a little scary.

Mickey helped them bring their suitcases in and they were soon installed in an airy, high-ceilinged bedroom—the bathroom had an old-timey tub in it—the tub even had claw feet. It was so long that either one of them could stretch out full length in it without touching the end.

"They must grow some tall people out here in Texas," Connie remarked. "That tub would hold Shaquille O'Neal."

Once they were alone in the room, Maggie flopped back on the bed, tired but not exactly sleepy.

Connie washed her face and then flopped down too.

"You aunt's a fuckin' dynamo," she told Maggie. "She told me she borrowed ten thousand dollars to build her first chicken gulag and now she's got twelve and employs forty people."

"Right, she's a dynamo," Maggie agreed. "It's sad about her daughter, though."

"Lot of things are sad," Connie reminded her. "You're not looking any too happy yourself."

Maggie shrugged. She unbuttoned her blouse but she didn't take it off.

"It's all just so unfamiliar," she said. "Maybe we're too old to be dealing with places that are unfamiliar."

"I don't believe it," Connie said. "You're supposed to be only as old as you think you are—didn't you hear Aunt Cooney say she was going to Thailand next week? They've got some new breed of chicken she wants to check out."

"Well, she's in the chicken business big time . . . I guess that makes sense," Maggie said.

"Mickey says she'd go anywhere in the world at the drop of a hat to check out a new kind of chicken."

"That Mickey's about the most beautiful thing I've seen in a while," Connie remarked. "And not only is he beautiful—he can really cook. I wonder if he's got a girlfriend."

"I hope you aren't thinking of seducing him," Maggie warned.

"I wasn't—I'm too wigged out to seduce anybody," Connie told her.

"Come to think of it, I never ate quail's eggs before," she added.

"I think we ought to start home tomorrow, or at the latest, the next day," Maggie suggested. "If Aunt Cooney's going to Thailand, she's probably got a lot of stuff to take care of first."

"I wish we could start home right now, even though I'm exhausted," Connie admitted. "One reason I'm exhausted is because

I'm not used to dealing with places that are just so fucking unfamiliar. If that makes me a bad traveler, so be it."

Maggie realized that she felt exactly the same way. They were on
a comfortable bed in a lovely, airy room, and yet she couldn't rid
herself of the feeling of being more or less lost in the world. For
some reason she had convinced herself that visiting Aunt Cooney—
a long-lost family member—would help her get her old self back;
but so far it wasn't happening. If anything, the reverse was happening. What it seemed like was that, in the wide open spaces of Texas,
even more of her old self was disappearing.

Frightened for a moment, feeling that she was in the process of
vanishing, she took Connie's hand.

"I think I'll call Kate after a while," she said. "Maybe Melanie's
had her period. That would end one crisis, at least."

Connie's answer was a gentle snore. Somehow, between one
heartbeat and the next, Connie could usually manage to go right on
to sleep.

4

JEANNIE WAS SORT OF RAPIDLY flipping through the front section of the
L.A. Times, looking to see what sort of civic outrages were being per-
petuated at the moment, when a headline on page four caught her eye:

THREE MURDERED IN HOLLYWOOD

There, below the headline, were pictures of two of the victims: Dr.
Tommaso Balducci and Ninotchka Giddings, his wife. The third
dead person, not pictured, was a black man named Diego Jones.

The story beneath the pictures was brief: it mentioned that Dr.
Tom had studied with Anna Freud; it also mentioned that
Ninotchka Giddings was a ranking lady bodybuilder who had once
been Miss San Bernardino. Of Diego Jones, the report said, "little is
known." All three had been gunned down outside the doctor's office
on Highland—gang involvement was suspected.

And that was it.

"Oh my God," Jeannie cried—she ran out the door to try and catch Fred, but she was a little too late. Fred was on his way to work. As usual he had forgotten to take his cell phone with him, so no help from Fred's direction could be expected for a while.

Fortunately she did manage to get Meagan, who had just dropped off her daughters at archery camp.

"No way! . . . You're kidding me!" Meagan said—but she realized a second later that the murder of Dr. Tom, as they had always called him, was hardly the kind of thing that Jeannie would joke about.

Shock, or something, hit—for a moment the street sort of swam before Meagan's eyes—not a good condition to be in if one were driving in Los Angeles. She immediately swung into the driveway of a parking lot of a Circle K and stopped.

"I'm parking," she told her sister. "I could have a bad wreck if I don't get myself under control, pronto."

Jeannie, meanwhile, had surfed through the news channels on TV, but of course there was nothing about the three murders on Highland Avenue. The murders had happened the day before and were already old news so far as TV was concerned. An old psychoanalyst, a lady bodybuilder, and a black man of whom little was known were not likely to get much airspace, not in L.A., not with the gangs constantly knocking off one another or anyone who happened to stray within their line of fire.

"Have you called Kate?" Meagan asked.

"Uh-uh," Jeannie said. "You know how she gets when you call her at work. Unless Armageddon is about to happen, I'm not calling Kate at work."

"This is bad, this is bad, this is bad!" Meagan said. "My hands are shaking. I need a latte to calm me down."

"Ordinarily a latte would speed you up," Jeannie pointed out. "But in this case, who knows? . . . Hold on . . . I'm getting a call."

The call was from Kate. A woman in her office had noticed the short piece about the three murders. Marge and Kate had been office mates and softball teammates for several years—at some point Marge must have heard Kate complain about her mother's dependence on an old Sicilian shrink—and somehow Marge remembered enough of the complaint to put two and two together when she saw the story in the paper.

"Oh my God, are we up a creek now," Kate told Jeannie. "I disapproved of that old fart from the word go, but the last thing I wanted is for him to be dead."

"The last thing any of us wanted was for him to be dead," Jeannie assured her. "Meagan's holding. This is really serious. Maybe we should get together after work and figure out how to break it to Mom."

"Agreed—okay if we come to your place?" Kate asked. "Howie can't stand conflict."

Jeannie thought that comment was worth pondering, but now was probably not the time to get into Howie's conflict avoidance.

"What if Mom calls?" Meagan asked, when Jeannie switched her back in. What if she just calls to report? If she were to call right this minute, I might just blurt it out."

"Don't just blurt it out," Jeannie said. "I'm turning my cell phone off and you might just want to do the same. We need to get this right."

As soon as Meagan hung up, though, Jeannie began to doubt her own advice. There was no absolutely correct way to inform their mother that her doctor and lover was dead. Maybe letting Meagan blurt it out was as good a way as any to get the sad message across.

She called Meagan back to tell her as much, but of course by then Meagan had already turned her cell phone off: all Jeannie could do was leave a voice mail.

A minute later Kate called again.

"This is the worst," Kate said. "Are you going to be at your house for a while?"

"Yeah, why?" Jeannie asked.

"I'm shaking like a leaf," Kate said. "I mean, this is bad. I think I'm gonna take off work."

"You, take off work?" Jeannie asked, blown away. Kate was the one member of the family who was fanatical when it came to her job—in sixteen years she hadn't missed a day. Every single year she got a little plaque for perfect attendance. The only time Kate had missed was to have babies, but that didn't stop the little plaques, because her company, which manufactured sports equipment, had extremely generous policies when it came to maternity leave.

"Katie, that's drastic," Jeannie said. "But come on over if you want to. Maybe I can locate Meagan and we can get together and figure this out."

"I hope so, I'm shaking like a leaf," Kate repeated.

5

IN THE LATE AFTERNOON, after Maggie and Connie had rested in their airy bedroom for a while, Aunt Cooney insisted that they pile in the big fire-truck red pickup and let her take them on a drive around her properties.

Connie was up for it, but Maggie still felt kind of blah. She didn't want to be a bad sport, though, so she put on her dark glasses and wrapped one of the scarves they had bought in Victorville around her head—and off they went.

"Can we peek into one of the chicken gulags?" Connie asked. "I've never seen any kind of sight like that."

"That's a little tricky, honey," Aunt Cooney told her. "If I did give you a peek you'd have to wear a gas mask and maybe even a medical suit, and that's because chickens have very weak immune systems. What you have to avoid when you're raising chickens on a big scale is anything that might cause an epidemic. If you've got one sick hen, the next thing you know you've got a million sick hens, ninety percent of which will keel over and die."

"Uh-oh," Connie said. "Sorry I asked. I don't really want to see into one *that* bad."

The denial came too late. In two seconds Aunt Cooney began to yell in Spanish and a minute later one of the little brown men came hurrying up to them with gas masks. He even showed them how to put them on, and a minute later they were looking at two hundred thousand chickens, all pecking away at some form of chicken feed.

Their peek only lasted a few seconds, which from Maggie's point of view was long enough. The mask had quickly made her claustrophobic, but she recovered pretty well once they were bouncing over the prairie breathing real air again.

Next they visited Aunt Cooney's buffalo, which looked exactly like buffalo looked in pictures; they muddled around, taking life easy, or at least it looked that way to Maggie and Connie.

"I nearly got serious about buffalo," Aunt Cooney confided. "Old Ted Turner pestered me about them for several years. He wanted me to take on a hundred thousand or so, and I nearly took the plunge, but I guess I just wasn't convinced that the public was ready for buffalo burgers. Besides, it's taken me thirty years to figure out how to raise chickens profitably; I ain't got thirty years to devote to the study of buffalo ranching. Feel like a swim?"

"A swim?" Connie asked. "Aren't we in a desert?"

"It ain't desert, it's plain, and I have got the perfect swimming hole," Aunt Cooney informed them. "I swim every day, you know, rain or shine, sleet or snow—no better exercise was ever devised."

They bounced over a ridge, and sure enough, a good-sized pond appeared, surrounded by a tall stand of trees.

"It's spring-fed, my swimming hole," Aunt Cooney informed them. "I bought a few towels—just peel down and jump in if you'd like to."

"Skinny-dipping? I don't know," Connie said. "What if someone were watching through binoculars?"

Aunt Cooney cackled at the notion.

"They'd see three naked women of indeterminate age," she said, before she undressed and plunged into her spring-fed swimming hole.

Maggie and Connie decided they didn't want to be sticks in the mud so they undressed near the spot where Aunt Cooney had peeled off her clothes.

Just as they were naked and about to jump in, a big green frog beat them to it. The giant frog appeared almost at Connie's feet and jumped into the water.

"Bullfrog," Aunt Cooney said, paddling around. "I think we're having frog legs for dinner, come to think of it."

"Not me, I'll just eat cereal," Connie said.

"She has frog phobia," Maggie informed her aunt.

"I'm even scared to look at them," Connie admitted, heading for the pickup, where she intended to wait.

Maggie had intended to strip off and swim a little but when Connie fled to the pickup she felt she should support her friend.

"I'm afraid to leave her alone," Maggie told her aunt. "She's capable of going into a tailspin over a frog that big."

"What about snakes? We got more snakes than we do bullfrogs," Aunt Cooney asked, treading water.

"Now you're getting into *my* phobias," Maggie admitted.

"Gosh, if you let little things like frogs and snakes keep you from enjoying life, what are you gonna do if there's a nuclear war?" Aunt Cooney inquired, before she gave up on Maggie and Connie and swam away.

6

WHEN THEY GOT BACK to the big house, Connie took an unusually long shower—it seemed to go on about as long as seven normal showers.

"Are you ever coming out?" Maggie yelled, finally. "What's taking you so long?"

"What's taking me so long is that I had to ride for miles in a pickup with a woman who had frog slobber on her—your aunt," Connie said, when she came out. She was wrapped in a very thick towel.

"I'll forgive your aunt, though, because she has such good towels." Somehow towels, good and bad, had come to occupy a central place in Connie's worldview.

"Frankly, your frog phobia is becoming a little ridiculous," Maggie told her. "Besides, Aunt Cooney said little frogs are dying off all over the world."

"Good," Connie remarked. "Once every last one of the slimy little fuckers is dead, I'll feel a lot better about going in the water."

"It's amazing that Aunt Cooney invested in chickens and made a lot of money," Maggie said. "My mother, her sister, never made a cent."

"Hurry up and dress," Connie said. "I want to see what Mickey's made for dinner."

In a few minutes they were downstairs eating wonderful, ripe homegrown tomatoes, with a little basil and mozzarella.

When Aunt Cooney informed Mickey that Connie had frog phobia and wouldn't eat frog legs, he immediately switched to a fallback entree: tiny little guinea hens stuffed with wild rice.

"It's a great blessing having a cook in the family," Aunt Cooney said. "You have no idea how I suffered before Mickey turned out to be a cook."

The three women were all drinking some powerful tequila Aunt Cooney had produced—it was clear that she had no use for low-grade products. Her towels were the best, her tequila was the best, and Mickey, her shy sweet grandson, was also the best. After their drive Aunt Cooney had shown them her free-range henhouse, where chickens were allowed to run around loose, pecking at bugs and ants. Some of the roosters looked so fierce that she and Connie gave them a wide berth.

While Maggie was wandering around the dining room after dinner, her third tequila in her hand, her cell phone rang. She had left her phone on the table, by Connie. A couple of times, earlier, she had tried to call Meagan but for some reason Meagan's cell phone was off. That was odd, because, of the three girls, Meagan was by far the most addicted to cell phone use. But then Meagan also had a scatterbrained side. She could have forgotten to recharge her battery or something. Maggie considered that she was still on vacation—she didn't feel the need to keep that close a check on family matters—it could even be that her girls were doing what she was always telling them to do: live their own lives, with minimal input from their mother.

Although Connie had finished her dessert she hadn't really stopped eating—she was now in the process of polishing off the wonderful tomatoes, savoring every juicy bite. She had a bite of tomato in her mouth when she grabbed Maggie's phone—the minute she swallowed, she clicked in.

"Hey," Connie said. "Hi, Meagan—want to talk to your mother?"

Maggie glanced over—later she would claim to have had a premonition, but whether it was some ESP premonition or just good instincts would have been hard to say. And what was the difference, anyway? Meagan's big voice usually carried so that Maggie could have heard every word even across a large room; but this time it didn't carry, a fact suspicious in itself. Connie had been about to stick her fork in another juicy bite of tomato but instead she looked over at Maggie with a look of total shock.

"Who's dead? Is it Dr. Tom?" Maggie asked. "I told him he ought to move—did the gangs get him, or what?"

"The gangs got him," Connie confirmed. Then she very carefully put down her fork and fainted dead away. The alert Mickey caught her as she slid out of her chair.

Aunt Cooney took the cell phone out of Connie's hand just as she was about to drop it.

"Hi, honey," she said, to Meagan. "We've got us a situation here. Connie's just fainted and your mother has had a big piece of bad news."

"Just tell Mom she's right," Meagan said. "Dr. Tom is dead and the gangs did get him."

"It's a sad ability women have," Aunt Cooney said. "Usually they know what the bad news is before they can be told in the normal way. I was that way about my daughter. I knew the precious thing was dead before anyone showed up to tell me.

"And now your mom's just proved my point," she added.

7

THE MOST DIFFICULT THING, Maggie found, was dealing with everyone's immense concern for her. The general assumption seemed to be that she was headed for a massive breakdown of some kind. Her daughters assumed something like that, and so did Auberon and Jeremiah and other members of Prime Loops, all of whom had been quick to convey their sympathies to her daughters—and to Connie, who was acting as Maggie's receptionist for the time being.

Connie, to her credit, didn't assume that Maggie was headed for a breakdown; Aunt Cooney didn't assume it, either. She took on the burden of explaining to Kate and Jeannie and Meagan that Maggie was in fact a resilient person. Of course she was deeply sad, but that didn't mean she was about to go off the deep end.

The most helpful thing that happened, in fact, was that Jeannie faxed Maggie Dr. Tom's obit, which had been in the *L.A. Times* just that day. In the nineteen years that she had been his patient she had never dared ask him any questions about himself—it was a big relief just to read the facts of his life in a newspaper. Not only was it a relief, it was also full of surprises. Ninotchka Giddings had been his fourth wife; all three of the others were living; he had eight children and twenty-four grandchildren. After studying with Anna Freud he had for a time been psychoanalyst to the stars—Hedy Lamarr and Dolores Del Rio, for two. In his youth he had been a sportsman, a big game hunter, and a renowned wing shot. He had even won the pigeon shoot at Monte Carlo twice.

By the time Maggie got the obit, he had already been cremated; his ashes were flown to Sicily, to be put in the family crypt.

"The pigeon shoot at Monte Carlo?" Connie asked.

"I'm impressed," Aunt Cooney said. "The pigeon shoot at Monte Carlo used to be a big deal when the jet set was first invented—Aly Khan and that bunch."

It was hard for Maggie, knowing him only in his last years, to think of Dr. Tom as a member of the international jet set—but then he *did* own Penthouse A at the Chateau Marmont, which was pretty jet-setty. Jeannie had also faxed the clipping of the little story about the murders, but the pictures didn't fax well. Maggie had hoped for a look at Ninotchka but in the photo she was just a black smudge.

Maggie soothed herself by reading the obit several times. About the tenth time she read it she noticed that one of Dr. Tom's ex-wives lived in Van Nuys. Her name was Natasha Boudberg.

"Maybe I'll go visit her at some distant time," Maggie said.

"I'd think about that," Connie advised. "Some ex-wives don't like being reminded of their husbands. It could be painful. Maybe Dr. Tom was the love of her life, or something."

"Naturally I'd call her first," Maggie said. She had a longing to talk with someone who had known Dr. Tom when he was younger, when he won pigeon shoots and advised great movie stars like Hedy Lamarr and Dolores Del Rio. Maybe she would just call Natasha Boudberg in the morning, and take her chances.

It was then that she realized she wasn't in Hollywood—it was a good long drive from Electric City, Texas, to Van Nuys, California. Also, the hour was late. Mickey, the cook, had rolled up in his blanket and was sound asleep on the table—Aunt Cooney's bottle of fancy tequila was empty. The three of them wandered into the kitchen, where Aunt Cooney made coffee, cracking open another bottle of tequila to lace it with.

"You loved him and he's dead," Connie said. "It's so sad *I* may crack up, if you don't."

"I was his patient, mainly," Maggie reminded her. "I didn't really try very hard to be anything else. You know how sometimes you know better than to get your hopes up? That's how I was with Dr. Tom. After all, he was married, which is a pretty good reason to be careful."

But Connie was remembering the happy look on Maggie's face after she finally succeeded in seducing Dr. Tom. In Connie's opinion Maggie had let her hopes soar pretty high—though maybe only briefly.

"It was two years before I could stand to be alone, after Adele was killed," Aunt Cooney said. "I didn't want to go to sleep, because of those terrible dreams. But in my third year I started sleeping, and then all I did was sleep. I'd sleep for four or five days."

At mention of sleep, Connie began to yawn.

"Are you sleepy, honey?" she asked Maggie.

"Not particularly, but I'll come up with you—I know you must be tired," Maggie said.

In her mind was the thought that somehow they must get home.

8

"I'M SURPRISED you didn't cry more," Connie said, when she woke up. The sun was bright in the large bedroom—it shone on the polished hardwood floors.

Maggie was rereading Dr. Tom's obituary.

"Isn't Monte Carlo where Grace Kelly lived after she became a princess?" Maggie asked.

"I think so, why?"

"If the pigeon shoot at Monte Carlo was such a big deal with the jet set, there's probably pictures of it somewhere," Maggie mentioned. "I'd just like to know what Dr. Tom looked like when he was younger."

She remembered that there had been some pictures in silver frames on the piano in Penthouse A, but she had been so nervous on that occasion that she hadn't looked at them. Penthouse A was probably already on the market, unless Dr. Tom had left it to one of his children.

"Crying is a healthy act—you usually cry at the drop of a hat," Connie reminded her.

"I cried when I heard he was dead."

"Not much."

"I cried enough—I can't turn into a waterspout just to please you," Maggie told her, a little impatiently.

"Just let me work through this in my own way," she added.

Secretly, though, she knew that Connie was onto something true—which was she had not been all that torn up at the news of Dr. Tom's death. In the first place it annoyed her that he hadn't taken her advice and moved to a safer building. But he hadn't listened—probably Sicilian princes were not in the habit of listening to women.

Somehow Maggie's annoyance displaced her sorrow, for a time. If you'd just listened to me, she wanted to say; after all, he had been listening to her babble for nineteen years. In the end, though, he ignored her and her good, commonsense advice; and because he had ignored her, his wife, Ninotchka, would not be moving to Oakland with the third-best javelin thrower in the world, and Diego Jones would not be dropping by Maggie's house once or twice a week to sell them excellent pot. In some ways Maggie thought she might miss Diego as much as she would miss Dr. Tom. He had been a polite presence for more than twenty years, and polite drug dealers in the Hollywood area were not to be sneezed at.

Meanwhile Connie was giving her little glances from time to time, glances Maggie did her best to ignore—it was hard to say from those glances whether Connie was more worried than she was annoyed, or vice versa.

"What do you want to do about getting home?" she asked.

Maggie let her mind rove around that question for a while. What she really wanted was something only to be found in science fiction movies: some kind of supersynthesizer that could just swish your molecules to another spot on the planet.

What she wasn't sure she could face, on the other hand, was two or three days on the 40 freeway—all those trucks, those hitchhikers, those long bleak distances. What if she got emotional while in heavy traffic? A wreck could happen and the two of them might be as dead as Dr. Tom, Ninotchka, and Diego Jones. Within the confines of Los Angeles—big confines—she considered herself an excellent driver, but the vast reaches of America could be spooky and scary.

"I wanta go soon," Maggie concluded. "We could fly, but if we do, how will we get the van home? I'm supposed to start my new job soon. How would I get to my new job without the van?"

"You're always preaching to the guys about riding the bus," Connie said. "I guess you could practice what you preach."

She said it meanly, too, which didn't surprise Maggie. She had been expecting some envy to surface, pretty soon.

"Are you pissed off because I have a job offer and you don't?" Maggie asked.

"Of course," Connie said—in her what-could-be-more-obvious tone.

"Marcus Choate is no fancy producer," Maggie reminded her. "He's pretty marginal, in my opinion."

Connie ignored that objection.

"You should never have disbanded the loop group," Connie said sourly. "We were just beginning to work together well."

"Oh, baloney," Maggie said. "We were just a B-movie loop group and you know it."

Connie stopped arguing, but she didn't stop looking resentful.

"I bet when Marcus gets his finances together he offers you a job too," Maggie said. "I can't do everything in a production office."

"Great—I'd be your assistant," Connie said, in her poutiest tones. "I'm always your assistant—how come you're never my assistant?" she asked.

"I *am* your assistant," Maggie said softly. "I assist you every day of my life, because you're my best friend and I love you.

"It just happens to be a nonpaying job," she added, hoping Connie could be made to see the humorous side of things.

After a little pause Connie did manage a rueful smile.

"I'm only this bitchy when I'm homesick," she said.

9

AT LUNCH MICKEY revealed that he had attended UCLA, which came as a big surprise to Maggie and Connie.

"That's where he caught the cooking bug," Aunt Cooney mentioned. "Old Wolfgang Puck infected him."

"Gee, Mickey . . . if that's so, maybe you'd like to drive our van back to California," Maggie said. "You could visit some of your friends.

"Of course we'd pay," she added.

"No way, José," Aunt Cooney said, in a rather rude tone. "I got to go to Thailand next week to look at some Burma chickens. Besides being my grandson and my cook, Mickey's my manager. If me and Mickey left at the same time, the chicken rustlers would come in and steal every one of my two million chickens. All twelve gulags would be gone."

"Steal two million chickens? How could anyone do that?" Connie asked, amazed.

"People who put their minds to stealing can steal anything," Aunt Cooney assured her. "Two million chickens is no challenge at all to a real chicken man."

Maggie had the sense that her aunt meant to keep her handsome grandson to herself. She was not going to let him go back to California, where willing women were as thick as fleas. Maggie and Connie themselves were willing women, for that matter.

The mere fact that Maggie had casually offered to pay Mickey to drive their van back to California had an immediate effect on Aunt Cooney's welcoming attitude. She began to look daggers at them, a fact Mickey was unaware of. He was in the kitchen, peeling pears for their dessert.

"It was just a thought—we're tired of the road," Maggie said, in a humble tone.

"Maybe one of the Mexicans could drive it," she added, discouraged at the thought that they might have to drive it themselves.

"Nope, right now I need every hand I've got, and I could use ten more, for that matter," Aunt Cooney said, emphatically. "Besides, any Mexican who was headed west would get snapped up by the Border Patrol somewhere along the way, which would mean I'd never see them again."

Then she glared at them—her good temper where the two of them were concerned seemed to be turning into bad temper, and rapidly.

"You little starry-eyed dolls must think I make a fortune in frying chickens by hiring *legal* Hispanics?" she said. "I wouldn't let a legal Hispanic on this place—before I knew it, one of the legals would set the law on me for using child labor or something silly like that."

"You use child labor?" Maggie asked, thinking how outraged Jeannie would be if she knew Aunt Cooney resorted to such practices.

"I did when I first tried raising laying chickens," Aunt Cooney said. "A little brown kid can take eggs out of a nest as well as a grown man. The way I see it, you're either a hog-at-the-trough capitalist or a goddam liberal do-gooder, such as the two of you I'm sitting here looking at."

Connie was annoyed by the remark.

"I'm not aware that we've done much good," she said.

Maggie was mostly puzzled. Why was Aunt Cooney all of a sudden so strident and hostile?

"Maybe we better just drive ourselves home," she said.

Then Aunt Cooney suddenly sagged; she put her head in her hands. While she had her head in her hands Mickey came in and served the pears, then went back to the kitchen to prepare the latte. The sight of his grandmother did not seem to disturb him.

"Do either of you believe in Darwin?" Aunt Cooney asked suddenly, looking up.

"The guy who invented evolution—sure," Connie piped up.

"He didn't invent it, he just described it," Aunt Cooney corrected.

"Main thing I like about his book is that he shows there's no mercy in nature. Now, anybody who's lived a long life in the Panhandle of Texas knows there's no mercy in nature. But not everybody lives in the Panhandle of Texas, and they may get the notion that maybe there's at least a little bit of mercy in nature. Wrong conclusion!

"And now it's time for the two of you to get packed," she added.

"I feel like we broke some law—only we didn't mean to," Maggie said, hoping her aunt wasn't going to grab a gun and shoot them, or anything.

"No, you didn't mean to transgress—I'm being rude and mean and unfair, and I know it," Aunt Cooney said. "But then I'm way too much of a Darwinian to worry about justice or fairness. What I am is an old lady who's red in tooth and claw, like Darwin said nature is in his great book."

The three of them sat in total silence while Mickey served the latte and carried out the dessert plates.

Aunt Cooney's eyes followed him as he went politely about his chores.

"If there's one law of nature you can bank on it's that young women, innocent or not, take young men away from old women," Aunt Cooney said. "That's a goddam natural law if there is a natural law."

"But we weren't thinking anything like that, Auntie," Maggie protested, getting a little ticked.

"A law of nature's a law of nature whether you were thinking about it or not," Aunt Cooney insisted. "If you don't linger over your packing you might make Albuquerque by sundown.

"And that would put you well on your way home," she added, in a more kindly tone.

10

MAGGIE HAD HER FEELINGS hurt the worst by Aunt Cooney's sudden hostility. After all, she was Maggie's one living aunt; but all of a sudden, because of an innocent comment, she had suddenly changed from nice to horrible.

"She's just a bossy old bitch who must think that owning two million chickens gives her the right to be rude to guests," Connie said. "Anyone who uses that much rouge is apt to be bitchy, in my opinion."

Maggie didn't answer. She was hurriedly stuffing her stuff into a big black airport bag. All she wanted was to escape Aunt Cooney's as fast as possible.

They made it as far as the van, flung their stuff in, and were about to pull away when Aunt Cooney had another sudden change of heart.

"I hate myself so for what I said to you nice girls that I could blow my ugly old head off," she said. "You two barely just got here and now I've run you off—my last living niece."

"That's okay, we need to get back anyway—I may have a new job," Maggie said.

"The fact is I was jealous of your mother all my life and that's why that ugly stuff came spilling out."

"Why were you jealous of Mom? I thought she was jealous of *you,*" Maggie inquired.

"She had a whole lot better boyfriends than any I was able to catch," Aunt Cooney said, wiping away her tears and a good bit of rouge as well.

"Your ma married a Congressional Medal of Honor winner, didn't she?" Aunt Cooney went on. "I just married two or three rodeo bums—most of them had been kicked in the head so many times by rodeo stock that they could barely think."

"Just because Daddy won the medal didn't mean they were perfectly happy in their marriage," Maggie pointed out.

"Oh, of course they weren't," Connie said. "Sally cheated on him constantly." Aunt Cooney agreed.

"Constantly? I didn't know it was constantly," Maggie said.

"Like mother, like daughter," Connie put in. She couldn't bear being left out of conversations—certainly not for long.

"I don't think I'm very much like my mother, thank you," Maggie protested. "I know I had affairs when I was married to Rog, but who wouldn't have?"

Maggie wanted to leave—she didn't want to sit there with the motor running while Aunt Cooney smeared her makeup all over the door of the van.

"Don't you have to come through L.A. on your way to Thailand?" Maggie asked. "Maybe you could visit us on your way back, if we manage to make it home."

"Maybe, but why would you ever want to see my ugly old face again—the way I acted today?" Aunt Cooney asked.

"Come on, it's not like you're an axe murderer," Connie told her, not in a kindly tone. A stranger, hearing her tone, might even get the notion that Connie did think Aunt Cooney might be an axe murderer.

"Connie, I'm sorry—I was a bad hostess!" Aunt Cooney admitted. "If I do come through from Bangkok, I'll take you girls down to that big swap meet in Harbor City and we'll see what we can find."

The mere prospect of buying things seemed to put Aunt Cooney in a friendly, cheerful mood.

"Harbor City? Never heard of it," Connie admitted.

"It's in the general vicinity of San Pedro," Aunt Cooney told them. "I won't be more specific because you girls might dash right down there and beat me to something good—a Cheyenne saddle, for example."

"Why does she think we'd buy a saddle?" Connie wondered, after the two of them had finally driven off. It was nice that good relations had been restored—Aunt Cooney, perfectly friendly, had babbled on for fifteen minutes before she finally took her scaly old arms off the car door.

"If we stayed here we'd have skin like that," Connie remarked. "It's because the water's too hard."

"Our skin may be like that anyway, when we're eighty-six years old," Maggie said.

"You didn't answer me—why would she think we'd buy a saddle?" Connie mentioned, but Maggie continued not to answer her, mainly because she had no idea why Aunt Cooney would think either of them would buy a saddle.

"Horses bite," Connie remarked, and then she dropped the subject of horses and saddles altogether.

In Borger, not far from Electric City, they noticed what seemed like a nice motel. It was called the Helium Courts and had a kind of neon balloon for a sign.

"Do you suppose this is where balloons were invented?" Connie wondered.

"Let's spend the night here," Maggie suggested. "I'm tired from all that emotion."

"It's five hours to sunset but who cares?" Connie said. "We don't have to use up every hour of sunset, do we?"

"No," Maggie ruled succinctly.

For dinner they went to Pizza Hut—after dinner Connie finished reading her copy of *Elle* magazine. Then she faded out, and was still faded when morning came. Maggie let the Weather Channel run all night, but even with that aid, she didn't sleep very well. She was thinking of all the cheating Aunt Cooney said her mother did; she wondered whether her father knew and whether it made him sad.

Book Four

RETURN OF THE LOOP GROUP

1

"WHO WAS IT THAT SAID you can't go home again?" Maggie wondered.

"Mel Gibson," Connie replied immediately. She was at the wheel. They had just blazed past the exit for Twentynine Palms and were definitely on the homestretch. Very soon, barring accidents, which both of them, being native Californians, knew could always happen, they would be easing through the familiar streets of Hollywood. Both were excited at the prospect—their excitement sort of had to contend with the fatigue of the long, long drive.

"It wasn't Mel Gibson, it was a writer—I don't think it was Steinbeck," Maggie said.

"Don't expect me to answer a literary quiz—I have to watch the road," Connie complained. "It would be a shame to get splattered when we're nearly home."

"I don't expect you to answer a literary quiz, for God's sake," Maggie said. "After all, it took you two thousand miles to read one copy of *Elle*."

"So what? It was the fall fashion issue," Connie told her. "There were a lot of clothes to look at. Anyway, that *was* a dumb remark. Of course you can go home again. You just have to get on the right freeway and avoid getting splattered."

"I don't think he was talking about roads," Maggie mentioned.

"Look, whatever he meant, it was a dumb remark," Connie replied. "Nobody's gonna tell me I can't go home again—after all, it's a free country."

Connie was never bossier than when smoking along a freeway doing about ninety-five—of course, driving fast was a turn-on for Maggie too. She herself sort of felt like the Queen of the Night when she happened to be speeding along in the high eighties or the low nineties, particularly if it was a good freeway—the 5 freeway, or maybe even the 101 if it wasn't the rush hour.

"I think what he meant was that by the time you actually get home, things might have changed," Maggie said.

"Changed how?" Connie asked, as persistent as she was bossy. "Las Palmas Street hasn't changed that much in our lifetimes— other than ramps for the handicapped at the corners, what's changed?"

"Well, people can get shot, for one thing, like Dr. Tom and Diego and Dr. Tom's wife," Maggie pointed out.

"I doubt that Dr. Tom's wife was ever on Las Palmas Street in her life," Connie argued—sometimes there was just no getting the last word with her.

Only a little more than an hour later they were smoking through Pomona and would soon be faced with some freeway decisions.

"I know you won't even consider going through Pasadena," Maggie said.

Connie snorted, which Maggie assumed meant no.

"I want to see those foxy skyscrapers all lit up," she said.

Then a rare miracle happened: they slipped right through downtown with not a single turned-over semi to block their path. Connie eased up on the speed—in minutes they were easing up to the curb at Maggie's house.

"Stay here tonight, it's so late," Maggie said. Connie looked sort of blah, she was coming down off her blazing drive.

"I was planning to," Connie said.

She looked at her friend and sighed.

"Sometimes I think I should just stay here forever—no guy's ever going to be as nice to me as you are," Connie said.

"And vice versa, probably," Maggie remarked. "Look at how we got all the way to Aunt Cooney's and back without having any big fights."

Maggie studied her house for a minute, to see if perhaps it had become more familiar to her, in her absence. In fact the van had become a kind of home to the two of them—to Maggie it seemed cozier than a house.

Then the two of them got out and stretched. The big drive of their lives was over—their journey into America—but they were still coming down from it. Maggie opened the rear doors—both of them looked wanly at the jumbled-up heaps of duffels and sacks and hand luggage that would eventually have to be unloaded.

"We could leave it till morning," Maggie suggested. It was two A.M.

"No way," Connie said. "The first gang that rumbled by would realize what a treasure trove this is."

"You're probably right," Maggie said, though she could not think of a single valuable thing that might be in the van. As if to emphasize the point about gangs, a low-rider cruised up De Longpre Avenue and sort of paused for a moment, as if to allow the occupants time to size up the possibilities of a block or two of Las Palmas where two ladies stood.

"There, see," Connie said.

"Don't rub it in," Maggie asked.

Wearily they began to attack the piles of clothes they had for some reason dragged to Texas and now had dragged back, ninety percent unworn.

At some point during her various trips in and out Maggie punched her message machine, only to discover that the memory was full.

"I have fifty messages," Maggie told Connie. "I just stopped wanting to check my machine, you know."

"I felt the same," Connie said. "I bet I have forty messages from that lying weasel Johnny Bobcat."

"I'm leaving mine till morning," Maggie decided, but then she thought she'd just play one, and the one turned out to be from Marcus Choate, her prospective new boss. Marcus had a deep polished voice—actually a kind of snobbish voice—but his voice didn't sound polished on the message. Instead his voice was shaky and ragged and he said he was in a little trouble and was calling from the L.A. County Jail—and would it be at all possible for Maggie to lend him five hundred dollars so he could make bail and, as he put it, "straight matters out"?

"Uh-oh," Maggie said. "I have a feeling I just lost my high-paying new job."

"Son of a bitch, prick, asshole, dickhead," Connie raged—she had just used her cell phone to call Johnny Bobcat, only to have a computer voice tell her that the number was no longer in service.

"Since you just called him a lying weasel, I don't see why you should care," Maggie told her, although she knew it was never that simple.

Both of them were too wired from their speedy drive to feel the least bit sleepy. Fortunately there was a bottle of gin in the fridge— they made a few sloppy martinis while contemplating the miserable heap of luggage in the living room—most of it was stuff they couldn't even remember why they had ever even wanted to own.

"Mel Gibson was kind of right—you can't go home again after all," Connie admitted. "I mean, you can go to the place that was home, but nothing you might have been getting your hopes up for will actually happen when you arrive."

"I couldn't have put it better myself," Maggie said. Then she flopped on her bed and watched the Weather Channel for a while.

2

"Pricks, jerks, assholes," Meagan shouted into her mother's uncomprehending ear. It was seven A.M.—Maggie had maybe been asleep two hours—it seemed in her groggy, road-fatigued state that she was hearing a replay of the very words Connie had been saying about the weaselly Johnny Bobcat just before she went to sleep. What Maggie seemed to have missed, while she was struggling to get awake, was the name of the prick, jerk, or asshole who had upset her daughter so.

"Conrad! I'm talking about Conrad! He left me!" Meagan repeated. She knew her mother had probably arrived home real late, but a cataclysmic family crisis was in progress and some motherly input was *really* needed, for once.

"And Fred left Jeannie and Howie left Kate, did you get that part?" Meagan asked.

Maggie had not got that part. Tired as she was, it all seemed a little surreal. In her opinion any husband was always a good bet to leave any wife, but why should her three mostly dependable sons-in-law leave the three charming young women they had been married to for pretty good lengths of time? And on the same day—could this have really happened?

Then, thanks to the miracles of modern telephony, Jeannie somehow managed to enter the conversation. Meagan seemed mostly stunned, but Jeannie was far from stunned: Jeannie was furious.

"The asshole motherfuckers planned this together!" she said. "They orchestrated it, they choreographed it, the slimy cocksuckers."

"Jeannie, if you're on this call, is Kate on it too?" Maggie asked.

"I just clicked in, the gang's all here," Kate said.

Connie, annoyed by all the noise, got up, pulled a sheet off the bed, and trudged into the living room to continue her sleep.

"Maybe you should just all come over," Maggie suggested. "The house is pretty messy but I could make some herbal tea and we could sit in the backyard and ignore the mess."

"I don't think herbal tea will do much to solve this one, Mom," Kate said. Of the three she was the most matter-of-fact, which was surprising. Kate had a tendency to flare.

Maggie was still attempting to suspend her disbelief.

"If this was the first of April I'd think it was an April Fools' joke," she said.

"Unfortunately it's July," Meagan reminded her.

Although it clearly was not April, Maggie was unwilling to immediately abandon the idea that the three errant husbands were just playing an elaborate prank.

"Maybe it's just a guy trick," she suggested. "Now that they've made you suffer, they're probably going to show up after a while and take you all out to some fancy restaurant or something," she suggested.

"She doesn't think it's for real," Jeannie said. "Did you tell her about the other women?"

"I did, but she was still kind of out of it—I don't know how much she grasped," Meagan admitted.

"What other women?" Maggie asked. She remembered having said to Connie at some point on their drive that Howie and Fred and Conrad were all about due for midlife crises. Why she came out with that remark, while they were in the middle of New Mexico, was a puzzler, particularly since she had only seen her sons-in-law once or twice since her surgery.

"I did miss whatever you said about the other women," Maggie said. "But I still think there could be less than meets the eye to this whole imbroglio. It could be that they're all having simultaneous midlife crises."

There was silence on the line for a few moments, as Meagan, Jeannie, and Kate considered that possibility.

"Anyone taking Viagra yet? Just curious," Maggie asked.

"You're forgetting the cruelty factor," Jeannie said, though in a more calm voice. "How many times have you heard of three husbands, married to three sisters, announcing at the same hour of the same day that they are leaving their wives for younger women?"

Maggie took her point—she hadn't known about the same-day, same-hour provision.

"That's one for the Guinness book of world records, I guess," she said.

Then a silence hung in the air.

"Is it Sunday? I've lost track of days," Maggie asked.

"Yes, Mom, it's Sunday, otherwise I'd be at work," Kate mentioned.

"Then just come over—just come over," Maggie said. "My ear's getting hot from holding the phone up to it."

3

CONNIE, GLAZED AND HUNGOVER, decided she couldn't face the combined misery of the Clary family in its hour of distress.

"I think I'll go to my place and call Danny," she said. "I want to know more about the head librarian—will you come with me to meet her, when the time comes?"

"Of course I will, but why would you want me to?" Maggie inquired.

"She's the *head* librarian—she might expect a lot of literacy or something," Connie replied. "What if she decides I'm a dumbbell or something?"

"You're fine and I'm sure she's nice and I'm sure she'll like you," Maggie told her. "See, now it's you who have something to be hopeful about—you don't have three daughters who've just been dumped by their ignorant stupid asshole husbands."

"I know, but I can't get in the habit of looking on the bright side," Connie confessed. "What if Marcus Choate did something really bad? Then you won't have a job and probably both of us will end up on the street."

"Get out, you're too pessimistic," Maggie insisted, and after a long search for the van keys, Connie drove away.

When she left, Maggie opened all the windows—the house smelled pretty musty. Then she made herbal tea.

Kate came in first. "I wish I had a tubful of herbal tea—I'd drown Howie in it, if I could find him," she said.

Jeannie and Meagan soon arrived; they all sipped tea and sat in lawn chairs in the backyard while Meagan cried. She looked as if she had been crying for days; Jeannie showed no signs of having cried at all; Kate fell somewhere in between.

"What bothers me most is that they were so deliberate about this—it's a little conspiracy of stupid dickhead husbands," Jeannie said. "And somewhere three little low-life sluts have got each of our husbands convinced that they're the hottest thing since Tabasco."

"I should have known—Conrad hasn't slept with me in three months," Meagan said, before sobbing some more.

Maggie listened sympathetically and now and then made a comment, not necessarily wise, while her daughters vented. The truth was, she felt pretty detached from the situation. The girls reveled in the injustices and humiliations their husbands had meted out to them over the years; Maggie didn't doubt that most of the charges were accurate, but then those were just the kinds of things that happened to people who were taking part in marriages. She could have told them some stories about Rog, their father, that would have curled their hair, but despite the secret family in Azusa, they still idealized their father—why attack him?

As the day wore on they all got hungry—Kate, who had done the least talking, ran up to Sunset and bought a bunch of sandwich stuff. She also bought some vodka and Bloody Mary mix; herbal tea gave way to Bloody Marys; talk kind of dried out, but the drinking went right on.

As the hour of five drew near, Maggie took advantage of the general drunkenness to slip away. Connie had returned, in the meanwhile, and was listening to all the stuff about husbandly behavior that Maggie had already heard.

What Maggie did was walk over to Highland, to the shabby old office building, a trip made in memory of Dr. Tom. Until the very hour of her usual visit approached she hadn't really missed him very much. She thought she might just return to the old spot at the old time—like a little swallow returning to San Juan Capistrano, she could return and be faithful to Dr. Tom in memory.

But the pilgrimage didn't really arouse much feeling in her; perhaps she was still just too tired from the drive. The entrance to the building, where she had often had to push her way through pushers and dopers and general riffraff, had a dirty yellow crime scene ribbon across it. So far as her daughters were aware, the LAPD had not found the killer—or killers. While she was standing, a little numb, outside the building, someone touched her elbow, and who should it be but Sam.

"Oh, Sam, hi—I just came to pay my respects to Dr. Tom," she said. "Did you go to the funeral?"

"Wasn't no funeral," Sam said. He was afoot, which was unusual, and he was a little less dapper than usual. Not derelict or anything—but maybe his suit could have used a trip to the cleaners.

"Soon as the po-lice got through with the body, they cremated Dr. Tom and shipped his ashes home," Sam said. "Now he's gone and the fancy days are over."

"Aren't you still driving?" Maggie asked.

"Oh no, I was Dr. Tom's driver and now he's gone," Sam said, with a touch of resignation in his voice. "I do a little bartending up at Musso's—enough to get by."

"Then I'll see you there—maybe when I come in you can protect me from Paolo," she said.

"No need, Paolo dropped dead," Sam told her. Then he smiled and tipped his cap to her and went on his way up Highland.

I don't know that I'm going to like being home as much as I thought I would, Maggie thought. Back at her house, Connie and the girls were still yakking, drinking, crying. Nobody had even noticed that Maggie had been away.

4

"LET'S TAKE BETS on which husband comes back first," Maggie suggested. She had not been interested in the sandwiches the first time Kate passed them around, but now hunger had arrived big time. She was loading up a nice fat pastrami on rye—the vodka had run out, so Connie was reduced to Virgin Marys.

"It'll be neck-and-neck between Howie and Fred," Maggie speculated. "Conrad, I'm thinking, may not come in from the cold for a while."

"The more kids there are, the less likely the husband is to come back," Connie posited. "I wish we had some more vodka."

"You know what, there *is* some more vodka," Maggie said. "I hid a bottle under the couch to keep Terry from guzzling it."

"Guess who I had a message from?" Connie asked, while Maggie was consuming her pastrami sandwich.

"Warren Beatty," Maggie guessed—a good all-purpose choice in her view.

"Nope, Rudy," Connie said, in a smug tone.

"Rudy? Sorry—I seem to be drawing a blank," Maggie admitted.

"Rudy, the guy who gave me the Prada handbag," Connie told her.

"Oh, that guy—you never told me his name, no wonder I couldn't remember."

"Well, you have been known to steal my boyfriends, particularly the generous ones," Connie told her. "What he said was he might have a job for me. Wouldn't it be odd if I got a job and you didn't? Kinda like reversal of fortune or something."

"Connie, I'd love for you to have a job—anytime, always," Maggie assured her. In fact, her feelings were hurt by the remark. So hurt that in a minute she started to cry.

"Cut it out, I didn't mean it," Connie said, horrified.

Even with that rapid apology Maggie couldn't immediately stop crying. It seemed as if the sorrow she had been expecting to feel when she stood outside Dr. Tom's old office building had refused to come at the right time—now it was all pouring out at the wrong time and upsetting her best friend.

When she finally did get her tears under control she explained matters to Connie as best she could, which probably was not actually very well.

However, Connie, contrite now, did her best to understand Maggie's stuttery explanations.

"You mean you actually snuck off from us—when?" she asked.

"When you were trying to cheer up my daughters—that was sweet of you," Maggie said.

5

"DON'T YOU BE pessimistic, now . . . just because I have a job and you don't," Connie warned.

"I haven't said a word, pessimistic or optimistic," Maggie pointed out.

"No, but you kind of have a pessimistic look in your eyes," Connie claimed. "You probably don't consider Rudy a serious producer because he only produces soaps."

"Did I say he wasn't serious?" Maggie asked. "And why would I have anything against soaps—after all, I used to work in them myself."

"I don't know, but you've still got that look," Connie insisted.

"I suppose I should have a face transplant, just to please you," Maggie allowed.

"Rudy would never do what Marcus Choate did," Connie told her.

"Good Lord, I hope not," Maggie said. "Anything involving child porn gives me the yucks."

From what she had been able to find out, Marcus himself had not been involved with child porn, but he had been caught blackmailing a famous gay actor who was into child porn and "much else," as Maggie's informant, Auberon Jarvis, put it. Auberon, justifiably proud of himself, now actually ran a loop group of his own. He even offered to make Maggie part of it if she got desperate.

"I hope I don't get desperate, but I'm certainly not closing any doors yet, either," Maggie told him. As for being Marcus Choate's assistant, that was a lost cause—Marcus was still in jail. Other charges had come to light and his bail had been increased.

Maggie was happy that Connie had landed an assistant's job with the generous Rudy Clipper, though she had a suspicion, based on long experience, that the assistant's job wouldn't last much longer than Rudy's sexual interest in Connie.

"He's from Chicago—his sexual interest is still going strong, so far," Connie reported.

"So far is two weeks," Maggie pointed out, trying to avoid a pessimistic tone. "Most guys plug away for two weeks. It's the six-month sag you have to watch out for."

Even with Rudy in her life, Connie continued to spend most of her nights at Maggie's, a habit Rudy Clipper, who was married, had no objection to.

"He's into daylight sex," Connie explained—Maggie tactfully refrained from pointing out that should Rudy now and then want nighttime sex, he had a wife available.

Maggie began to notice an odd thing: her house—the house she had lived in all her life—no longer felt like her house except when Connie was there with her. One night Rudy's wife happened to be out of town, so he took Connie on an all-night date. Alone in her house for the first time in weeks, Maggie felt herself getting suddenly blue, then sad. She hastily put up her tent and crawled into it, but she didn't feel any more right in the tent than she had in the house; what she would have liked to do was to smoke some dope and calm down, but Diego Jones was dead, she had no dope, and she didn't feel bold enough to go up to Sunset or Hollywood Boulevard and make a buy.

Her anxiety didn't quite reach the level of a full-blown panic attack, but it was serious anxiety nonetheless. Her lifelong house no longer felt like *her* home—not unless Connie was in it with her. For most of the time since the sixth grade, when she and Connie became friends, Maggie had sort of considered that she had to be the rock of stability that Connie could depend on. But now, feeling a little shaky, she had to wonder if there had been another reversal of fortune: maybe now it was Connie who had become *her* rock of stability.

Of course, by the next night, Rudy Clipper's wife was back from out of town and Connie was back at Maggie's. In the course of the day Maggie had cautiously procured some pot and they smoked it. With Connie there her house seemed familiar again.

"Make any calls today—job-interview-type calls?" Connie inquired. Maggie shook her head.

"Why not?" Connie asked. "We've been back two weeks now. Are you just going to sit on your ass from now on, or what?"

"I'm shifting through my options," Maggie told her. "Please don't pressure me."

"If I don't, who will? I don't want you losing your grip," Connie said. "What about that old fart at Fox who's been in love with you for thirty years at least—wouldn't he at least give you some scripts to write coverage on or something?"

"Oh, Erik Asti, probably he would," Maggie conceded. And in fact she had always been exceptional when it came to writing coverage: she could quickly and clearly summarize a book or a script, evaluate its salient features, give some thoughts on castability, anticipate location needs, budget, star roles, and the like; and she could do it in plain, simple language that studio executives could immediately grasp.

"Erik Asti and Dr. Tom had one thing in common, beautiful table manners," Maggie remarked. "I guess that's because they were both from Europe, you know."

"They had another thing in common—money," Connie pointed out.

"I fully intend to get a job," Maggie said. "It's just that you may have to support me until my head clears."

"Till what?"

"Till my head clears," Maggie repeated.

"Is your mind cloudy? I don't understand," Connie asked.

"I don't either—it's just something that is," Maggie said.

6

A MONTH INTO THE NEW ERA—the era of Connie supporting Maggie—Connie began to get seriously worried about her friend. Rudy

Clipper and she were still going strong—he had even bought her one or two more expensive presents—so it wasn't a money thing. So far as money went, she knew she probably owed Maggie Clary hundreds of thousands of dollars. Long ago, when Connie had had a pretty bad cocaine habit, Maggie had covered at least a hundred of her bad checks and never asked for a penny back—and besides that, there had been a good many random loans through the years, none of them paid back. Usually these occurred when her boyfriend stole her paycheck or emptied her wallet or—on one occasion—bullied her into signing over her savings, all three hundred dollars of them, and every time Maggie had slowly helped her struggle back to at least a low level of solvency. So it wasn't a money thing—it was more like an apathy thing: Maggie's apathy. For one thing she had found, absent Diego, a safe connection and was smoking a lot of pot—not the worst thing to be doing. Still, it wasn't likely to produce a job.

Even right after the hysterectomy, in Connie's opinion, there hadn't been *this* much of a sag in Maggie's spirits. Ten days after the surgery she was at work with the loop group again. She hadn't seemed happy, of course; she didn't seem quite herself, but at least she was working—and in their world, working was the line that separated the living from the dead—or at least the healthy from the sick.

"Do you think it could maybe be the aftershock of Dr. Tom getting killed?" Connie asked Jeannie. She had finally become worried enough to consult one of Maggie's daughters, the brightest and most normal of whom, in her view, was Jeannie.

"Who am I to judge—or maybe it should be *how* am I to judge?" Jeannie said.

The deli they were lunching at at least had excellent chicken salad.

"Did Fred ever show back up?" Connie inquired.

"He tried to come back, but right now I'm in a punishment mode," Jeannie said. "At the moment he's living with an old army buddy—his little chicklet dropped him, of course."

"This may seem silly, but I think we should try to get Maggie into counseling," Connie said. "After all, what she's mainly lost was her shrink."

"If not counseling, maybe an exercise group, at least," Jeannie suggested. "You heard what Kate did to Howie, I guess?"

"Nope," Connie admitted.

"She showed up at his construction site and beat the piss out of him in front of the foreman—who had no idea until that morning that Howie had deserted his wife and kids. The foreman turned out to be big on family values—he wouldn't even let Howie up on his crane until he promised to try and make it up with Kate."

"Does Kate really want Howie to make it up?" Connie asked.

"I don't know—I've never been able to fathom my big sister," Jeannie said.

"What about Meagan and Conrad?" Connie asked, feeling that she might as well get a comprehensive report.

"Conrad is still at large and Meagan has a suitor, but don't tell Mom," Jeannie said. "Met your future daughter-in-law yet?"

"I did, I liked her, your mother went with me," Connie told her. "Danny's the happiest I've ever seen him."

"Is she pretty?"

"Not pretty—appealing, though," Connie said. "Flat-chested, but you can't have everything."

"Is she real highbrow, or what?" Jeannie asked. She liked Danny Bruckner, despite his addictions—it had always been in the back of her mind to make a pass at him sometime, but since he was engaged to a not really pretty but appealing librarian, it was probably too late for that sort of thing to occur between them.

"Actually she's a Lakers fan, we talked about Kobe and Shaq and stuff," Connie said. "Boy, was that a relief. She says she sits right behind Jack Nicholson, only about a hundred seats up."

"Ha," Jeannie said. "Fred's so desperate that he offered to get us season tickets to the Lakers games, but I think I can live without basketball easier than I can live with my Fred."

Pretty soon the excellent chicken salad and a latte or two had been consumed; Jeannie and Connie found themselves out of anything much to say.

"I hope I haven't taken up too much of your time," Connie said. "I just wanted you to know that I'm a little worried about your mother."

"And I want you to know that we're all grateful she has you," Jeannie said. "If she didn't have you she'd probably be in the nuthouse by now."

"Don't even think about it," Connie said.

7

ON BAD DAYS, when she couldn't even work up to dipping leaves out of the pool, Maggie began to wonder how one went about getting into a good nuthouse. Never before in her life had she been so out of it as to neglect her little pool—the pool her father the war hero dug with his own hands. Even from her back porch she could see that the surface of the water was almost covered with leaves; but she could not devote even ten minutes to dipping them out.

She got her address book and sort of skimmed through it. Over the years she had known various people who had spent time in nuthouses—maybe one of them would know something about the procedures for admittance.

Loyal as Connie was, Maggie knew it could not be much fun living with a cabbage such as herself, a woman so out of it that she could not even handle pool care in a very small pool. Probably her daughters, and Connie as well, would feel better if she was safely parked in a nuthouse somewhere. One afternoon she got out her laptop and immediately discovered that there was a nice private psychiatric hospital right in Brentwood—she pulled up beautiful pictures of the place and then checked out the cost, which was fifteen hundred dollars a day for inpatient care.

"So much for the nuthouse solution," she said aloud.

Then she bethought herself of convents—people overburdened

with the cares of this world sometimes went into convents, she remembered. But the notion of going into a convent did not survive for long. What if the nuns expected her to pray, something she had never known how to do? And in the second place, what sort of cares did she think she was burdened with? She lived in her own home, supported by a wonderful friend. What was the big deal? Even though she had no job at the moment, she was well liked in Holly-wood—she could find a job, if she pushed.

She had no lover, either—but did it really matter now? The last man she had desired was dead—why couldn't she just let love go?

Of course, a new guy could always waltz into her life, as Rudy Clipper had waltzed into Connie's; but then Connie had managed to keep a willingness or openness or something—a quality that Maggie could no longer summon the slightest iota of.

In place of that kind of willingness had come a sadness, unwanted, unsummoned, deep as the bone, and far out of propor-tion to anything she had actually suffered, recently or ever. It came like the Santa Ana wind; sometimes she had to grip the arms of her chair to keep the winds of sadness from completely blowing her away.

Ridiculous, ridiculous, ridiculous! she told herself.

And it was ridiculous; but that didn't mean it wasn't real.

8

"YOU LOOK SUICIDAL—are you?" Connie asked. She had popped in the door and caught Maggie off guard.

"I don't have the energy to suicide myself," Maggie told her, truthfully.

"Besides which I did something," she added. "I actually called Erik Asti and made a lunch date . . . how's that?"

"Excellent," Connie told her. It was Friday night and she herself was not in the best of tempers: for the first time ever, Rudy Clipper had stood her up.

"You might know—and I put on my best duds, as you can see," Connie said.

In fact, Connie looked dazzling—Maggie wondered if she herself would ever look that dazzling again. She owned some clothes that were just as nice as those Connie had on, but did she still have a self with the capacity to dazzle?

"My date with Erik will be a test," Maggie mentioned, but Connie, not unnaturally, was still fuming about her own problems.

"Maybe his wife showed up unexpectedly," Maggie suggested.

"Nope, she's gone to Chicago to her grandfather's funeral," Connie said. "I was with Rudy when she called from O'Hare to tell him she had arrived safely."

"If it was O'Hare," Maggie said.

"Of course it was O'Hare—her grandfather was a big mobster or something."

"Maybe Rudy felt guilty and went to Chicago on the red-eye," Maggie suggested—she was determined to run through the hopeful possibilities first.

"If you knew him you'd know he's not the guilty type," Connie said. "He's more like the pussy-hound type."

"I don't think you should jump to conclusions," Maggie told her.

"And I don't think you should sit there looking suicidal," Connie shot back. "Get up from there and let's go to dinner."

The suggestion—a perfectly normal one—took Maggie aback.

"Do what?" she asked.

"Go-to-dinner!" Connie repeated, sort of spelling it out. "I'm all dressed up with no place to go. At least we could go to Musso's and eat some clams.

"Come on, come on, Mag!" she insisted. "Cha-cha-cha." And she did a little dance, which somehow touched Maggie—why not do what her friend wanted, for once?

"Okay, you win, I'll try to find something to wear," Maggie said.

She went through her closet and managed to find a decent dress, but when she started to put on makeup she couldn't remember how.

She suddenly felt unconfident. Her hand shook when she picked up an eyebrow brush.

Connie, coming in to hurry her up, found her sitting at the makeup table, looking sort of numb, or paralyzed, or something.

"What's wrong now?" she asked.

"I forget how to apply makeup," she admitted.

"What?" Connie said. "You've been putting on makeup since you were twelve years old—you've done it millions of times—how can you forget how to do it?"

"I know, I used to do it in my sleep," Maggie said. "In fact, I used to do it in my sleep when we where chasing around with the loop group."

"And you did it driving, too," Connie reminded her. "You even did it when we were on the 405—it's a wonder we weren't all killed. The 405 freeway is no place to do your stupid eyes."

"I'll get it, I just lost confidence for a minute," Maggie told her.

"We're just going to Musso's—it's not the Oscars or something," Connie said. "You don't need much."

"But you're wearing eye shadow and everything—I have to at least try," Maggie said. "Besides, I have to meet Erik Asti in the executive commissary at MGM tomorrow. He's just the sort to notice bad makeup."

"Just hurry," Connie urged, trying Rudy on her cell one more time.

Then somehow the technique of applying makeup suddenly came back to Maggie. The old skill returned from wherever it had been; she started with her eyes and worked down. The result was not as good as Connie's makeup, but it was more than good enough for a clam dinner at Musso's.

To Maggie's surprise, once she had been propelled into action by Connie, she found that she liked being in a famous Hollywood restaurant again. She changed her mind at the last minute and ordered oysters Rockefeller rather than clams; and what's more, Jerry, the night maître d', who had known both of them for years, was so glad to see them that he laid on free champagne.

9

ERIK ASTI WAS THE ONLY male of Maggie's acquaintance who got regular manicures. He had an apartment in the Beverly Wilshire hotel
and had a private manicurist who came there to do his fingernails
once a week. Maggie couldn't help wondering if he got pedicures too,
but the only way she was ever going to find out what his toes looked
like was to sleep with him, which so far hadn't happened, although
Erik had made several mild fluttery passes over the years.

"Darling, you look *splendide,*" he said, when she finally managed
to penetrate to the executive commissary, where Erik suddenly
sprang up from his usual banquette.

"Has anyone ever told you you look like Paulette Goddard?" he
asked, while helping her into her seat.

"Never," Maggie said, though in fact Erik himself always told
her she looked like Paulette Goddard—it was his seduction line,
and if they happened to be alone, was usually followed by a fluttery
little pass.

Of course, that couldn't happen in the sanctity of the executive
commissary at MGM.

Once settled in and equipped with a martini—one thing you
could count on in an executive commissary was very correctly made
martinis—Maggie noticed that Erik Asti didn't look ninety anymore: he looked more like one hundred and ten. His neck was very
thin and his eyes so sunken in their sockets that they didn't really
seem to be attached to him. What would happen if one of them
rolled out when he bent to sip his soup?

That macabre thought somehow struck her as funny. She gulped
a swallow of martini, which went down wrong. It was all she could
do not to splutter.

"Are you all right?" Erik asked.

"I'd be better if I had a job," Maggie told him. She noticed that
his fingernails were just as well kept as ever. His eyes, though

sunken, were still smart eyes. She couldn't remember how many languages he was supposed to speak—one of the reasons he still had an office at Metro was in case Ingmar Bergman or Fellini or someone like that showed up; Erik Asti could totter out and speak to them in their own language.

"I can't give you a job but I can give you money if you're broke," Erik said.

All of a sudden, irrationally, Maggie felt totally perked up. Here she was in the MGM executive commissary, having lunch with a much respected old man who had worked with D. W. Griffith and Charlie Chaplin and who knows who else; she was wearing her Armani and had taken pains with her makeup, and her pains must have worked because Erik hadn't uttered a word of criticism, something he would have done if the tiniest flaw had displeased him.

"No way I'm taking money from you, honey," Maggie told him. "I write pretty good coverage—I think I wrote some for you before. I thought you might have a script or two that needed covering."

"We should have been lovers at some point," Erik said, suavely ignoring her job pitch.

"I don't know how come we missed," Maggie told him, and it was true. More than once the possibility that she and Erik Asti would become lovers had been sort of hanging there. At one point his fingernails alone were almost enough to get her—but for no particular reason, the big act didn't quite happen.

"There were near misses, though," she said, not wanting to hurt his feelings.

"Did anyone ever tell you you look like Paulette Goddard?" Erik asked.

Maggie looked at him closely and noticed that the smarts had dimmed in his ancient eyes; he was an old man no longer wanted, repeating old seduction lines—but impeccably dressed, at least.

It's good that he kept up the manicures, she thought, as she was driving home.

10

THE MYSTERY OF WHAT HAPPENED to Rudy Clipper was soon solved—
he had taken his wife to Paris in hopes of regaining her good graces.
Chloe, the busybody receptionist at the third-string talent agency
next door to Rudy's office, informed Connie of this after she came
nosing around for the third or fourth time.

"How did he get out of his wife's good graces?" Connie asked.
She was wondering if it could have anything to do with her.

"By fucking the maid, among others," Chloe pointed out, in her
usual mean tone.

"Gee, I wonder if I'll still have a job when he gets back," Connie
mused. Chloe turned down a thumb, as if she were a Roman emperor
condemning a fallen gladiator to death.

"That soap got canceled," Chloe explained.

"What? Soaps never get canceled!"

"*Thy Neighbor's Wife* did," Chloe assured her. "Now nobody in that
office has a job, including Rudy. Whether he still has a wife remains
to be seen."

If that wasn't enough, when Connie got home, Maggie was in the
backyard crying.

"What the fuck are you crying about now!" she demanded to
know, in her enough-is-enough tone.

Maggie just handed her *Variety*. The minute Connie saw the
headline—*Worked with Griffith and Chaplin*—Connie knew why
Maggie was crying. Erik Asti, who had indeed worked with Griffith
and Chaplin, had shot himself.

"He did it neatly, I bet," Maggie remarked, drying her tears. "He
was always very neat."

"Well, shit—but it says he was one hundred and one," Connie
pointed out. "He had a whole century. That's more than most people
have."

"True, but he never had me," Maggie told her. "Now that it's too
late I sort of wish that I'd slept with him.

"Now I'll never know whether his toenails were as good as his fingernails," she added.

"What?" Connie said, looking revolted. "What kind of reason is that for sleeping with a guy?"

"You're not turning into a foot fetishist, I hope," she added, a minute or two later.

"Nope, I'm not," Maggie assured her.

Then Connie spilled out the scoop about Rudy being in Paris with his wife and the soap being canceled.

"Of course, Chloe is a fat lying whore, maybe none of it is true," Connie speculated.

However, in the very next morning's *Hollywood Reporter* Maggie noticed a one-paragraph item mentioning that the soap *Thy Neighbor's Wife,* producer Rudy Clipper, had been canceled.

"Still, that doesn't necessarily mean you're fired," Maggie pointed out. "The guy probably has some other shows in the works—most producers do."

"I don't care, I never want to see the stupid son of a bitch again," Connie said. "Why didn't he take *me* to Paris? Why do men always think they have to make it up with their *wives?* Why don't they ever try to make it up with *me?*"

"Because they're creatures of habit," Maggie told her. "Look at Fred. He finally made it up with Jeannie."

"Big whup. Jeannie never let Fred slow her down anyway."

"No, but the kids missed him," Maggie said.

11

THE DOUBT ABOUT whether Connie still had a job was soon resolved; she didn't. The office next to Chloe's no longer had a Clipper Productions bar on the door. There was a new bar that said Anaconda Productions.

"I hope they don't make movies about snakes," Connie mentioned, when she got home.

Maggie had all her credit cards spread out on the table and was attempting to calculate how much she could charge before they were all maxed out.

Connie immediately spread out *her* cards and they figured their resources up at the same time. The results were totally discouraging: the two of them were only six hundred dollars from doomsday, the bottom of the credit card barrel.

"As hard as I've worked, I wonder why I never quite got ahead," Maggie speculated. "When does Social Security kick in?"

"Not for a while yet," Connie said. "I think you better call every single name in your address book and see if you can't get a job."

"You could do the same with your address book," Maggie said, meaning it as a joke. Connie's address book consisted of a few phone numbers for old boyfriends, most of whom, like Johnny Bobcat, had long since moved on to different phone numbers.

Still, Connie's suggestion was practical enough, the main problem being that it had become really difficult to reach the actual human being you were calling. By the time Maggie had worked her way through the *A*s, *B*s, and *C*s, she had only managed to reach five actual people: three secretaries and two old producer friends, both of whom were very friendly but neither of whom had a job for Maggie.

The other calls all reached voice mail or message machines, a fact so disappointing that Maggie couldn't bring herself to launch into the *D*s.

"It's like I'm my own telemarketer and I'm not making any calls sales," she told Connie.

"I just hope we don't have to be waitresses," Connie lamented. "I was a waitress twice and I hated it.

"I've been thinking of selling my condo but Danny doesn't want me to—he feels sentimental about it," she said. "Of course, they're going to live in Betsy's house, but Danny still doesn't want me to sell that smelly old condo. Which reminds me."

"Which reminds you of what?"

"I have to buy a new dress for the wedding—nothing I have is suitable," Connie said. "And you have to buy one too—nothing you have is suitable, either."

Maggie had to admit that that was probably true. Betsy, the librarian Danny was marrying, was a pretty conservative dresser—and conservative had not been the guiding principle of either Maggie or Connie when they bought clothes. Provocation, if anything, was the guiding principle.

"I've never let myself get this broke," Maggie admitted. "I know it's because of my slump."

"It *is* because of your slump," Connie agreed. "For a while I had Rudy and things were okay, but now I don't have Rudy and they aren't."

"Here's a thought—what if we had a huge garage sale?" Maggie suggested. "Both our places are full of crap. Between us we must have a hundred pounds of costume jewelry alone."

"What? Not on your life!" Connie insisted. "I love my costume jewelry. I love it."

"Okay, but there are other things that could go," Maggie pointed out. "Old shoes for example."

"Not me, not mine!" Connie insisted. "I'm not putting my beautiful shoes out on a card table for a lot of people with dirty feet to try on."

And there, for the moment, the economic situation stalled.

12

THE TWO OF THEM WERE watching Letterman when suddenly there was a knock on the door—it could even be described as an urgent knock—urgent enough, at least, that both Maggie and Connie jumped off the couch, bewildered—both had been maybe half asleep.

"Who is it?" Maggie asked, but the urgent knocker was knocking some more, so loudly that whoever it was probably didn't hear her question.

"Who is it?" she asked, more loudly.

"I think I ought to get the gun—the one we forgot to take to Texas," Connie mentioned.

"Just wait a minute, please," Maggie told her—she'd peeped around the curtain and managed to make out that the urgent knocker was none other than Auberon Jarvis.

"It's only me, Auberon! Please open," Auberon pled, just as Maggie opened the door.

Auberon, shaking badly—as badly as if he were having an attack of the DTs—stumbled in and thrust an immense mass of papers into Maggie's hands.

"Hey, what's this?" she asked, although a glance told her that it was mostly paperwork of a sort that the boss of a loop group was likely to accumulate.

"These are the call sheets and the directions for the next two weeks," Auberon said, looking over his shoulder out the open door. He was obviously in a deep state of anxiety.

"Are you having one of your panic attacks, Auberon?" Connie asked. "I've never seen you this anxious."

"Worse . . . far worse, dearies," he said. Ever gallant, he gave each of them a peck on the cheek.

"The loop group's yours again," he said. "Flourish, prosper, enjoy—I'm on my way out of town and fear I will be gone some time."

"Is this about a boy?" Maggie asked—she had a funny feeling it was.

"You've nailed it," Auberon said. "I thought he was just a gutter-snipe but he turns out to be the black sheep of a very important family. Very important."

"I wish you'd outgrow that stuff, Auberon," Connie told him. "This is not the first time this has happened."

"No, but it will be the last, if I don't get going," Auberon said. "Good luck with the loop group, sweeties."

"How old is he?" Maggie asked, just for her own information.

"He claimed fourteen but I fear it's more like nine," Auberon said, as he hurried out the door.

Before Maggie could really even shut the door, Auberon was back.

"He was in my car but now he's not—lock all your doors, please," he said. "Little Pat has very sticky fingers."

Then he was gone. Connie locked the back door, Maggie the front.

"I think we should load the gun," Connie said.

"Connie, he's nine," Maggie reminded her. "We can't be shooting a nine-year-old, and besides, he's from a rich family."

"Nine-year-olds kill tons of people," Connie pointed out.

"I wonder where Auberon will go?" Maggie asked. "Did you see how the poor guy was shaking?

"I mean, I know he's depraved as hell, but I still feel sorry for him," she said.

13

LETTERMAN WAS ALMOST OVER before the police showed up. Their arrival was not exactly a surprise, since the sound of the police helicopter sweeping the neighborhood had been keeping them both awake.

Connie followed Maggie to the door—she didn't want to be alone with little Pat on the loose.

The large policeman who stood on the porch when Maggie opened the door happened to be Tub Smith, the same officer who had spared Maggie when she was drunk and clinging to a parking meter.

A tough-looking boy in jeans and no shirt was in the grip of two policemen; the policemen had big flashlights, but at least the search helicopters had gone away.

"Now don't rush me," Tub said. "I know I know your name, ma'am, but I'm having a little trouble calling it up."

"Maggie—we only met once, and that was over by the Chateau when I was drunk," Maggie reminded him. "Diego Jones introduced us."

Officer Tub nodded. "Old Diego, a dapper dude—he was here and now he's gone," he said. "Ever see this young man here, who has somehow been separated from his shirt?"

Maggie and Connie shook their heads. They had just had their first glimpse of little Pat.

"We fished him out of that little tent in your backyard," Tub said. "Man, that's a nice little tent. If I had me a tent that good I'd be off to Big Bear."

"It's from L.L. Bean, I ordered it all the way from Maine," Maggie told him proudly.

"Do say? All the way from Maine," Tub said.

Maggie and Connie were dreading the next question, which they assumed would be about Auberon. After all, little Pat would surely tell them that Auberon had brought him to their house.

Tub Smith gave the two of them a thoughtful look. Maggie was prepared to lie like crazy, to protect Auberon, and Connie felt the same way; but Officer Smith surprised them.

"Sorry to wake you ladies up," he said. "Have a good night."

Then he turned to go.

"Officer Smith," Maggie asked, "did you ever find out who killed Dr. Tom and his wife and Diego Jones?"

Officer Smith shook his head.

"No, ma'am," he said. "It was a misty night. Somebody just walked up and shot them, took their cash, and kept walking. It was what you might call a fatal encounter."

"I see, good night," Maggie said.

14

AFTER SUCH A LATE, strange night it was not easy for the two of them to get themselves out the door at seven-fifteen, but somehow they did it. Connie drove and Maggie plotted a course to the various pickup points. Jeremiah Moore, as usual, they collected first. He was superglad to see them; he admitted that working with Auberon had been pretty stressful. There were two new guys, Karel and Andy, both of whom became shy when they discovered they were traveling with women. Jesús had resurfaced, along with his little brother Angel, who was nearly as cute as a real angel. They made the studio on Pico just in time, they looped, and Maggie drove everybody home, while Connie mostly snored.

No sooner had they walked in the door than the phone rang—in their dog-tired state neither of them really wanted to answer it. They had set the message machine for eight rings, the maximum; very few people in speedy Hollywood had the patience to listen to a phone ring eight times—usually they gave up around five or six.

"Don't answer—when somebody calls us, it means trouble," Connie pointed out, not inaccurately.

"Mom . . . Mom . . . come on, Mom, pick up, I know you're there," Meagan said. "Please pick up."

Connie watched, reproach in her eyes, to see if Maggie was going to break, though the outcome, as she well knew, was a foregone conclusion.

Maggie picked up.

"What, sweetie?" she asked.

"I don't know," Meagan said. "Howie went back to Kate and Fred went back to Jeannie. Why won't Conrad come back to me?

"Do you suppose there's something wrong with me?" Meagan asked. "I know I don't have big boobs, like Kate."

"Neither does Jeannie, which doesn't keep her from getting plenty of guys," Maggie pointed out.

"I know, but there must be something the others have that I don't," Meagan lamented. "My self-esteem is sinking fast."

Maggie sighed; Connie looked even more reproachful because Maggie was indulging her youngest daughter even though they had had a bad night followed by a hard day.

"Did I call at a bad time?" Meagan asked.

"Sort of," Maggie admitted. "We had a terrible night—Auberon got in some trouble. We've had to take over his loop group at short notice. The fact is, we're both pooped."

"I'm sorry," Meagan said. "I know I shouldn't burden you with my troubles. After all, I'm a grown woman."

"When I'm fresh, which I hope will be tomorrow, it's fine," Maggie told her. "Right now I'm too tired to give sensible advice where husband and wife are concerned."

There was awkward silence—Maggie almost went to sleep holding the phone to her ear. She heard Meagan gulp, as if she might be about to cry, but then Meagan said a quick "Bye" and hung up.

Instantly the phone rang again.

Connie, looking disgusted, wandered off to the bathroom.

Maggie, after wondering briefly why she could never not pick up—after all, maybe she'd won the lottery—picked up.

"Well, did my little group perform to standard?" Auberon asked.

"They did fine—I think the producer was pleased," Maggie said.

Then she got one of her uncanny feelings—Auberon had asked a normal question in a normal voice but somehow she still had an inkling that it wasn't a normal call.

"Are you in jail?" she asked—why not cut to the chase?

"Right, L.A. County," Auberon admitted.

"I guess the reason the cops didn't ask about you was because they already had you, right?" Maggie guessed.

"I didn't even make it to Cahuenga," Auberon admitted.

"I didn't see anything in the papers," Maggie said. "I guess that's because little Pat was from that important family."

"You're batting a thousand today," Auberon said. "They're going to cut me off any moment now. I need a big favor."

"What?"

"I need you to get my car out of the police pound and sell it so I can make bail," he said. "Otherwise I'll be here until I rot.

"I should have figured out sooner that that little brute was a rich kid," he added. "I should have kept looking until I found a real guttersnipe. They're hardly in short supply."

Just then Connie wandered in, a toothbrush in her mouth. She had already put on her pajamas. She was brushing her teeth at a very slow rate.

"He's in jail, that's why they didn't ask about him," Maggie informed her. Connie lifted an eyebrow.

"How much is the bail?" Maggie asked.

"More than my car is worth but could you please try?" he added. Then there was a click.

"He wants us to sell his car," Maggie reported.

"Okay, but when? We have to work every day this week."

"I don't know when," Maggie said. "Is there anything to eat in this house?"

Connie made a quick tour of the kitchen.

"Two avocados," she said.

15

Maggie usually left her mail for weekends. An untidy pile would accumulate on the kitchen table, getting smeared with mustard or grape jelly or whatever smearables were in the process of being consumed. Eventually, Saturday afternoon maybe, Maggie would probe the pile warily. If she saw anything with a major department store's name on it—Sears, Dillard's, you name it—she would generally just drop the envelope in the wastebasket—what could it be but long overdue bills?

The week of looping had seemed unusually hectic because the two of them were out of practice. Pretty much the last thing Maggie wanted to do on Saturday was probe in a big disgusting pile of mail.

Another thing she didn't want to do was attempt to extract Auberon's car from the police pound, particularly since they had admitted on a subsequent call that the car had at least two thousand dollars' worth of overdue traffic tickets charged against it. Tired as they were, it was easy to rationalize ignoring Auberon's plight.

"He's so picky they'll get tired of him and let him out," Connie reasoned. "The cops aren't gonna want to put up with Auberon indefinitely just because he fucked some little piece of jailbait."

That position seemed reasonable enough to Maggie—anyway, they had only worked a week and didn't have the money to pay off all those tickets.

"Auberon's a grown man," Connie repeated. "I'm not saying he's mature."

While Maggie was sort of circling the big pile of mail she happened to notice an envelope that looked sort of fatter and richer than all the other envelopes. She pulled it out and held it up to the light, but the paper was far too thick for that to work. The envelope was from a jewelry store on Rodeo Drive, in Beverly Hills.

"Gosh, the stores on Rodeo must be getting desperate if they think they should send me a come-on," she said.

Connie's personal method for dealing with mail was to go over to her place every Sunday and throw it all away. She did it mainly as a favor to the postman, who got irritated if he had to stuff new mail on top of old mail day after day.

"I hate Rodeo Drive," Connie informed her. "And the reason I hate it is because I can never afford a single thing that's for sale on it."

Maggie opened the fat envelope, expecting nothing more exciting than the announcement of a sale. She was so sure that that was what the envelope was about that she was about to toss it unread and would have if her eye had not caught the name of Erik Asti.

Then she read the letter and gasped.

"He left me a jewel, I can pick it up anytime," she said.

"Who, Dr. Tom?"

When Connie said the name, Maggie felt a little pang, a sudden wish that the jewel had been left to her by Dr. Tom, of whom she possessed not a single memento, unless she counted his obit, and even that was faxed. Of course, Dr. Tom had all those children and ex-wives—it was silly of her to expect anything—maybe his picture of Anna Freud or something?

But Erik Asti, who actually left her the jewel, had been muttering sweet nothings to her for thirty years but had never really touched her, other than maybe a hug or something in some public place; then she remembered that he had once kissed her hand—the gesture startled her so that she had almost jerked her hand away, though of course kissing a lady's hand was a perfectly normal thing for a correct European gentleman to do.

"Son of a bitch," Connie said, when she read the letter—she meant it in a nice way, of course, though Connie was incapable of not being at least a little jealous when Maggie received a gift and she didn't.

"I wonder what kind of jewel it will be," she asked. "Maybe pearls. He looked to me like the kind of old guy who might give pearls."

"I guess pearls are nice, but they aren't very sexy," Maggie commented. "Though some nice pearls would be appropriate to wear to Danny's wedding."

"You said yourself you never even came close to sleeping with the guy," Connie pointed out. "Why would he give you a sexy jewel?"

"Well, I think he always wanted to sleep with me," Maggie told her. "I saw him maybe a hundred times and he just never got around to making a pass."

"He was probably just shy—you should just have grabbed his dick and gone for it," Connie remarked. "You wouldn't catch me going out with some old dude a hundred times unless there was some fucking."

"Not even if he took you to really nice places—Le Dôme or somewhere like that?" Maggie inquired. "Not even if he ordered hundred-dollar bottles of wine?"

"Do I look like a wine snob?" Connie asked.

"We have to go grocery shopping this weekend," Maggie said. "I'm exhausted and we ate those avocados."

"Just use the phone book," Connie advised. "There must be at least one hundred take-outs in this part of town.

"Let's get Chinese?" Maggie suggested.

"What's wrong with Thai?" Connie wanted to know.

"If you mean that Thai place on Melrose, they take too long to deliver," Maggie told her. "I'll be asleep before the food comes."

"Maybe for once they'd speed it up, if I asked them," Connie speculated.

"Miss Optimism," Maggie said. They ordered Thai.

16

THE PEOPLE IN THE JEWELRY STORE on Rodeo Drive took their time buzzing Maggie in, though she considered that she was dressed nicely, or neatly at the very least. The man who met her when she finally got inside the door looked at her as if she were some particularly disgusting leftover that had been in the fridge a few weeks.

"May we help you?" he asked, in a voice that suggested he'd rather just kick her out.

"I was a friend of Mr. Asti's," Maggie told him. Even though she had the letter in her purse the man was so chilly that she began to feel insecure; probably it was all some kind of mistake—maybe the jewel was really meant to go to Paulette Goddard, if she was still alive.

Nevertheless, there she was, so she extracted the letter and handed it to the tall, chilly man.

"Oh yes, lucky you," the man said, and disappeared, leaving her with the three women, none of whom said a word. Maggie was almost afraid even to look at the jewelry in the cases, for fear the women would pounce on her like a pack of skinny greyhounds.

The man came back with a little black velvet box, and a sheaf of papers Maggie was required to sign, though not until she had produced every piece of identification she had with her.

The tall man showed her driver's license to the three silent women and there was a good deal of looking back and forth, from the license to Maggie.

"I really am me," Maggie said, a couple of times, but the others just ignored her comment.

Finally, once all the papers had been signed and scrutinized, the black velvet box was handed over.

"Now I'm scared to open it," Maggie confessed. "What is it?"

"Why, an emerald," the tall man said. "A fine one too. It's unset, but we'll be happy to set it for you, if you'd like."

Maggie opened the box and took a peek. The emerald was so beautiful she felt a little weak. Never in her life had she owned anything to approach it.

"In view of its size it could be either a ring or a pendant," the man said. "What do you think?"

"I'd like to look at it a few days, before I decide," Maggie told him. "I've never owned anything this beautiful."

"Few of us have," the man said, handing her his card. "I'd suggest the simplest possible setting."

"Thank you, I've gotta get out of here," Maggie said. She felt for a moment that she might faint, and she didn't want to faint in the snippy store.

It took them no time to buzz her out.

17

"This is the first thing we've had worth stealing," Connie commented, after they had both stared at the emerald for a while.

"*You* have something worth stealing," she amended.

"Oh, you can wear it all you want to, once we figure out how to set it," Maggie said. "Maybe you could even wear it to Danny's wedding."

"No, I couldn't—I don't want to upstage Betsy," Connie said. "After all, she's the bride and it should be her day."

Then she burst into tears and cried for maybe three minutes, at the thought that her son would soon belong to another woman, and a head librarian at that.

"A jewel like this is something we could be murdered for," Maggie said. For some reason the sight of the emerald—a very valuable object, obviously—was making her very tense and paranoid.

"You should maybe just put it in your safe deposit box," Connie advised.

"Come on—I don't have a safe deposit box," Maggie pointed out. "I've never owned anything valuable enough to put in one."

"You should try to get one, pronto," Connie suggested. "That emerald could be the answer to your financial problems. I bet you could pawn it for a lot."

"I don't think I deserve this emerald—I never went to bed with the guy," Maggie repeated for maybe the tenth time. "Maybe I should pawn it and pay off Auberon's tickets and help him get out of jail."

Connie looked stunned. "Hey, calm down," she said. "It's just a rock—a nice rock, but still a rock."

"It's not just a rock, it's something I don't deserve. I don't want it!" Maggie said, becoming more frantic by the minute.

"You take it," she said, thrusting the box at Connie. "I give it to you. I don't want it! I don't want it!"

Then, despite herself, she began to spiral out of control. She felt like she might fly apart—she was descending into panic, the same kind of panic she felt the Sunday afternoon when there had been the small earthquake—two-point-two on the Richter scale by her neighbor Gwen's estimate. She thought she might scream and run out and hide in her tent, where actually she had found a syringe the morning after little Pat had hidden there—somehow the police overlooked it.

"I don't want it, I don't want it," she kept repeating, getting a little louder every time, so that finally she was almost screaming and she might have kept screaming until someone came and carried her off in a straitjacket had Connie not grabbed her by the shoulders and given her a good shaking, a hard shaking, hard enough that her teeth clattered and she had to gasp for breath, at which point she stopped yelling about the emerald she didn't want.

"You know something, that's enough out of you," Connie said, in a firm but not unfriendly voice.

"It's your emerald," she added. "You even have the papers on it. If you don't want the fucking thing, sell it!"

"I'm afraid of it," Maggie told her. "It's bad luck to have expensive things you don't deserve.

"Thank you for shaking me," she added. It was surprising how calm Connie had been able to stay while she herself descended into the great wild space of paranoia.

"What are friends for?" Connie replied, with a nice smile. "I hope you'll do the same for me the next time I have a fit."

Maggie was thinking that there *had* been a reversal of fortune in their lives. She had once been the strong one—now it seemed as if Connie were the strong one and she herself the unstable one; maybe the reversal of fortune had been coming ever since her hysterectomy; Connie having the good sense to shake her until she stopped yelling about the emerald she didn't want was just the latest manifestation of it.

"Do you think I'm going crazy, Connie?" Maggie asked. "Don't lie—if you think I'm going crazy, just say so."

Connie threw up her hands and gave Maggie one of her what-am-I-going-to-do-about-you looks.

"You are *not* going crazy," Connie told her. "And I know crazy because my mother went crazy and my baby sister was crazy practically from the moment she was born.

"My dad wasn't exactly what you'd call sane, either," she added, whirling a finger around her ear.

"I don't want to be crazy," Maggie said. It was a sentiment that she had been meaning to deliver for months because, sometimes in the dark of night and sometimes in the midst of the brightest, sunniest, smog-free day, she felt herself kind of slipping down an inner slope of some kind, and where she was slipping was toward a form of instability at the very least—with outright insanity probably being the very worst that would happen. And yet Connie, who had had her own periods of instability if not worse, said it wasn't so; and who did she trust in this world more than Connie? The answer to that was no one. If you couldn't trust a person who had been your best friend since the sixth grade you might as well give up on the whole notion of trust.

"Please let me give you the emerald," she said—why not try once more?

"No, dear," Connie said. "In the first place a nice old man gave it to you."

"But I never slept with him."

"Oh, shut up about not sleeping with him," Connie said, looking a little exasperated. "Is sex supposed to be the only pleasure a woman can give a man? You had lots of lunches with the guy. For all you know those lunches were the happiest moments of his life."

That notion had never occurred to Maggie.

"I never looked at it that way," she admitted. "I mean, I know he enjoyed the lunches—I guess I'm just surprised that he enjoyed them an emerald's worth."

"People get their kicks in different ways," Connie reminded her. "Having lunch with you is better than what Auberon does, wouldn't you say?"

"Sure . . . I'll buy that," Maggie agreed. "Can you believe that dirty little boy left a syringe in my tent?"

"Little fucker," Connie said.

18

FINDING A HIDING PLACE for the emerald was the next problem.

"Remember what Aunt Cooney said—good thieves operate by instinct," Maggie told Connie, while they were racking their brains over what might make a safe hiding place.

"If stealing two million chickens is no problem for them, how long do you think it would take them to ferret out this stupid emerald?" she asked.

"Hey, don't call it stupid," Connie protested. "Even if you don't want it, it's still the most beautiful thing either of us has ever owned or ever will own."

Finally they wrapped it up good and buried it in a flowerpot, beside a half-dead petunia. Once the emerald was buried, Maggie spent a half hour smoothing the dirt over the hiding place.

"Don't make it too smooth—it looks unnatural," Connie told her. "A good thief will spot that in ten seconds."

Maggie tried to ruffle up the soil a little but neither of them was pleased with the result.

They went to bed anyway, but Maggie tossed and turned all night, worrying about the emerald. Connie slept soundly, woke up first, and immediately saw that the flowerpot had been disturbed.

"Oh my God, it's gone . . . I wonder what else is missing," she said.

"Nothing is missing—I got up in the night and hid the emerald in the peanut butter jar," Maggie told her.

"Oh great, suppose the burglar happened to be hungry," Connie complained. "So he makes himself a peanut butter sandwich and finds your emerald."

"I don't think I can stand to own this emerald any longer," Maggie said. "What if I just sold it back to those creeps Erik bought it from?"

"Well, maybe you should," Connie allowed.

"We could pay off our credit card debt," Maggie reasoned.

"Right—and maybe there'd be enough left over for us to buy classy wedding dresses for Danny's wedding," Connie allowed.

"That's a thought, only not too classy. We don't want to upstage the bride, remember?

"I guess it would be a miracle if it were worth *that* much, but wouldn't it be great if there were enough left over to make a down payment on a new van for the loop group?" Maggie fantasized.

"Good idea, the van's on its second transmission, remember," Connie reminded her. "The bottom's gonna fall out one of these days and then where will we be?"

19

FORTUNATELY MAGGIE remembered that the tall chilly man at the snooty jewelry store had given her his card, which she dug out of the papers that proved the emerald was really hers, a gift from Mr. Erik Asti.

The name on the card was DeCourcy Brown—part of the name was fancy and part of the name was even more normal than Maggie's own last name, Clary. When she called the jewelry store DeCourcy Brown himself answered. The minute Maggie told him she might be interested in selling the emerald he at once stopped being chilly.

"How nice of you to think of us," he said, "the more so considering how rude we were."

"Thanks, I don't get the rudeness," she told him. "What's the point of being that rude?"

"You'd understand it if you happened to run a fancy store on Rodeo Drive," DeCourcy Brown told her. "Actually I'm just a Midwestern slob from South Dakota."

"Oh, you're no slob—that was a terrific suit you had on," Maggie told him.

"Sweetie, if we keep chatting like this we'll soon be in love," he said. "When would you like to bring in the nice green stone?"

"It would have to be Saturday, I work all week," she told him— when she got to the store on Saturday DeCourcy Brown himself buzzed her in before she even had time to ring the bell.

This time the three women, thin as whippets, even smiled at her, but better than the smiles and DeCourcy Brown's friendly manner was the fact that he immediately offered her forty thousand dollars for the emerald.

"How much?" Maggie asked, thinking she had misunderstood.

"Forty thousand—could you be content with that?" he asked.

"I not only can be content with it, I can be ecstatic about it," Maggie assured him.

"Just owning it made me paranoid," she confessed, out of the blue. "I had a panic attack—my best friend had to shake me to get me to calm down."

"Well, we can cure that permanently," DeCourcy Brown said. A minute or two later he handed Maggie a check for forty thousand dollars.

It was such an unbelievable turn of events that Maggie's hand shook a little when she slipped the check into her purse.

"Did you know Mr. Asti?" she asked, hoping she wasn't breaking the Rodeo Drive rules by asking such a question.

"No, but one of our older secretaries remembers that he used to come in often during the forties," he said. "Apparently he didn't forget us, for which I'm grateful."

"No more grateful than I am," Maggie assured him.

"He was always elegant but I never quite knew whether he was rich," she said, with an inquiring look. "For all I know he was so rich he could have given away dozens of emeralds."

DeCourcy looked around to make sure the three whippetlike women weren't in earshot before he answered.

"Not from us, he didn't," he said in a low tone. "You got the only emerald, but there was a good-looking younger man who was given a very nice watch.

"It wasn't on the level of your emerald," he told her quickly. "But the young man *was* very good-looking and it was a *very* nice watch."

"Oh," Maggie said. "Okay."

There was a silence. Then, impulsively, she stuck out her hand and DeCourcy Brown shook it.

"It's been nice knowing you," she told him. "I didn't think it was going to be, at first, but it has."

"What a nice compliment, thanks," he said.

"Seems like you'd sell more stuff if you were more friendly from the get-go," Maggie told him. "Or is that wrong?"

"Actually, it *is* wrong," he said, "though it's a perfectly normal assumption to make. What you have to factor in is that this *is* Rodeo Drive. Customers expect merchants to be snooty."

"Okay," Maggie said, not wholly convinced.

DeCourcy Brown wasn't through.

"The other thing you have to factor in is that a lot of rich people are masochists," he said. "You have to humiliate them a little before they'll buy anything."

"Yuck, that kind of stuff gives me the creeps," she said, but she gave him a nice smile before he buzzed her out the door.

20

"All that freaking out you did over not sleeping with the guy who gave you the emerald was wasted freaking out," Connie said, a little smugly, once she learned about the good-looking young guy and the watch.

"The old dude was probably gay all the time," she added.

"You don't know that—he might have liked women at some point," Maggie countered.

Then they quietly dropped the question of Erik Asti's sexuality, if any, and let themselves contemplate the glorious fact that they had a forty-thousand-dollar check to carve up.

"Okay, let's get a pencil and paper and figure this out," Maggie insisted. "Let's add up the credit card debt before we go wild with this money."

"We just added it up last Sunday," Connie reminded her. "Where'd that piece of paper go?"

"It was so depressing I threw it away," Maggie said. "Every time I saw the total I had dreams about being behind bars with Auberon. And when we add it up again, it will still be depressing."

That obvious prediction proved true.

"Well, okay, that still leaves twenty-five thousand, about," Connie said. "How much do you want to allow for dresses to Danny's wedding?"

"How would I know how much to allow?" Maggie asked. "I've never been good with budgets, you know that."

"I don't know if I'm good at them or not because I never made one," Connie admitted.

Then Connie began to look miserable, for no reason that Maggie could see.

"What's wrong, Con?" she asked.

"Everything!" Connie told her.

"Be more specific," Maggie coaxed.

"This is really *your* money—it's your behest from an old geezer who had the hots for you and never did anything about it," Connie said—her dejection seemed to grow ever deeper.

"Why am I talking as if some of it's *my* money?" she asked. "None of it's *my* money. It's all *your* money!"

Then she burst into tears.

"I'll never in a million years have this much money," Connie wailed.

"You know something, what's mine is yours now," Maggie said. "What's mine is yours."

She had been meaning to say something like that for some time, but just hadn't got around to it, quite.

"No it *isn't* mine, you're just being nice," Connie insisted.

Maggie took a deep breath, as if she were about to dive into very deep and unfamiliar waters.

"I don't know if you've noticed but we live together now," Maggie said. "You never spend the night at your place, and you know what? I don't want you to. You started staying here to help me when I was low, and sometimes I'm still low. I still miss my little womb. If you hadn't been so devoted, I think I would have cracked up.

"So, could you just not shake your head when I say what's mine is yours?" she continued.

Connie dried her eyes. She looked at Maggie a long time, but didn't answer. Then they hugged.

"You might change your mind if I see a dress I really like for Danny's wedding and it costs too much," Connie pointed out.

"Bullshit!" Maggie assured her. "I will not change my mind and there's one way to test it."

"How?"

"Nordstrom," Maggie said.

Connie looked startled. "You mean go shopping?" she asked, brightening a little.

Then minutes later, in the van that was on its second transmission, they were on their way to Nordstrom, and when the wedding between Danny and Betsy finally took place, everyone agreed that Connie and Maggie, resplendent in their provocative new duds, were the best-dressed, foxiest two women in the church.

"So much for good intentions," Maggie said, as the limo was taking them home. "We upstaged the bride."

Connie, who had cried copiously through the service, and who had hugged everyone at the wedding at least twice, shrugged off this charge.

"She's got my Danny," she said. "What more could she want?"